The Bughouse Affair

BY MARCIA MULLER AND BILL PRONZINI

NOVELS
Double
Beyond the Grave
The Lighthouse

SHORT STORY COLLECTIONS
Duo
Crucifixion River

NONFICTION
1001 Midnights

The Bughouse Affair

A CARPENTER AND QUINCANNON MYSTERY

Marcia Muller

Bill Pronzini

A TOM DOHERTY ASSOCIATES BOOK  NEW YORK

THE BUGHOUSE AFFAIR

Copyright © 2012 by the Pronzini-Muller Family Trust

A Forge Book
Published by Tom Doherty Associates, LLC
175 Fifth Avenue
New York, NY 10010

www.tor-forge.com

Forge® is a registered trademark of Tom Doherty Associates, LLC.

Library of Congress Cataloging-in-Publication Data

Muller, Marcia.
   The Bughouse affair / Marcia Muller and Bill Pronzini. — 1st ed.
      p. cm.
   "A Tom Doherty Associates book."
   ISBN 978-0-7653-3174-8 (hardcover)
   ISBN 978-1-4299-9721-8 (e-book)
 1. Private investigators—California—San Francisco—Fiction.
2. Women detectives—California—San Francisco—Fiction. 3. San
Francisco (Calif.)—History—19th century—Fiction. I. Pronzini, Bill.
II. Title.
   PS3563.U397B84 2013
   813'.54—dc23
                                                    2012024910

First Edition: January 2013

Printed in the United States of America

0 9 8 7 6 5 4 3 2 1

For Alix and Jessie,
who probably wouldn't read it
even if they knew how

The Bughouse Affair

1

QUINCANNON

It was late morning of a warmish early fall day when Quincannon, in high good spirits, walked into the handsomely appointed offices he shared with his partner. Sabina had opened the window behind her desk, the window that overlooked Market Street and bore the words CARPENTER AND QUINCANNON, PROFESSIONAL DETECTIVE SERVICES. A balmy breeze off San Francisco Bay freshened the air in the room, carrying with it the passing rumble of a cable car, the clatter of dray wagons, the calls of vendors hawking fresh oysters and white bay shrimp in the market across the street, the booming horn of one of the fast coastal steamers as it drew into or away from the Embarcadero.

Sabina was reading one of the city's morning newspapers. Unlike many women in this year of 1894, she read them front to back, devouring political and sensational news along with the social columns and features aimed at her sisters. She glanced up at Quincannon, smiled, and immediately returned her attention to the newsprint. This gave him the opportunity to feast his gaze on her—something he never tired of doing—without fear of reprimand.

She was not a beautiful woman, but at thirty-one she possessed a mature comeliness that melted his hard Scot's heart. There was strength in her high-cheekboned face, a keen intelligence in eyes the color of dark blue velvet. Her seal-black hair, layered high and fastened with one of the jeweled combs she favored, glistened with bluish highlights in the pale sunlight slanting in at her back. And her figure . . . ah, her figure. Slim, delicately rounded and curved in a beige cotton skirt and white blouse with leg-o'-mutton sleeves. Many men found her attractive, to be sure—and as a young widow, fair game. But if any had been allowed inside her Russian Hill flat, he was not aware of it; she was a strict guardian of her private life.

They had been partners in San Francisco's premier investigative agency for over three years now. When they had met by chance in Silver City, Idaho, he had been an operative of the United States Secret Service investigating a counterfeiting operation, and she had been a Pink Rose, one of the select handful of women employed as investigators by the Pinkerton International Detective Agency, at the time working undercover to expose a pyramid swindle involving mining company stock. Circumstances had led them to join forces to mutually satisfactory conclusions, and resulted in an alliance that had prompted Quincannon to wire her at the Pinkerton Agency in Denver shortly after his return to San Francisco:

I AM CONSIDERING RESIGNATION FROM SERVICE TO ESTABLISH PRIVATE PRACTICE STOP WOULD YOU BE IN-

TERESTED IN MOVE TO SF TO JOIN THIS VENTURE QMK
STRICTLY BUSINESS OF COURSE

Her reply had come the next afternoon:

YOUR OFFER PLEASANT SURPRISE STOP YES I WOULD
CONSIDER IF EQUAL PARTNERSHIP WHAT YOU HAVE
IN MIND STOP STRICTLY BUSINESS OF COURSE STOP IF
YOUR ANSWER AFFIRMATIVE I WILL REQUEST LEAVE OF
ABSENCE TO COME TO YOUR CITY FOR DISCUSSION
OF TERMS

Two weeks later, she had arrived by train and ferry, and not
long afterward the joint venture had been established and their
offices leased and opened for business. Quincannon had no
regrets where their professional relationship was concerned;
it had turned out to be more compatible and successful than either of them had foreseen. A man engaged in the time-honored
profession of manhunter couldn't ask for a more capable associate. He could, however, eventually ask for more than a
"strictly business" arrangement and an occasional luncheon
and a few dinners that had ended with nothing more than a
chaste handshake.

He knew she was fond of him, yet she continually spurned
his advances (which may at first have been slightly less than
honorable, he admitted to himself, but were now more wistful
than lecherous). This not only frustrated him, but left him in a
state of constant apprehension. The thought that she might accept a proposal of either dalliance or marriage from anyone
other than John Quincannon was maddening. . . .

He was still visually feasting on her when she glanced up and caught him at it. "Well, John?"

The words brought him out of his reverie. He cleared his throat, and said, "I was merely taking note of the fact that you look lovely this morning."

Her smile bent at the corners. "Soft soap so early? Really."

"A genuine compliment, I assure you."

"With the usual underlying motives."

"Can I help it if I find you alluring? I do, you know."

"So you've told me any number of times."

"Truth can't be repeated often enough."

"Nor can blarney, apparently."

Quincannon sighed, shed his Chesterfield and derby, and went to his desk, which was set catercorner to Sabina's. He sat for a moment fluffing his beard, watching her read. His whiskers were so dark brown as to be almost black, and when he assumed one of his ferocious scowls, the combination gave him the appearance of an angry and dyspeptic pirate—a look he cultivated in his dealings with yeggs, thimbleriggers, and other miscreants. A fierce demeanor was sometimes as effective a weapon as the Navy Colt he carried.

"Idle hands, eh, my dear?" he said when Sabina turned another page in the newspaper.

"Hardly, John. These are the first few moments I've had to myself all morning. Not only have I finished the reports, invoices, and other paperwork you find so tedious, but I've taken on a new client over the telephone."

"Have you, now? And who would that be?"

"Mr. Charles Ackerman, owner of the Haight Street Chutes Amusement Park."

"Ah. A new and wealthy client," Quincannon said approvingly. Ackerman not only owned and operated the Chutes, but was a prominent attorney for both the Southern Pacific Railroad and the Market Street and Sutter Street railway lines. "What service does he want us to perform?"

"To relieve him of the headache of a clever pickpocket. Several Chutes patrons have been robbed in the past few days, despite increased security measures, and his business is suffering as a result."

"And the coppers, naturally, have failed to identify much less arrest the dip." In Quincannon's view, shared by a number of other local citizens, San Francisco's police force was composed largely of fat-headed incompetents only slightly less corrupt than the denizens of the Barbary Coast.

"Yes. I have a one o'clock appointment with Mr. Ackerman's manager, Lester Sweeney, to begin my investigation."

"Will you need my assistance?"

Sabina shook her head. "I'm perfectly capable of handling the matter myself. The pickpocket is a woman."

"Well and good, then. But perhaps you'll share an early lunch with me before your appointment? The table d'hôte at the Hoffman Café is particularly good on Tuesdays—"

"I already have a luncheon engagement."

"With whom, may I ask?"

"You may not."

"Well . . . a business meeting, is it?"

"As a matter of fact, no."

"Your cousin? Another woman friend?" Concern had risen in him, scratching like a thorn at his jealousy.

"Really, John, it's none of your concern." With her usual

deftness, she changed the subject. "You have work of your own, haven't you? The consultation with Jackson Pollard?"

Quincannon worried in silence for a few seconds before he replied. "Already attended to. Earlier this morning, in his office."

"Do you agree with his theory about the burglaries?"

"I do. He's a shrewd bird, when he sets his mind to it."

"How many names on the list?"

"Six. The three who have already had their homes burglarized, plus three other prominent citizens—all Great Western policy holders. Pollard is likely right that the housebreaker is in possession of a similar list. Possibly from an unscrupulous Great Western employee, though he disputes that notion, or through other nefarious means."

"He's paying our usual fee?"

"For the prevention of any more burglaries, yes. With a handsome bonus for the recovery of all the stolen goods in the first three crimes."

"How handsome?"

The answer to that question brought a gleam to Quincannon's eye and restored his good spirits. "One thousand dollars."

Sabina raised an eyebrow. "Pollard offered that much?"

"Not at first. The power of persuasion is one of my many gifts, as you know."

"The more so when it involves the root of all evil."

"You make it sound as though I'm consumed by greed."

"Well?"

"Not so. I admit to a thrifty Scot's desire for financial security, but my motives are pure. The pursuit of justice. The righting of wrongs against society and my fellow men."

"The spreading of hogwash."

He pretended to be wounded. "A great man is often misunderstood, even by his intimates."

Sabina made a sound close to an unladylike snort and returned to her reading. The newspaper's front page was turned toward him, and he glanced at the headlines. None of the stories they heralded was of any professional interest. A soireé at the Japanese tea garden that had been built for the Mid-Winter Fair in Golden Gate Park. A three-alarm fire in the Western Addition. The gist of yet another speech by Adolph Sutro, who was running for mayor on the Populist ticket, promising to end widespread City Hall corruption. As if he stood a chance of doing so. Politics. Bah!

Quincannon busied himself with his stubby briar and pouch of shag-cut tobacco, and soon had the air filled with fragrant clouds of smoke. Fragrant to him, anyhow. Sabina wrinkled her nose and would have opened the window if the sash weren't already up.

When he had the pipe drawing to his satisfaction, he gave his attention to the list of Great Western clients. A few judicious inquiries should tell him which of the three remaining names was most likely the next victim of the phantom housebreaker. Tonight, if all went according to his plan, the scruff would no longer be anonymous.

He was about to use the telephone to make the first of his inquiries when Sabina began to chuckle. She possessed a fine chuckle, throaty and melodious, and an even finer laugh; both had the power to stir him in uncomfortable ways.

"What do you find so amusing in . . . which paper is that?"

"The *Examiner*. Mr. Bierce's 'Prattle' column."

As he might have known. Sabina was an admirer of San Francisco's resident pundit and merciless, often vicious critic of all that others held dear: Ambrose Bierce—Bitter Bierce, as he was more widely known. Quincannon found the man's scribblings insufferably arrogant, as evidenced by his definition of an egoist as "a person of low taste, more interested in himself than in me." Sabina had once voiced the opinion, tongue in cheek, that Quincannon's aversion to the man stemmed from the fact that he was something of a curmudgeon himself and chafed at the competition. Patent nonsense, of course. True, he was not one to suffer fools and knaves, and often grumbled at the foibles of others, but the milk of human kindness had yet to sour in him as it had in Bitter Bierce.

Sabina said, "I know how you feel about Mr. Bierce, but I think you'll find this entry amusing."

"Will I? I doubt it."

" 'In a city in which anomalous occurences abound,' " she read, " 'none would seem more peculiar than the presence among us of an ambulatory dead man. No less a personage than the world's most-celebrated detective, Mr. Sherlock Holmes, reportedly done in by a plunge from atop a waterfall in Switzerland three years ago, is alleged to have achieved a miraculous resurrection and found his way across thousands of miles of land and sea to our fair city, where he is spending a leisurely period of recuperation, or perhaps reanimation, at the home of a prominent family. If these rumors should prove factual and the secret of the Great Man's revivification is widely disseminated, cemeteries everywhere will soon empty and the general population swell to riotous proportions.

" 'There is, however, a less preternatural explanation for

this phenomenon. It may well be that the person answering to
the name of the London sleuth is in fact that rival aspirant to
public honors, an impostor—a latter-day claimant in deerstalker
hat and gray cape to the throne left vacant by the passing of His
Imperial Majesty, Joshua Abraham Norton. More crackbrains
walk among us than dead men, as may be seen on any evening's
stroll along the Cocktail Route.'"

Joshua Abraham Norton. A gent known locally as Emperor
Norton, the self-proclaimed "Emperor of these United States
and Protector of Mexico," whose antics had captured the imag-
ination of San Francisco's citizens some thirty years earlier,
long before Quincannon's arrival in the city. Among Norton's
numerous proclamations were an "order" that the United States
Congress be dissolved by force, and ridiculously impossible
"decrees" that a bridge be built across and a tunnel under San
Francisco Bay. A crackbrain, to be sure.

"For once, Bierce and I agree," Quincannon said. "There is
no disputing his last statement."

"No. But wouldn't it be wonderful if Sherlock Holmes were
still alive and visting in San Francisco?"

"Wonderful? Bah."

"Why do you say that?"

"World's most-celebrated detective. In whose opinion besides Bitter Bierce's?"

"You've read of Holmes's exploits, surely. His companion
and biographer, Dr. John Watson, has written numerous accounts that have been all the rage here as well as in England."

"I've better things to do with my time," Quincannon said.
He was not about to admit that he had, in fact, read some of Dr.
Watson's hyperbolic writings. "Sherlock Holmes . . . faugh!

The man may have achieved a small measure of fame, but fame is fickle and fleeting. In a few years, his exploits will be forgotten."

"Whereas the detections of John Quincannon are bound to be writ large in the annals of crime."

Quincannon, who did not have a humble bone in his body and who considered himself the finest detective west of the Mississippi, if not in the entire United States, failed to notice the note of gentle sarcasm in her voice. He said in all seriousness, "I should hope so. Meaning no disrespect to your detective skills, my dear."

"Oh, of course not. You know, you should cultivate a biographer such as Dr. Watson. Perhaps Mr. Ambrose Bierce would agree to the task."

"Bierce? Why Bierce?"

"Well," Sabina said, "prattle *is* his stock-in-trade."

2

SABINA

After John had left the office for parts unknown, Sabina put on her straw picture hat and skewered it to her upswept dark hair with a Charles Horner hatpin of silver and coral. The pin, a gift from her cousin Callie on her last birthday, was one of two she owned by the famed British designer. The other, a butterfly with an onyx body and diamond-chip wings, had been a gift from her late husband and was much too ornate—to say nothing of valuable—to wear during business hours.

Momentarily she recalled Stephen's face: thin, with prominent cheekbones and chin. Brilliant blue eyes below wavy, dark brown hair. A face that could radiate tenderness—and danger. Like herself, a Pinkerton International Detective Agency operative in Denver, he had been working on a land-fraud case when he was shot during a raid and succumbed to his wounds. It troubled Sabina that over the past few years his features had become less distinct in her memory, as had those of her deceased parents, but she assumed that was human nature. One's memories blur; one goes on.

At times, however, the memories had a stronger pull than at

others. This morning she could not dismiss recollections of the year when she had been a girl Friday (a term she loathed) in the Pinkerton Agency's offices in Chicago. Her father had also been a Pinkerton operative and had died at the age of forty-nine, not in the line of duty but rather ignobly of gout; Sabina had secured her position through her father's partner when the need to work to support her sickly mother became apparent. And it was there that her talent for detective work had engaged the interest of branch manager Stephen Carpenter, who began courting as well as mentoring her. By the onset of the new year, Sabina was on her way to becoming a full-fledged "Pink Rose," as the women operatives proudly called themselves.

The Pink Roses were few in number, yet respected as excellent detectives. Forty years earlier, the first of them, a widow named Kate Warne, had entered the Chicago offices of the agency and requested of Allan Pinkerton that he give her a position—not as a member of the clerical staff, but as an operative. Mrs. Warne overcame Pinkerton's objections, was given the position on a trial basis, and acquitted herself outstandingly from the first. She had been instrumental in uncovering a plot to assassinate Abraham Lincoln as he rode the train from Illinois to Washington, D.C., to take the oath of office after his election, and had herself accompanied him all the way to the nation's capital.

It was rumored that Mrs. Warne had engaged in a long-standing love affair with Allan Pinkerton, but if the rumors were true, the affair had been well shielded and never publicly corroborated. John seemed not to know about this, or at least had never spoken of it to her, and of course she had been careful not to mention it herself. She had enough difficulty fending off his advances without a possible precedent to spur him on.

Within a year of their marriage, she and Stephen had been transferred together to the agency's Denver headquarters, where occasionally they worked as a team, but most often on separate cases that utilized their individual talents. Until the unthinkable happened, and Sabina found herself a widow.

In her grief she had taken a leave of absence from the agency and for a time withdrawn from society, even from herself. She spent long days and nights in the too-quiet flat she and Stephen had occupied in a large brick house in the city, doing little, feeling nothing. Neglecting her appearance, burrowing in bed for entire days, not eating until hunger drove her to gorge herself and then regurgitate.

Then, at her lowest point, Frieda Gosling became her savior.

Frieda, the wife of another Pinkerton operative and a friend of both hers and Stephen's, entered the flat against Sabina's protests, sat her down, and in stern but compassionate tones delivered both a lecture and a message from the Pinkerton office. Did Sabina expect to wallow in grief and misery for the rest of her life? A fine monument to Stephen's memory that would be. Wouldn't he want her to start embracing life again, and return to her duties in the profession for which she was best suited? If she chose the latter, Frieda said, the agency had urgent need of a Pink Rose to work an undercover assignment in Silver City, Idaho, on a case involving a mining stock swindle.

Sabina had taken her friend's words to heart and never

regretted it. For not only had her return to Pink Rose status given her renewed purpose, it had been in Silver City that she'd met John Quincannon, then with the United States Secret Service, and eventually embarked on her new and rewarding life in San Francisco. She and Frieda had remained close, exchanging frequent letters and small gifts at Christmastime.

Now she scrutinized her reflection in her hand mirror and concluded that she looked more like a respectable young matron than a detective setting out to snaffle a pickpocket. Satisfied, she left the office to keep her luncheon date with Callie at the Sun Dial, a popular spot with the ladies.

Sabina held a relatively unique position for a woman in San Francisco: as a widow and the co-owner of a highly respectable business, she was free of many of the strictures imposed on single and married women alike. While the ladies of the city poured tea and offered sweets during weekly "at homes," Sabina traveled the far more interesting, if sometimes dangerous, byways and districts from the notorious Barbary Coast to luxurious Nob Hill. In the course of her investigations she met people of undisputed good standing as well as those of dubious and ill repute. To her second cousin, Callie French, with whom she'd resumed a childhood friendship when she moved West, and with whom she was in fact lunching today, these were dangerous activities inviting folly.

Callie, like Sabina, had been born in Chicago, but her family had moved to California when she was only five. For a time they'd lived in Oakland, the city across the Bay, then settled on Nob Hill when her father was promoted to the regional headquarters of the Miners Bank. Callie had been a debutante—one of the "buds" of society who were presented at the cotillions—

and had married a protégé of her father's in a lavish wedding that had reputedly cost fifty thousand dollars, an unheard of amount for the day. She was Sabina's entrée into the workings of the upper classes and the ways of the city's elite.

But Sabina also moved unharmed through far less genteel surroundings, as if protected by an invisible shield of armor. Perhaps it was her confident manner or perhaps it was because with Stephen's death the worst that could happen to her had already occurred. On that matter, she didn't care to speculate.

When she entered the Sun Dial, she spied Callie at a corner table in the bright, airy main room. Sunlight spilled down through one of the large skylights, giving Callie's intricately braided and coiled blond hair a golden sheen. She greeted Sabina effusively as always, with a hug and a burst of chatter. "There you are, my dear! How are you? In fine fettle, I hope. Here, let me help you with your cloak. They say the chicken dish is exceptional today, but I'm thinking of the veal chop."

While Sabina studied the menu, Callie plied her with questions about John. How was he? Had she changed her mind about seeing him outside the office? No? Why not? He was such a charming man, so polite and well mannered in spite of his ferocious beard.

Sabina smiled inwardly. Callie was a firm believer in marriage, thanks to the success of her own union, and made no bones about the fact that she thought Sabina ought to marry again. Nothing would have made her happier than a Carpenter and Quincannon matrimonial as well as business match. If Sabina ever even hinted at such a possibility, Callie would immediately order champagne and a string quartet for the wedding.

Not that such a hint would ever be forthcoming, but if Sabina had spoken forcefully against the notion, it would only have hurt Callie's feelings. Her cousin could be frivolous and at times downright silly, but she was loyal and had a good, well-meaning heart. Sabina prized their friendship.

The coq au vin didn't appeal to her, nor did the veal chop, but a seafood pasta struck the right note. When she ordered it, Callie said, "Oh, how I envy you. If I ate starch for lunch, I'd have to let my corset out."

"Nonsense."

"Nonsense to you, perhaps. You've never needed to wear a corset."

"Not yet, at least."

Callie leaned forward and lowered her voice. Sabina knew what was coming, for her cousin had an enormous interest in her work—and an equally enormous penchant for gossip. "Tell me, dear. What sort of cases are you and John investigating now?"

"You know I can't tell you that."

"You and your silly rules about client confidentiality. At least tell me this: is there any danger in what *you're* doing?"

"No, none."

"Are you sure? You know how I worry about you."

"Yes. But needlessly."

"I wish I could be certain of that. It's *such* a dangerous profession you've chosen. . . ."

Sabina said quickly, to forestall any painful reminder of what had happened to Stephen, "No more dangerous than crossing a busy street. Or devouring that veal chop you ordered."

Callie sighed. "Not to mention the chocoloate torte I'm considering for dessert."

After she and Callie parted outside the restaurant, Sabina hailed a cab that carried her down Van Ness Avenue and south on Haight Street. The journey was a lengthy one, passing through sparsely settled areas of the city, and all unbidden she found herself thinking about John instead of Stephen. No doubt because of Callie's none-too-subtle matchmaking . . . and yet, her thoughts seemed to turn to her partner more and more often lately, at odd moments, in spite of her vow to keep their relationship strictly professional.

He had left the office grumbling because of her refusal to tell him with whom she was having lunch, and because she had also refused an invitation to dinner at Marchand's French restaurant. Sabina, a practical woman, had thus far turned down nearly all of John's frequent invitations. Mixing business with even the simplest of pleasures was a precarious proposition; it could imperil their partnership, an arrangement with which she was quite happy as it stood.

Another reason she spurned his advances was that she was unsure of what motivated them. Plain seduction? She had no interest in a dalliance with her partner or any other man. A more serious infatuation? As she had often told Callie, she was unwilling to enter into another committed relationship—especially one with John of all possible swains—while the lost love of her life remained bright in her memory. Whatever poor John's intentions, he was simply out of luck.

Sometimes working with him tried her patience, and not only because of his persistence in trying to obtain her favors. His preening self-esteem, though often justified, could be exasperating. Yet she knew him well enough to understand that it was more a façade than his true nature, masking an easily bruised ego and a deep-seated fear of failure. Of course, he would never admit to being either vulnerable or insecure. Or to the fact that she was his equal as a detective. His pride wouldn't allow it.

Yet John also had many good qualities: courage, compassion, sensitivity, kindness, a surprising gentleness at times. And she had to admit that she did not find him unattractive. Quite the opposite, in fact . . .

The Chutes Amusement Park, on Haight Street near the southern edge of Golden Gate Park, had only been open a short while and was still drawing large daily crowds. Its most prominent feature was a three-hundred-foot-long Shoot-the-Chutes: a double trestle track that rose seventy feet into the air. Passengers would ascend to a room at the top of the slides, where they would board boats for a swift descent to an artificial lake at the bottom. Sabina craned her neck to look up at the towering tracks, saw the boats descending, heard the mock terrified screams and shouts of the patrons. She had heard that the ride was quite thrilling—or frightening, according to one's perspective. She herself would enjoy trying it.

In addition to the water slide, the park contained a scenic railway that chugged merrily throughout its acreage; a mirrored, colorful merry-go-round with a huge brass ring; various carnival-like establishments—fortune-tellers, marksmanship booths, ring tosses, and other games of chance—and a refreshment stand offering hot dogs, sandwiches, and lemonade. Vendors with carts moved among the crowd, dispensing popcorn and cotton candy. A giant scale defied men to test their strength—"hit it hard enough with a wooden mallet to make the bell at the top ring," the barker in charge intoned, "and win a goldfish for your lady." Sabina suspected trickery: a man built like a wrestler accompanied by a homely woman missed the mark, but another as thin as a slat accompanied by a dark-haired beauty came away with two fish.

Ackerman had told Sabina she would find his manager, Lester Sweeney, in the office beyond the ticket booth. She crossed the street, holding up her flowered skirt so the hem wouldn't get dusty, and asked at the booth for Mr. Sweeney. The man collecting admissions motioned her inside and through a door behind him.

Sweeney sat behind a desk that seemed too large for the cramped space, adding a column of figures. He was a big man, possibly in his late forties, with thinning red hair and a complexion that spoke of a fondness for strong drink. When at first he looked up at Sabina, his reddened eyes, surrounded by pouched flesh, gleamed in appreciation. To forestall any unseemly remarks she quickly presented her card, and watched the gleam fade.

"I didn't know they'd be sending a woman," he said. "Mr. Ackerman told me it would be one of the owners of the agency."

"I am one of the owners."

He looked at the card again. "Well, well. These days . . . well. Please sit down, Mrs. Carpenter."

"Thank you." Sabina sat on the single wooden chair sandwiched between the desk and the wall.

"You'll pardon me if I expressed reservations," Sweeney said. "You look so, ah, refined—"

"As do many of your patrons, from what I've observed. One of the advantages for a woman in my profession is to be able to blend in. And few would expect a detective to be female."

"True," he admitted, "true."

"To business, then. These pocket-picking incidents have occurred over the past two weeks?"

"Yes. Five in all, primarily in the afternoon. Word has begun to spread, as I'm sure Mr. Ackerman told you, and we're bound to lose customers."

"You spoke with the known victims?"

"Those who reported the incidents, yes. There may have been others who didn't."

"And none was able to describe the thief?"

"Other than that she's a woman who disguises herself in different costumes, no. Nor have our security guards been able to find any trace of her after the incidents."

"Were the victims all of the same sex?"

He nodded. "All men."

"Did they have anything in common? Such as age, type of dress?"

Sweeney frowned while he cudgeled his memory. The frown had an alarming effect on his face, making it look like something that had softened and spread after being left out in the direct sun. In a moment he shook his head. "Various ages, various types of dress. Picked at random, I should think."

"Possibly. Do you have their names and addresses?"

"Somewhere here." He shuffled through the papers on his desk, found the list, and handed it to her. Sabina read it through, then tucked it into her reticule and rose from the chair. "You'll begin your investigation immediately, Mrs. Carpenter?"

"Yes. I'll notify you as soon as I have anything to report."

3

SABINA

John's vast storehouse of knowledge of San Francisco's under-world had helped Sabina familiarize herself with most of the city's female dips and cutpurses. Fanny Spigott, dubbed "Queen of the Pickpockets," who with her husband, Joe, "King of the Pickpockets," had not long ago audaciously—and unsuc-cessfully—plotted to steal the two-thousand-pound statue of Venus de Milo from the Louvre Museum in Paris; Lily Hamlin ("Fainting Lily"), whose ploy was to pretend to pass out in the arms of her victims; Jane O'Leary ("Weeping Jane"), who lured her marks by enlisting them in the hunt for her "missing" six-year-old, then lifted their valuables while hugging them when the precocious and well-trained child accomplice was found; Myra McCoy, who claimed to have the slickest reach in town; and "Lovely Lena," true name unknown, a blonde so bedazzling that it was said she blinded her male victims. Un-fortunately, none of these, nor any others of their sorority, was working the Chutes today.

Sabina's roaming two-hour search had taken her on a tour of the park grounds on the scenic railway, and for a thrilling boat ride down the Chutes waterway—so thrilling that, despite the generous meal she'd eaten at the Sun Dial, she had rewarded her bravery with a cone of vanilla ice cream. No person or activity had struck her as suspicious until she spied a youngish, unaccompanied woman wandering among those clustered around the merry-go-round. The way in which the woman moved and looked over the men in the crowd struck Sabina as furtive. She grew even more alert when the woman sidled up next to a nattily dressed man in a straw bowler, closer than a respectable lady would venture to a stranger. But when he turned and raised his hat to her, she quickly stepped away.

Sabina moved nearer.

The woman had light brown hair, upswept under a wide-brimmed straw picture hat similar to Sabina's that was set low on her forehead so that her face was shadowed. She was slender, outfitted in a white shirtwaist and cornflower blue skirt. The only distinctive thing about her attire was the pin that held the hat to her head. Sabina—a connoisseur of hatpins—recognized it even from a distance as a Charles Horner of blue glass overlaid with a pattern of gold.

When the slender woman glanced around in a seemingly idle fashion, Sabina had a glimpse of rather nondescript features except for a mark on her chin that might have been a small scar. If it was a scar . . .

After a few seconds the woman's gaze seemed to focus on a man to her right. She took a step in his direction, but when he reached down to pick up a fretting child, she didn't approach him. Instead she veered away toward a fat burgher in a fawn-colored waistcoat, only to stop abruptly when a young girl hurried up and took hold of his arm.

The actions of a pickpocket, for certain; Sabina had observed how they operated on a number of occasions. They prowled a crowd, chose a would-be mark, studied the possibilities carefully before proceeding. The hatpin woman had backed off when two promising marks were joined by another person. It was much easier to rob an unaccompanied individual in a public place.

But who was she? Not any dip known to Sabina. And yet that blemish on her chin, the plain features, and the brown hair were familiar. . . .

The woman sauntered along, scanning the sea of faces, looking only at members of the opposite sex. Men were easier marks than those of her own sex, who were likely to cry out when they felt their purse strings cut or clutched upon. Also, men were assumed to carry larger amounts of cash and more easily sold valuables.

Apparently she saw no other prospects to her liking along the midway, and eventually approached a group of revelers clustered in front of an ice-cream wagon. She paused there, then approached a portly man who glared at her when she brushed up close beside him. She moved gracefully away, paused again outside the group, then abruptly turned to cast a long sweeping glance behind her as if sensing that she was being watched. Sabina pretended interest in a sticky-faced, weeping child who had been jostled into dropping her cotton candy, until the hatpin woman turned again and moved off at a quickened pace. Sabina followed as inconspicuously as she could without losing sight of her.

The woman's destination soon became apparent—the park

gates between Cole and Clayton. By the time she reached them, she was moving as quickly as though she were being chased.

Guilty, Sabina thought.

There was a row of hansom cabs waiting outside the gates of the park. The woman with the distinctive hatpin claimed the first in line; Sabina entered the second, asking the driver to follow the other hack. He regarded her with perplexed curiosity, no doubt unused to gentlewomen making such requests, but he neither objected nor refused. A fare was a fare, after all.

Sabina smiled wryly as she settled back. She'd seen the same bemusement on John's face. The new century was rapidly approaching and with it what the press had dubbed the New Woman; very often these days the female sex did not think or act as they once had. Men didn't necessarily dislike the New Woman—at least the progressively intelligent among them didn't—but in general they failed to understand her. What did she want? Sabina had heard them asking one another on more than one occasion. Wasn't the American woman—particularly those in cosmopolitan San Francisco—among the most prized, revered, and coddled in the world?

What they were unable to grasp was that many women were no longer content with being treated as fragile pieces of china and were tired of being considered intellectual inferiors. Such treatment, to one of Sabina's temperament, was both demeaning and insulting.

The hatpin woman's cab led them north on Haight and finally to Market Street, the city's main artery. There she disembarked near the Palace Hotel—as did Sabina—and crossed Market to Montgomery. It was five o'clock, and businessmen of all kinds were streaming out of their downtown offices, many on their way to travel what the young blades termed the Cocktail Route.

The pickpocket's destination was of no surprise to Sabina. A professional thief operated in more than one venue, and while there were plenty of potential marks at the Chutes, the Cocktail Route was a virtual dip's paradise.

From the Reception Saloon on Sutter Street to Haquette's Palace of Art on Post Street to the Palace Hotel Bar at Third and Market, the influential men of San Francisco trekked daily after five, partaking of fine liquor and bountiful "free lunches." More like banquets, these lavish tables consisted of cheeses, platters of sausages and salamis, hams, small sardines, pickles, green onions, and rye and pumpernickel breads. Later came the hot dishes; terrapin cooked in its shell with cream, butter, and sherry being the most favored of all.

It was along this route that friends met, traveling in packs like so many well-trained—and sometimes ill-trained—dogs. In the various establishments, business was transacted and political alliances formed. Women were not admitted, and often, Sabina's cousin Callie had told her, messenger boys scampered to take notes to wives waiting at dinner that stated that their husbands would be "unfortunately detained" for the evening. The festivities often continued with lavish dinners and, for the recklessly adventurous and immoral, visits to the Barbary Coast or the parlor houses in the Uptown Tenderloin, followed by stops at the Turkish baths and culminating with breakfast—and more champange, of course—at various restaurants throughout the city.

As a respectable woman, Sabina had had no chance to frequent such establishments, but she had ample knowledge of them from Callie and from John's tales of the days when he had been a hard-drinking Secret Service operative unabashadly savoring the liquors and fine wines, the rich foods and seductive women of this glittering city.

The hatpin woman was now well into the crowd on Montgomery Street—known as the Ambrosial Path to cocktail hour revelers. Street characters and vendors, beggars and ad-carriers for the various saloons' free lunches, temperance speakers and the Salvation Army band, all mingled with well-dressed bankers and attorneys, politicians and physicians. The men called out greetings, conferred in groups, some joining, some breaking away. Conviviality was in the air. It was as if these men had suddenly been released from burdensome toil—although many did not reach their offices until late morning and then indulged in long recuperative luncheons.

Sabina made her way through the Ambrosial Path throngs, never losing sight of the pickpocket's blue hat, brushing aside the importunings of a match-peddler. The woman moved along unhurriedly, scanning for marks as she had at the Chutes, and after two blocks turned left and walked over to Kearney Street at the edge of the Barbary Coast.

There the gaslit street scene was even livelier. Saloons, shooting galleries, auction houses, discount clothiers, and painless dentists lined the block; gaudy signs proclaimed PROF. DIAMOND, COURSES IN HYPNOTISM and THE GREAT ZOCAN, ASTRAL SEER and DR. BLAKE'S INDESTRUCTIBLE TEETH. And there were sellers and pitchmen of all sorts—fakirs, snake charmers, news vendors, organ players, matrimonial agents, plug-hatted touters of

Marxism and Henry George's Single Tax. The only difference between the pitchmen and a pickpocket or footpad, Sabina thought, was that they employed quasi-legitimate means to relieve individuals of their money.

Her quarry continued to walk at a leisurely pace, stopping once to finger a bolt of Indian fabric and then again to listen to a speaker extol the dubious virtues of phrenology. Momentarily she lost her in the crowd, then spotted her again edging up close beside a gentleman in a frock coat. Hurrying, Sabina drew near just as the man cried out and bent over at the waist, his silk hat falling to the sidewalk.

The crowd swarmed around him as he straightened, his face frozen in a grimace of pain. Sabina, elbowing her way forward, saw him reach inside his coat, and suddenly anger replaced pain. "My gold watch," he shouted, "it's been stolen! Stop, thief!"

But no one was fleeing. Voices rose from the group around him, heads swiveled in alarm and confusion, bodies formed a moving wall that prevented Sabina from reaching or pursuing her quarry.

When she finally extricated herself, the blue hat was nowhere to be seen. The pickpocket had found an ideal mark, struck, and swiftly vanished into the crowd.

4

QUINCANNON

The house at the upper westward edge of Russian Hill was a dormered and turreted pile of two stories and some dozen rooms, with a wraparound porch and a good deal of gingerbread trim. It was set well back from the street and well apart from its neighbors, given seclusion by shade trees, flowering shrubs, and marble statuary. A fine home, as befitted the likes of Samuel Truesdale, senior vice president of the San Francisco Maritime Bank. A home filled with all the treasures and playthings of the wealthy.

A home built to be burglarized.

Thirty feet inside the front gate, Quincannon shifted position in the deep shadow of a lilac bush. From this vantage point he had clear views of the house, the south side yard, and the street. He could see little of the rear of the property, where the bulk of a carriage barn loomed and a gated fence gave access to a carriageway that bisected the block, but this was of no consequence. The housebreaker might well come onto the property from that direction, but there was no rear entrance to the house and the night worker's method of preferred entry was by door, not first- or second-story windows; this meant he would have to come around to the side door or the front door, both of which were within clear sight.

No light showed anywhere on the grounds. Banker Truesdale and his wife, dressed to the nines, had left two hours earlier in a private carriage, and they had no live-in servants. The only light anywhere in the immediate vicinity came from a streetlamp some fifty yards distant, a flickery glow that did not reach into the Truesdale yard. High cirrostratus clouds made thin streaks across the sky, touching but not obscuring an early moon. The heavenly body was neither a sickle nor what the scruffs called a stool-pigeon moon, but a near half that dusted the darkness with enough pale shine to see by.

A night made for burglars and footpads. And detectives on the scent.

A raw wind had sprung up, thick with the salt smell of the bay, and its chill penetrated the greatcoat, cheviot, gloves, neck scarf, and cap Quincannon wore. Noiselessly he stomped his feet and flexed his fingers to maintain circulation. His mind conjured up the image of steaming mugs of coffee and soup. Of a fire hot and crackling in his rooms on Leavenworth Street. Of the warmth of Sabina's flesh on the scant few occasions he had touched her, and the heat of his passion for her . . .

Ah, no. None of that now. Attention to the matter at hand, detective business first and foremost. Why dwell on his one frustrating failure instead of contemplating another professional triumph? Easier to catch a crook than to melt a stubborn woman's resistance.

A rattling and clopping on the cobbled street drew his attention. Moments later a hack, its side lamps casting narrow funnels of light, passed without slowing. When the sound of it faded, Quincannon grew aware of another sound—music, faint and melodic. Someone playing the violin, and reasonably well, too.

He listened for a time, decided what was being played were passages from Mendelssohn's *Leider.* He was hardly an expert on classical music, or even much of an aficionado, but he had allowed himself to be drawn to enough concerts to identify individual pieces. Among his strong suits were a photographic memory and a well-tuned ear.

More time passed at a creep and crawl. The wind had died down some, but he was so thoroughly chilled by then he scarcely noticed. Despite the heavy gloves and the constant flexing, his fingers felt stiff; much more time out here in the night's cold, and he might have difficulty drawing his Navy Colt if such became necessary.

Blast this blasted burglar, whoever he was! He was bound to come after more spoils tonight; Quincannon was sure of it, and his instincts seldom led him astray. So what was the yegg waiting for? It must be after nine by now. Wherever banker Truesdale and his missus had gone for the evening, chances were they would return by eleven. This being Thursday, Truesdale's presence would surely be required tomorrow morning at his bank.

Quincannon speculated once more on the identity of his quarry. There were scores of house burglars in San Francisco and environs, but the cleverness of method and skill of entry in this case narrowed the field to but a few professionals. Of those known to him, the likeliest candidates were the Sanctimonious Kid and Dodger Brown. Both were suspected to be in the Bay

Area at present, but neither had done anything to attract attention to themselves. In any case, the swag seemed to have been planted for the nonce, since none of the stolen items had surfaced. Likely the thief's plan was to dispose of it all at once, in a bundle, after he had gone through most if not all of the six names on the target list.

Quincannon relished the prospect of convincing him otherwise, almost as much as he relished the thought of collecting the fat fee and bonus from Great Western Insurance.

The violin music had ceased; the night was hushed again. He flexed and stomped and shifted and shivered, his mood growing darker by the minute. If the burglar gave any trouble, he would rue his foolishness. Quincannon prided himself as possessing guile and razor-sharp wits, but he was also a brawny man of Pennsylvania Scots stock and not averse to a bit of thumping and skull dragging if the situation warranted.

Another vehicle, a small carriage this time, clattered past the property. Shortly a figure appeared on the sidewalk, and Quincannon tensed expectantly—but it was only a citizen walking his dog, and soon gone.

Hell and damn. Had he been wrong that the burglar would strike again so soon? Or been wrong in his choice of the Truesdale home as the next probable target? Both were possible, though it was already a surprise to him that the yegg hadn't chosen the banker's vulnerable home as one of his first three objectives.

Ah, but he *wasn't* wrong on either count. That became evident in the next few seconds, when he turned his gaze from the street to the inner yard and house.

Someone was moving over there, not fifty yards from Quincannon's hiding place.

His senses all sharpened at once; he stood immobile, peering through the lilac's branches. The movement came again, a shadow drifting among stationary shadows, at an angle from the rear of the property toward the side porch. Once the figure reached the steps and started up, it was briefly silhouetted—a man in dark clothing and a low-pulled cap. Then the shape merged with the deeper black on the porch.

Several seconds passed. Then there was a brief flicker of light—the beam from a dark lantern such as the one in Quincannon's pocket. This was followed by the faintest of scraping sounds as the intruder worked with his tools.

Once again stillness closed down. The scruff was inside the house now. Quincannon stayed where he was, marking time. No light showed behind the dark windows. The professional burglar worked mainly by feel and instinct, using his lantern sparingly and shielding the beam when he did.

When Quincannon judged ten minutes had passed, he left his hiding place and cat-footed through shadows until he was parallel with the side porch stairs. He paused to listen, heard nothing from the house, and crossed quickly, bent low, to a tall rhododendron planted alongside the steps. Here he hunkered down on one knee to wait.

The wait might be another ten minutes; it might be a half hour or more. No matter. Now that the crime was in progress, he no longer minded the cold night, the dampness of the earth where he knelt. Even if Truesdale owned a safe not easily cracked, no burglar would leave premises such as these without spoils of some sort. Art objects, silverware, anything of value that could be carried off and eventually sold to one of the many fences operating in the city. Whatever this lad emerged with, it would be enough to justify a pinch.

Whether Quincannon turned him over to the city police immediately or not depended on the scruff's willingness to reveal the whereabouts of the swag from his previous jobs. Stashing and roughhousing a prisoner for information was unethical, if not illegal, but Quincannon felt righteously that in the pursuit of justice, not to mention a substantial fee and bonus, the end justified the means.

His wait lasted less than thirty minutes. The creaking of a floorboard pricked up his ears, creased his freebooter's beard with a smile of anticipation. Another creak, the faintest squeak of a door hinge, a footfall on the porch. Now the burglar descended the steps into view—short, slender, but turned out of profile so that his face was obscured. He paused on the bottom step, and that was when Quincannon levered up and put the grab on him.

He was much the larger man, and there should have been no trouble in the catch. But just before his arms closed around the wiry body, the yegg heard or sensed danger and reacted—not by trying to run or turning to fight, but by dropping suddenly into a crouch. Quincannon's arms slid up and off as if the man were greased, pitching him off balance. The housebreaker bounced upright, swung around, blew the stench of sour wine into Quincannon's face while at the same time fetching him a sharp kick on the shinbone. Quincannon let out a howl, staggered, nearly fell. By the time he caught himself, his quarry was on the run.

He gave chase on the blind, cursing sulphurously, hobbling for the first several steps until the pain from the kick ebbed. The burglar had twenty yards on him by then, zigzagging toward the bordering yew trees, then back away from them in the direction of the carriage barn.

In the moonlight he made a fine, clear target, but Quincannon did not draw his Navy Colt. Since the long-ago episode in Virginia City, when he had accidently caused the death of a woman and her unborn child, and suffered mightily as a result, he'd vowed to use his weapon only in the most dire of circumstances—a vow he had never broken.

Before reaching the barn, his man cut away at another angle and plowed through a gate into the carriageway beyond. Quincannon lost sight of him for a few seconds, then spied him again as he reached the gate and barreled through it. A race down the alley? No. The scruff was nimble as well as slippery; he threw a look over his shoulder, saw Quincannon in close pursuit, suddenly veered sideways, and flung himself up and over a six-foot board fence into one of the neighboring yards.

In a few long strides Quincannon was at the fence. He caught the top boards, hoisted himself up to chin level. Some fifty yards distant was the backside of a stately home, two windows and a pair of French doors ablaze with electric light; the outspill combined with pale moonshine to limn a jungle-like garden, a path leading through its profusion of plants and trees to a gazebo on the left. He had a brief glimpse of a dark shape plunging into shrubbery near the gazebo.

Quincannon scrambled up the rough boards, rolled his body over the top. And had the misfortune to land awkwardly on his sore leg, which gave way and toppled him to his knees in damp grass. He growled an oath under his breath, lumbered to his feet, and stood with ears straining to hear. Leaves rustled and branches snapped—his man was moving away from the gazebo now, toward the house.

The path was of crushed shell that gleamed with a faint, ghostly radiance; Quincannon drifted along parallel to it, keeping to the grass to cushion his footfalls. Gnarled cypress and thorny pyracantha bushes partially obscured the house, the shadows under and around them as black as India ink. He paused to listen again. There were no more sounds of movement. He resumed his forward progress, eased around one of the cypress trees.

The man who came up behind him did so with such silent stealth that he had no inkling of the other's presence until a hard object poked into and stiffened his spine, and a forceful voice said, "Stand fast, if you value your life. There's a good chap."

Quincannon stood fast.

5

QUINCANNON

The man who had the drop on him was not the one he'd been chasing. The calm, cultured, British-accented voice, and the almost casual choice of words, told him that.

He said, stifling his anger and frustration, "I'm not a prowler."

"What are you, then, pray tell?"

"A detective on the trail of a thief. I chased him into this yard."

"Indeed?" His captor sounded interested, if not convinced. "What manner of thief?"

"A blasted burglar. He broke into the Truesdale home."

"Did he, now? Mr. Truesdale, the banker?"

"That's right. Your neighbor across the carriageway."

"A mistaken assumption. This is not my home, and I have only just this evening met Mr. Truesdale."

"Then who are you?"

"All in good time. This is hardly the proper place for introductions."

"Introductions be damned," Quincannon growled. "While we stand here confabbing, the thief is getting away."

"Has already gotten away, I should think. If you're what you say you are and not a thief yourself." The hard object prodded his backbone. "Move along to the house and we'll have the straight of things in no time."

"Bah," Quincannon said, but he moved along.

There was a flagstone terrace across the rear of the house, and when they reached it he could see people in evening clothes moving around inside a well-lighted parlor. His captor took him to a pair of French doors, ordered him to step inside. Activity in the room halted when they entered. Six pairs of eyes, three male and three female, stared at Quincannon and the man behind him. One of the couples, both plump and middle-aged, was Samuel Truesdale and his wife. The others were strangers.

The parlor was large, handsomely furnished, dominated by a massive grand piano. On the piano bench lay a well-used violin and bow—the source of the passages from Mendelssohn that had been played earlier, no doubt. A wood fire blazed on the hearth. The combination of the fire and steam heat made the room too warm, stuffy. Quincannon's benumbed cheeks began to tingle almost immediately.

The first to break the frozen tableau was a small, round-faced gent with Lincolnesque whiskers and ears that resembled the handles on a pickle jar. He stepped forward and to one side so that he faced the Englishman. If the fellow was an Englishman. Quincannon was not at all sure the cultured accent was genuine.

"Where did this man come from?" the large-eared gent demanded. "Who is he?"

"On my stroll in the garden I spied him climbing over the fence. He claims to be a detective on the trail of a pannyman. Housebreaker, that is."

"I don't claim to be a detective," Quincannon said sourly. "I *am* a detective. Quincannon's the name, John Quincannon."

"Doctor Caleb Axminster," the large-eared fellow said. "What's this about a housebreaker?"

The exchange drew the others closer in a tight little group. It also brought the owner of the English voice out to where Quincannon could see him for the first time. He wasn't such-a-much. Tall, excessively lean, with a thin, hawklike nose and a prominent chin. In one hand he carried a blackthorn walking stick, held midway along the shaft. Quincannon scowled. It must have been the stick, not a pistol, that had poked his spine and allowed the scruff to escape.

"I'll ask you again," Dr. Axminster said. "What's all this about a housebreaker?"

"I chased him here from a neighbor's property." Quincannon shifted his gaze to the plump banker. He was not a man to mince words, even at the best of times. "Yours, Mr. Truesdale."

Mrs. Truesdale gasped. Her husband's face lost its healthy color. "Mine? Good Lord, man, do you mean to say we've been robbed?"

"Unfortunately, yes."

"Of what, do you know? What was stolen?"

"A question only you can answer."

"Little enough, I pray. My wife's jewelry and several stock certificates are kept in the safe in my office, but the thief couldn't have gotten into it. It's burglarproof."

No safe, in Quincannon's experience, was burglarproof. But he allowed the statement to pass without comment, asking instead, "Do you also keep cash on hand?"

"In my desk . . . a hundred dollars or so in greenbacks . . ." Truesdale shook his head; he seemed dazed. "You were on my property?"

"I was, with every good intention. Waiting outside."

"Waiting? I don't understand."

"To catch the burglar in the act."

"But how did you know . . . ?"

"Detective work, sir. Detective work."

The fifth man in the room had been silent to this point, one hand plucking at his middle as if he were suffering the effects of too much rich food. He was somewhat younger than the others, forty or so, dark-eyed, clean-shaven, with a nervous tic on one cheek; his most prominent feature was a misshapen knob of red-veined flesh, like a partially collapsed balloon, that seemed to hang unattractively between his eyes and a thin-lipped mouth. He aimed a brandy snifter at Quincannon, and said in aggrieved tones, "Thieves roaming everywhere in the city these days, like a plague, and you had the opportunity to put one out of commission and failed. If you're such a good detective, why didn't you catch the burglar? What happened?"

"An unforeseen occurrence over which I had no control." Quincannon glared sideways at his gaunt captor. "I would have chased him down if this man hadn't accosted me."

"Accosted?" The Englishman arched an eyebrow. "Dear me, hardly that. I had no way of knowing you weren't a prowler."

Mrs. Truesdale was tugging at her husband's arm. "Samuel, shouldn't we return home and find out what was stolen?"

"Yes, yes, right away."

"Margaret," Axminster said to one of the other women, a slender graying brunette with patrician features, "find James and have him drive the Truesdales."

The woman nodded and left the parlor with the banker and his wife in tow.

The doctor said then, "This is most distressing," but he didn't sound distressed. He sounded eager, as if he found the situation stimulating. He produced a paper sack from his pocket, popped a horehound drop into his mouth. "But right up your alley, eh, Mr. Holmes?"

The Englishman bowed.

"And yours, Andrew. Eh? The law and all that."

"Hardly," the man with the drinker's nose said. "You know I handle civil, not criminal, cases. Why don't you introduce us, Caleb? Unless Mr. Quincannon already knows who I am."

Quincannon decided he didn't particularly like the fellow. Or Axminster, for that matter. Or the gaunt Englishman. In fact, he did not like anybody tonight, not even himself very much.

"Certainly," the doctor said. "This is Andrew Costain, Mr. Quincannon, and his wife, Penelope. And this most distinguished gentleman from far-off England . . ."

"Costain?" Quincannon interrupted. "Offices on Geary Street, residence near South Park?"

"By God," Costain said, "he *does* know me. But if we've met, sir, I don't remember the time or place. In court, was it?"

"We haven't met anywhere. Your name happens to be on the list."

"List?" Penelope Costain said. She was a slender, gray-eyed, brown-curled woman some years younger than her husband—

handsome enough, although she appeared too aloof and wore too much rouge and powder for Quincannon's taste. "What list?"

"Of actual and potential burglary victims, all of whom own valuables insured by the Great Western Insurance Company."

This information seemed to make her husband even more dyspeptic. He rubbed nervously at his middle again as he asked, "Where did such a list come from?"

"That remains to be determined. Likely from someone affiliated or formerly affiliated with Great Western Insurance."

"And Truesdale's name is also on the list, I suppose. That's what brought you to his home tonight."

"Among other things," Quincannon said.

Axminster sucked the horehound drop, his brow screwed up in thought. "Quincannon, John Quincannon . . . why, of course! I knew I'd heard the name before. Carpenter and Quincannon, Professional Detective Services. Yes, and your partner is a woman."

"A woman," the man called Holmes said. "How curious."

Quincannon skewered him with a sharp eye. "What's curious about it? Both Mrs. Carpenter and her late husband were valued operatives of the Pinkerton Detective Agency."

"Upon my soul. In England, you know, it would be extraordinary for a woman to assume the profession of consulting detective, the more so to be taken in as a partner in a private inquiry agency."

"She wasn't 'taken in,' as you put it. Our partnership was by mutual arrangement."

"Ah."

Quincannon demanded, "What do you know of private detectives, in England or anywhere?"

"He knows a great deal, as a matter of fact," Axminster said with relish. He asked the Englishman, "You have no objection if I reveal your identity to a colleague?"

"None, inasmuch as you have already revealed it to your other guests."

The doctor beamed. He said as if presenting a member of British royalty, "My honored houseguest, courtesy of a mutual acquaintance in the south of France, is none other than Mr. Sherlock Holmes of 221 B Baker Street, London, England."

Sherlock Holmes, my eye, Quincannon thought. This must be the fellow Bitter Bierce had written about in his column in this morning's *Examiner*—the crackbrain posing as the legendary detective.

He said, "Holmes, eh? Not according to Mr. Ambrose Bierce."

Axminster made sputtering noises. "Bierce is a poisonous fool. You can't believe a word the man writes."

"I assure you, Mr. Quincannon, that I am indeed Sherlock Holmes." The Englishman bowed. "At your service, sir."

"I've already had a sampling of your 'service,'" Quincannon said irascibly. "I prefer my own."

"Nous verrons."

King's English, and now French. Bah.

"Sherlock Holmes died in Switzerland three years ago. Resurrected, were you, as Bierce inferred?"

The Englishman ignored the last comment. "Reportedly died. Dispatched at Reichenbach Falls by my archenemy,

Professor Moriarity. Officially I am still deceased. For private reasons I've chosen to let the misapprehension stand, until recently confiding in no one but my brother, Mycroft. Not even my good friend Dr. Watson knows I'm still alive."

"If he's such a good friend, why haven't you told him?"

Holmes, for want of another name, produced an enigmatic smile and made no reply.

Axminster said, "Dr. John H. Watson is Mr. Holmes's biographer as well as his friend, as you must know, Quincannon. The doctor has chronicled many of his cases: 'A Study in Scarlet,' 'The Red-Headed League,' 'The Sign of Four,' the horror at Baskerville Hall, the adventure of the six orange pips. . . ."

"Five," Holmes said.

"Eh? Oh, yes, five orange pips."

The stuffily overheated room was making Quincannon sweat. He stripped off his gloves, unbuttoned his greatcoat, and swept the tails back. At the same time he essayed a closer look at the man who claimed to be Sherlock Holmes. For an impostor, he seemed to fit the role of the Baker Street sleuth well enough as described in Dr. Watson's so-called memoirs. Despite his gaunt, almost cadaverous appearance in evening clothes, his jaw and hawklike nose bespoke intensity and determination, and his eyes were sharp, piercing, lit with what some might consider a keen intelligence. Quincannon's opinion was that it was the glow of madness.

The bright eyes were studying him in return. "I daresay you've had your own share of successes, sir."

"More than I can count."

"Oh, yes, Mr. Quincannon and his partner are well known locally," the doctor said. "Several of their investigations involving seemingly impossible crimes have gained notoriety. If I remember correctly, there was the rainmaker shot to death in a locked room, the strange disappearance on board the Desert Limited, the rather amazing murder of a bogus medium. . . ."

Holmes said, "I would be most interested to know the methods you and your partner employ."

"Methods?"

"In solving your cases. Aside from the use of weapons, fisticuffs, and such surveillance techniques as you employed tonight."

"What happened tonight was not my fault," Quincannon said testily. "As to our methods . . . whatever the situation calls for. Guile, wit, attention to detail, and deduction, among others."

"Capital! My methods are likewise based on observation, in particular observation of trifles, and on deductive reasoning—the construction of a series of inferences, each dependent upon its predecessor. An exact knowledge of all facets of crime and its history is invaluable as well, as I'm sure you know."

Bumptious, as well as a candidate for the bughouse. Quincannon managed not to sneer.

"For instance," Holmes said, smiling, "I should say that you are unmarried, smoke a well-seasoned briar, prefer shag-cut Virginia tobacco, spent part of today in a tonsorial parlor and another part engaged in a game of straight pool, dined on chicken croquettes before proceeding to the Truesdale property, waited for your burglar in a shrub of *Syringa persica,* and . . . oh, yes, under your rather gruff exterior, I perceive that you are well read and of a rather sensitive and sentimental nature."

Quincannon gaped at him. "How the devil can you know all that?"

"There is a loose button and loose thread on your vest, and your shirt collar is slightly frayed—telltale indications of our shared state of bachelorhood. When I stood close behind you in the garden, I detected the scent of your tobacco; and once in here, I noted a small spot of ash on the sleeve of your coat, which confirmed the mixture and the fact that it was smoked in a well-aged briar. It happens, you see, that I once wrote a little monograph on the ashes of one hundred forty different types of cigar, pipe, and cigarette tobacco and am considered an authority on the subject.

"Your beard has been recently and neatly trimmed, as has your hair, which retains a faint scent of bay rum, hence your visit to the tonsorial parlor. Under the nail of your left thumb is dust of the type of chalk commonly used on the tips of pool cues, and while billiards is often played in America, straight pool has a larger following and strikes me as more to your taste. On the handkerchief you used a moment ago to mop your forehead is a small, fresh stain the color and texture of which identifies it to the trained eye as having come from a dish of chicken croquettes. Another scent which clings faintly to your coat is that of *Syringa persica,* or Persian lilac, indicating that you have recently been in close proximity to such a flowering shrub; and inasmuch as there are no lilac bushes in Dr. Axminster's garden, Mr. Truesdale's property is the obvious deduction.

"And, finally, I perceive that you are well read from the slim volume entitled *Poems* tucked into the pocket of your coat, and that you have a sensitive and sentimental nature from the identity of the volume's author. Emily Dickinson's poems, I am given to understand, are famous for those qualities."

There was a moment of silence. Quincannon, for once in his life, was at a loss for words.

Axminster clapped his hands, and exclaimed, "Amazing!"

"Elementary," Holmes said.

Horse apples, Quincannon thought.

Penelope Costain yawned. "Mr. Holmes has been regaling us with his powers of observation and ratiocination all evening. Frankly I found his prowess with the violin of greater amusement."

Her husband was likewise unimpressed. He had refilled his glass from a sideboard nearby and now emptied it again in a swallow; his face was flushed, his eyes slightly glazed. "Mental gymnastics are all well and good," he said with some asperity, "but we've stayed well away from the issue here. Which is that my name is on that list of potential burglary victims."

"I wouldn't be concerned, Andrew," Axminster said. "After tonight's escapade, that fellow wouldn't dare attempt another burglary."

Quincannon said, "Not immediately, perhaps. He may well suspect that I know his identity."

"You recognized him?"

"After a fashion."

"Then why don't you go find him and have him arrested?" Costain demanded.

"All in good time. He won't do any more breaking and entering tonight, that I can guarantee."

Mrs. Costain asked, "Did you also guarantee catching him red-handed at the Truesdales' home?"

Quincannon had had enough of this company; much more

of it and he might well say something he would regret. He made a small show of consulting his stem-winder. "If you'll excuse me," he said then, "I'll be on my way."

"To request police assistance?"

"To determine the extent of the Truesdales' loss."

Dr. Axminster showed him to the front door. The Costains remained in the parlor, and the counterfeit Sherlock Holmes tagged along. At the front door the fellow said, "I regret my intervention in the garden, Mr. Quincannon, well-intentioned though it was, but I must say I found the interlude stimulating. It isn't often I have the pleasure of meeting a distinguished colleague while a game's afoot."

Quincannon reluctantly accepted a proffered hand, clasped the doctor's just as briefly, and took his leave. Nurturing as he went the dark thought of a different game, one involving *his* foot, that he would have admired to play with the Axminsters' addled guest.

6

SABINA

Before leaving her Russian Hill flat on Wednesday morning, Sabina set out a bowl of milk for the young cat she'd recently adopted, Adam—so named because he was the first in what she hoped would be a long succession of pets—and opened the bedroom window a few inches so he could come and go as he pleased. She had never sheltered an animal before, but Adam provided companionship and comfort against the cold of the night.

"Don't stray too far," she told him as he brushed against her ankles. "You're much safer here, with a nice soft featherbed to sleep on."

I must be daft, she thought, speaking this way to a creature that can't possibly understand me. Yet she felt that the cat, in its own way, seemed to understand her moods, especially that of loneliness. And she was lonely often of late, even more so than usual since Stephen's death, for reasons that were not quite clear to her. Perhaps she ought to accept one of John's frequent invitations to dinner and a performance at the opera house. . . .

MARCIA MULLER AND BILL PRONZINI

She'd contemplate the notion later. At the moment there was business to attend to.

As usual she was the first to arrive at the agency office. John came in a short while later. Sabina had a sharp eye for his moods; one long look at his gloomy visage prompted her to say, "I take it your surveillance at the Truesdale home last night was unproductive."

"Oh, the yegg came skulking, right enough."

"But you weren't able to nab him?"

"It wasn't my fault that I didn't." Her partner shed his Chesterfield and derby, hung them on the clothes tree, and retreated behind his desk where he tamped his pipe full of tobacco and set fire to it with a lucifer. "Unique scent," he muttered. "Monograph on a hundred and forty different types of tobacco ash. Faugh!"

"What's that you're grumbling about?"

"Confounded lunatic. Not only did he cost me the housebreaker's capture, he did his level best to make a fool of me with a bagful of parlor tricks."

"Lunatic?"

"That blasted Englishman pretending to be Sherlock Holmes."

Sabina raised an eyebrow. "You mean the fellow Mr. Bierce wrote about yesterday?"

"None other." He puffed furiously on his pipe. "Sherlock! What kind of name is that?"

"John. Exactly what happened last night?"

She listened gravely while he explained in detail accurate to a fault. When he was done, she said, "Well, the Englishman may be an impostor—"

"May be!"

"—but it sounds as though he's well versed in the methods employed by the genuine Sherlock Holmes."

"Bah. A mentalist in a collar-and-elbow variety show at the Comique could perform the same tricks."

"Nevertheless," Sabina said, "he must be adept at his role to have fooled Dr. Axminster and his guests into believing him."

"Crackbrains can be sly as the devil. This one also happens to be a pompous, arrogant show-off."

She suppressed a smile, thinking of John's lofty opinion of his own detective skills. "Arrogance was one of Mr. Holmes's traits, judging from Dr. Watson's memoirs."

"Yes? Well, it's hardly the mark of a successful detective. I am every bit as skilled as he was reputed to be and I've blessed little arrogance in *my* makeup."

Sabina again managed not to smile. "Poor John. You did have rather a difficult evening, didn't you?"

"Difficult, aye, but not wasted. Dodger Brown's the man I'm after, sure enough. When he slipped my clutches on the Truesdale property and swung around to kick me—"

"Kick you? I thought you said you slipped on the wet grass."

"Yes, yes. But how he got away is of no consequence. The important fact is that he was of the right size and reeked of cheap wine. Dodger Brown's weakness is foot juice."

"Yes, I remember."

"Where's the dossier on him?"

"Your left hand is resting on it."

"So it is." He caught up the paper, read aloud from it as he sometimes did with such documents—more to himself than to her. "Dodger Brown, christened Hezekiah Gabriel Brown, born in Stockton twenty-nine years ago. Orphaned at an early age, ran off at thirteen, fell in with a bunch of rail-riding yeggs, and immersed in criminal activity ever since, exclusively home burglary in recent years. Arrested numerous times and put on the small book by the coppers in San Francisco, Oakland, and other cities. Served two prison terms, the last at Folsom for stealing a pile of green-and-greasy from an East Bay politician. Description: slight of build, thinning brown hair, vulpine features. Known traits: close-mouthed, seldom works with confederates. Known confidantes: Clara Wilds, extortionist, otherwise none. Known habits: a taste for Chinese prostitutes and frequenter of parlor houses that employ same; regular customer of cheap-jack gambling halls and Barbary Coast wine dumps. Current whereabouts unknown." He lowered the dossier, nodding thoughtfully. "Little enough information, but perhaps enough."

Sabina said, "If he recognized you last night, he may have already fenced his swag and gone on the lammas."

"I don't think so," John said. "It was too dark for him to see my face any more clearly than I saw his. For all he knows, I might have been a neighbor who spotted him skulking or the owner home early. A greedy lad like the Dodger isn't likely to cut and run when he's flush and onto a string of profitable marks."

"After such a narrow escape, would he be bold enough to try burgling another home on the insurance company's list?"

"As like as not. He's none too bright and as arrogant in his yegg's fashion as that daft Holmes impostor. It was a bughouse caper that landed him in Folsom prison two years ago. He's not above another, I'll wager."

"So then you'll reconnoiter again tonight at another of the residences on Great Western's list?"

"Aye, and I'll put the fear of God into him if he comes. Scruffs like the Dodger can be made to confess their sins."

"Strongarm tactics, John?"

He pretended to be mildly offended at the suggestion. "The threat of violence is often as effective as the use of it," he said sagely.

"You intend to avoid Jackson Pollard for the time being, I suppose?"

John nodded. "Not only cash was stolen last night, but also a valuable necklace the banker's wife neglected to lock away in their safe. I suggested Truesdale wait before filing a claim with Great Western, but he refused. Pollard won't take kindly to the claim."

"No, he won't."

"If he should call while you're here, tell him that blasted English impostor is responsible for the night's fiasco and I'm busy working to atone for his interference."

That wouldn't placate him, Sabina knew. Great Western's claims adjustor was not a tolerant man. Bungling was bungling, in his view, no matter what the reason or excuse.

"It's not likely either of us will have to talk to him today," she said. "I'll be leaving shortly and I expect to be gone the rest of the day."

"Your pickpocket investigation?"

"Yes. I spotted the woman at the Chutes yesterday afternoon and followed her to the Ambrosial Path on Kearney Street. She struck again there before I could stop her, and vanished into the crowd." Sabina added ruefully, "So you're not the only one who suffered a setback last evening."

"Were you able to identify her?"

"No. She wore a hat and clothing fashioned to obscure her features and conceal the shape of her body. She seemed familiar, though—I did get close enough to determine that. I'll know her the next time my path crosses hers. And when it does, she won't get away from me again."

"Nor Dodger Brown from me," John vowed.

7

QUINCANNON

Even in daylight hours Quincannon walked soft and wary, and made sure his Navy Colt was fully loaded, when he entered the heart of the nine square blocks that comprised the Barbary Coast.

The district, named for the coast of North Africa where Arab pirates attacked Mediterranean ships, housed every imaginable type of crime and vice and the thousands of thieves, cutthroats, footpads, swindlers, crooked gamblers, shanghaiers, and hordes of prostitutes who carried them out. Sudden death lurked in its crowded streets and buildings, the danger so great that no coppers in uniform ventured there after dark except in twos and threes and heavily armed with pistols, Bowie knives, and skull-bashing truncheons a foot long. Only the most notorious felons were pursued and caught by the police, and of those, few were ever punished for their crimes.

For the most part, though he was known as a detective, Quincannon was tolerated in the district. He had lived and worked in the city long enough to make the acquaintance of several Barbary Coast denizens, among them members of the underclass who were willing to sell information for cash; he caused no trouble and gave no grief while within its boundaries; and if he chanced to be after one of the scruffs who inhabited the Coast, he made the fact known to such prominent members of the ruling class as Ezra Bluefield—men who were not averse to giving up one of their own in return for money or favors. Sabina didn't quite approve of these sometimes less-than-scrupulous dealings, but she admitted that more often than not they produced results, and trusted him not to cross a line that would endanger the agency's reputation.

His first stop on today's venture into the Coast was Jack Foyles' on Stockton Street, a known hangout of Dodger Brown's. Foyles' was a shade less disreputable than most wine dumps, if only because it was equipped with a small lunch counter where its habitues could supplement their liquid sustenance with stale bread and a bowl of stew made from discarded vegetables, meat trimmings, bones, and chunks of tallow. Otherwise, there was little to distinguish it from its brethren. Barrels of "foot juice" and "red ink" behind a long bar, rows of rickety tables in three separate rooms lined with men and a few women of all types, ages, and backgrounds, a large open-floored area to accommodate those who had drunk themselves into a stupor. Porters who were themselves winos served the cheap and deadly drink in vessels supplied by junkmen—beer glasses, steins, pewter mugs, cracked soup bowls, tin cans. There was much loud talk, but never any laughter. Foyles' customers had long ago lost their capacity for mirth.

No one paid Quincannon the slightest attention as he moved slowly through the crowded rooms. Slurred voices that spanned the entire spectrum of society rolled surflike against his ears:

lawyers, sailors, poets, draymen, road bums, scholars, factory workers, petty criminals. There were no class distinctions here, nor seldom any trouble; the drinkers were all united by failure, bitterness, disillusionment, old age, disease, and unquenchable thirst for the grape. If there was anything positive to be said about wine dumps, it was that they were havens of democracy. Most customers would be here every day, or as often as they could panhandle or steal enough money to pay for their allotment of slow death, but a few, not yet far gone, were less frequent visitors—binge drinkers and slummers who found the atmosphere and the company to their liking. Many of these were crooks of one stripe or another, Dodger Brown among them.

But there was no sign of the Dodger today. Quincannon questioned two of the porters; one knew him and reported that Brown hadn't been to Foyles' in more than a week. Did the porter know where the lad might be found? The porter did not.

Quincannon left Foyles' and continued on his rounds of the devil's playground. During the daylight hours, the district seemed quiet, almost tame—a deceit if ever there was one. Less than a third as many predators and their prey prowled the ulcerous streets as could be found here after sundown; the worst of the rapacious were creatures of the night, and it was the dark hours when the preponderence of their victims—mainly sailors off the ships anchored along the Embarcadero—succumbed to the gaudy lure of sin and wickedness.

Some of the more notorious gambling dens and parlor houses were open for business, as were the more scabrous cribs and deadfalls, but they were thinly populated at this hour. And mostly absent was the nighttime babel of pianos, hurdy-gurdies, drunken laughter, the cries of shills and barkers, and the shouts and screams of victims. Quincannon was anything but a prude, having done his fair share of carousing during his drinking days, but the Coast had never attracted him. He preferred to satisfy his vices in more genteel surroundings.

Near Broadway there was a section of run-down hotels and lodging houses. He entered one of the latter and had words with the desk clerk, a runty chap named Galway with whom he'd done business before. Galway admitted to having seen Dodger Brown a time or two in recent weeks; he thought the Dodger might be residing at Foghorn Annie's, one the seaman's boarding houses on the waterfront.

Just outside the Barbary Coast on Montgomery Street, Quincannon found a hack—he and Sabina both preferred cabs to trolleys and cable cars when clients were paying expenses—and was shortly delivered to the Embarcadero. The trip turned out to be a waste of time. Scruffs were known to seek shelter among seafaring men now and then, by pretending to be former sailors themselves or by paying extra for the protective coloration. Dodger Brown was known at Foghorn Annie's, but not as a current resident. Visits to two other houses in the area produced neither the Dodger nor a clue to his whereabouts.

Hunger prodded Quincannon into a waterfront eatery, where he made short work of a dozen oysters on the half shell, a large bowl of fish stew, and a slab of peach pie. His appetite had always been prodigious. He had inherited all of his father's lusty appetites, in fact, along with his genteel Southern mother's love for poetry. Sabina had once remarked that he was a curious mixture of the gentle and the stone-hard, the sensitive and the unyielding. He supposed that was an accurate assessment, and the reason, perhaps, that he was a better detective than Thomas L. Quincannon, the fearless rival of Allan Pinkerton in the nation's capital during the Civil War. He knew his limitations, his weaknesses. His father had never once admitted to being wrong, considered himself invincible—and had been shot to death while on a fool's errand on the Baltimore docks. John Frederick Quincannon intended to die in bed at the age of ninety. And not alone, either.

Another hack returned him to the outskirts of the Barbary Coast. He found and spoke with three more individuals who had sold him information in the past—a Tar-Flat hoodlum named Luther James, a bunco steerer who went by the moniker of Breezy Ned, and a "blind" newspaper vendor known as Slew-foot. None of them had anything worthwhile to sell this time.

Enough of roaming the Coast, Quincannon decided. The time had come to call on Ezra Bluefield again. He had already approached the man once within the past week, seeking information on the house burglaries and possible fencing of the loot, and Bluefield grew testy when he was asked for too many favors. But if there was one lad in the devil's playground who could find out where Dodger Brown was holed up, it was Bluefield.

Quincannon walked to Terrific Street, as Pacific Avenue, the district's main artery, was called, turned into an alley, and entered a large building in mid-block. A sign in bloodred letters above the entrance proclaimed the establishment to be the SCARLET LADY SALOON. A smaller sign beneath it stated: EZRA BLUEFIELD, PROP.

At one time the Scarlet Lady had been a crimping joint, where seamen were fed drinks laced with laudanum and chloral hydrate and then carted off by shanghaiers and sold to venal shipmasters in need of crews. The Sailor's Union of the Pacific had ended the practice and forced the saloon's closure, but only until Bluefield had promised to give up his association with the shanghaiers and backed up the promise with generous bribes to city officials. The Scarlet Lady was now an "honest" deadfall in which percentage girls, bunco ploys, and rigged games of chance were used to separate seamen and other foolhardy patrons from their money.

As usual, Bluefield was in his office at the rear. He was an ex-miner who had had his fill of the rough-and-tumble life in various Western goldfields and vowed to end his own rowdy ways when he moved to San Francisco and opened the Scarlet Lady. He had taken no active part in the crimping activities, and was known to remain behind his locked office door when brawls broke out, as they often did; the team of bouncers he employed were charged with stifling trouble and keeping what passed for peace. It was his stated intention to one day own a better class of saloon in a better neighborhood, and as a result he cultivated the company and goodwill of respectable citizens. Quincannon was one of them, largely because he had once prevented a rival saloon owner from puncturing Bluefield's hide with a bullet.

Bluefield was drinking beer and counting profits, two of his favorite activities. The profits must have been considerable, for he was in a jovial mood and seemed not to mind being visited again so soon.

"I've nothing for you yet, John, my lad," he said. "You know I'll send word when I do."

"I'm the one with news today," Quincannon said. "The housebreaker I'm after is Dodger Brown."

"The Dodger, is it? Well, I'm not surprised. How did you tumble?"

"I came within a hair of nabbing him in the act last night. He escaped through no fault of mine."

"So he knows you're onto him?"

"I don't believe he does, as dark as it was."

"He'll still be in the city then, you're thinking."

"Or somewhere in the Bay Area."

Bluefield raised his mug of lager with one thick finger, drank, licked foam off his mustached upper lip. The mustache was an impressive coal-black handlebar, its ends waxed to rapier points, of which he was inordinately proud. "And mayhap old Ezra can find out where he's hanging his hat, eh?"

"If anyone can, it's you."

"You flatter me, Quincannon. Not that I mind."

"Then you'll put out word on Dodger Brown?"

"I will. For a favor in return."

"Name it."

"There is a saloon and restaurant just up for sale in the Uptown Tenderloin. The Redemption, on Ellis Street."

"I know it. A respected establishment."

"I'm looking to buy it," Bluefield said. "It's past time I put this hellhole up for sale and leave the Barbary Coast for good. There'll never be a place better suited or better named for the likes of me to own so that I can die a respectable citizen. I have the money, I've made overtures, but the owners aren't convinced my intentions are honorable. They're afraid I have plans to turn the Redemption into a fancy uptown copy of the Scarlet Lady."

"And you've no such plans."

"None, lad, I swear it."

"Is it a letter of reference you're after?"

"It is. Your name carries weight in certain quarters in this city."

"No greater weight than yours in other quarters."

"The letter in exchange for my help, then?"

"You'll have it tomorrow, by messenger."

Bluefield lumbered to his feet and thumped Quincannon's back with a meaty paw. "You won't regret it, lad. You and Mrs. Carpenter will always have free meals at Ezra Bluefield's Redemption."

Quincannon had never once turned down the offer of anything for free—anything reasonably legitimate, that was—nor would his thrifty Scot's blood ever permit him to do so. But it wouldn't do to press his luck with a man of Bluefield's mercurial temperament.

"I'll settle for the whereabouts of Dodger Brown," he lied glibly.

"Within forty-eight hours," Bluefield said, "and that's a bloody promise. Even if it means hiring a gang of men to comb through every rattrap from here to China Basin."

8

SABINA

Sabina spent the rest of the morning in pursuit of information from the pickpocket's victims and their families, following a route she had mapped out after studying the list Lester Sweeney had given her.

Her first destination was the residence of Mr. William Buchanan on Green Street near Van Ness Avenue. Mr. Buchanan was not at home, the maid who answered the door told her. He and Mrs. Buchanan had gone to their country house on the Peninsula for two weeks.

The driver of the hansom she'd hired and left waiting took her next to Webster Street in the Western Addition, where she had somewhat better luck. The house there was large and well kept, and its owner, John Greenway, the man who had been robbed of a wallet containing nearly forty dollars, chanced to be home. He greeted Sabina cordially, and when she presented her card and stated her purpose in calling, he showed her into the front parlor where he introduced her to his wife, who was quite obviously expecting a child.

"Of course we'll help in any way we can," he said then, "but

I'm afraid there isn't much we can tell you. I didn't see the woman who robbed me. Mrs. Greenway did, but only a fleeting glimpse."

Mrs. Greenway nodded. "She was rather tall and wore a white hat with a sun veil that covered part of her face. That's all I remember about her."

"What were the circumstances of the theft?" Sabina asked.

"We had ridden the water slide and stopped at the refeshment stand for a glass of lemonade," Greenway said. "The ride was ill-advised—it made Mrs. Greenway feel unwell. There was a large crowd watching a juggler near the gates, and while we were passing through it the woman bumped into me and I felt a sudden sharp pain in my side. It caused me to stumble and fall to one knee. My wife and a young fellow in the crowd helped me up, and that was when I discovered the theft."

"What caused the sharp pain you felt?"

"I don't know. I thought at the time that it was a gastric attack, a result of the food we'd eaten combined with the ride, but upon reflection it seemed more a jabbing or pricking sensation."

A jabbing or pricking sensation. Sabina had overheard the frock-coated victim on the Cocktail Route last evening make a similar complaint, which he attributed to having eaten too many oysters on the half-shell at the Bank Exchange. Coincidence? Or a clever pickpocket using some sharp object to distract her mark—an object such as a hatpin?

No one came to the door at either of the next two victims' residences, but at a small Eastlake-style Victorian near Washing-

ton Square, Sabina was greeted by the plump young daughter
of Mr. George Anderson. Her father was at his place of business, the Orpheum, a vaudeville house on O'Farrell Street, she
said, and her mother was out shopping. Did she know anything about the robbery of her father at the Chutes? Oh, yes,
she had witnessed it.

In the small front parlor, Ellen Anderson rang for the housekeeper and ordered tea. It came quickly, accompanied by a plate
of ginger cookies. Sabina took one as Miss Anderson poured
and prattled on about how exciting it was to make the aquain-
tance of a lady detective.

Sabina directed her back to the business at hand by asking,
"Were you alone with your father when his purse was stolen?"

"No, my mother and my brother were also there. But they
didn't see what happened."

"Tell me what you saw, please."

"We were near the merry-go-round. It was very crowded,
children waiting to board and parents watching their children on the ride. Allen, my brother, was trying to persuade
me to ride with him. He's only ten years old, so a merry-go-
round is a thrill for him, but I'm sixteen, and it seems so very
childish. . . ."

"Did you ride anyway?"

"No. But Allen did. We were watching him when suddenly
my father took hold of his middle, groaned, twisted round, and
staggered a few paces. Mother and I both thought he'd had a
seizure. We managed to keep him from falling, and when we'd
righted him he found all his money was gone."

"What caused him to take hold of his middle?"

"He didn't know. Gastric distress, he supposed."

"Does he normally suffer from digestive problems?"

Ellen Anderson shook her dark ringlets. "But earlier we'd eaten hot sausages at the refreshment stand."

"Did his distress continue afterward?"

"Father's not one to talk about his ailments, but . . . no, I don't believe so. We assumed the sausages were what affected him and that the thief had taken advantage of the moment."

Not so, Sabina thought. And definitely not a coincidence that the dip's victims had all suffered sharp pains before being relieved of their valuables. There was little doubt now that the woman's method of operation was to inflict physical pain on her victims, as well as the kind caused by the loss of their valuables.

Two more fruitless stops left her with a final name on the list: Henry Holbrooke, on Jessie Street. Jessie was something of an anomaly as the new century approached—a mostly residential street that ran for several blocks through the heart of the business district, midway between Market and Mission. Old, crabbed houses and an occasional small business establishment flanked it, fronted by tiny yards and backed by barns and sheds.

The muslin curtains in the bay window of Henry Holbrooke's house were open, but Sabina's ring was not immediately answered. She twisted the bell again, and after a few moments she heard shuffling footsteps and the door opened. The inner hallway was so dark that she could scarcely make out the person standing there—a thin woman of upper middle age dressed entirely in black.

"Mrs. Holbrooke?"

"Yes." The woman's voice cracked, as if rusty from disuse.

Sabina gave her name and explained her mission. The woman made no move to take the card she extended.

"May I speak with your husband?" Sabina asked.

"My husband is dead."

"My condolences. May I ask when he passed on?"

"Ten days ago."

That would have been less than a week after he was robbed of his billfold at the Chutes. He had been one of the pickpocket's first victims.

"May I come in, Mrs. Holbrooke?"

"I'd rather you didn't. I've been . . . tearful. I don't wish for anyone to see me after I've been grieving."

"I understand. But could you tell me the cause of your husband's death?"

Mrs. Holbrooke hesitated before answering. Then, with a sigh, "An internal infection."

"Had he been ill long?"

"He had never been ill. Not a day in his life."

"What was the cause of the infection?"

"The doctor didn't know. He really wasn't a very good physician, but we couldn't afford a better one after the two hundred dollars was stolen. My husband died here, in my arms. I was forced to sell my jewelry—what little I had left—so he could have a decent burial."

"I'm so sorry," Sabina said sincerely. "May I ask why he carried so much money on an outing at the amusement park?"

"My husband never went anywhere without our cash reserves

in that old beaded leather billfold of his. He was afraid to leave the money at home—this neighborhood is not what it once was. And he distrusted banks."

Sabina was in sympathy with the former reason but not the latter. Henry Holbrooke would still be alive if he had kept their funds in a bank.

The older woman leaned heavily on the doorjamb; like Jessie Street, she gave the impression of slow disintegration. "If you apprehend the thief, is there any chance you'll recover the money?"

Most likely it had already been spent, but Sabina said, "I'll make every effort to do so."

"If you do recover any of it, will you please return it to me? I ask not so much for myself, but for Henry's memory. It pains me that I'm not able to purchase a decent marker for his grave."

"Of course."

Sabina took her leave. It would have been cruel to share her grim thoughts with Henry Holbrooke's widow, but it seemed probable that the infection her husband had died from had been caused by the deep jab of a sharp and unclean hatpin. In which case the woman responsible was not only a pickpocket but a murderess.

It was just one o'clock when Sabina dismissed the hansom driver near the gates to the Chutes Amusement Park. The place was not quite as crowded as the day before, she found, either because word of the thefts had spread or because the afternoon was cloudy and there was a chill breeze swirling in from the ocean. If the hatpin dip appeared again today, she ought to be relatively easy to spot.

But she didn't appear. At least Sabina saw no one who employed the woman's methods of picking her marks. She may have come early and left early, or come briefly and found no potential victim to her liking during the three hours Sabina roamed the grounds. Or stayed away entirely because of the weather. In any event there was no report of a robbery at the Chutes that day. A brief conversation with Lester Sweeney in his office confirmed it.

Shortly past four by the small gold watch she kept pinned to the bodice of her shirtwaist, Sabina left the Chutes and hired another hansom to take her downtown. She was tired, and stuffed uncomfortably full of sausage, ice cream, and cotton candy, having overindulged out of frustration during her wanderings. She didn't relish another long walk along the Cocktail Route, but since the pickpocket had successfully preyed there last night, it seemed likely to be one of her regular haunts.

Perhaps so, but Sabina saw no sign of the woman anywhere between Sutter Street and the Palace Hotel, or on the crowded Ambrosial Path where last night's robbery had taken place. There were far more men abroad, and the women among them were noticable, but the pickpocket was adept at costume disguise. Sabina might easily have missed her in the streams of businessmen, gay blades, *nymphes du pavé,* and adventuresome young ladies who packed the sidewalks.

At six o'clock, as weary and chilled as she was, Sabina considered going home to Russian Hill. But Stephen had instilled tenacity of purpose in her during her time with the Pinkertons, and the fact that she was after a murderess as well as a pick-pocket was an added incentive to continue her search awhile longer. Her quarry, for reasons of her own, might have decided against prowling anywhere today or tonight. But she might also have decided to ply her trade in yet another place that afforded profitable pickings, such as the nightly bazaar on Market Street opposite the Palace Hotel—a place worth investigating.

9

SABINA

The open field at dusk was brightly lit by lanterns and torch-lights, and packed with gaily colored wagons presided over by an array of pitchmen; phrenology and palmistry booths; the usual hodgepodge of temperance speakers, organ grinders, balloon and pencil sellers, beggars, and ad carriers passing out saloon handbills for free lunches; and a constant flow of gawk-ers and curiosity seekers, which Sabina joined. Music filled the air from many sources, each competing with the other. The loudest was the Salvation Army band pouring forth its solemn repentance message.

From the wagons men hawked both well-known and ob-scure patent remedies: Tiger Balm, Miracle Wort, Burdock's Blood Bitters, Turkish Pile Ointment, Dr. Sage's Catarrh Rem-edy, Lydia Pinkham's Vegetable Compound for Ladies. Others offered services on the spot: matrimonial advice, spinal re-alignment, head massages. Sabina, who had attended the ba-zaar with John after moving to San Francisco—a must, he'd said, for new residents—recognized several of the participants: the Great Ferndon, Herman the Healer, Rodney Strongheart.

The din rose as a shill for Dr. Wallmann's Nerve and Brain Tonic stood in his red-and-yellow coach to extol the alleged virtues of the product. "This miracle tonic," he intoned, "cures all bilious derangements, including but not limited to dyspepsia, costiveness, erysipelas, palpitations of the heart, and persistent and obstinate constipation, and drives out the foul corruption that contaminates the blood and causes decay. It stimulates and enlivens the vital functions, being as it is a pure vegetable compound and free from all mineral poisons. It promotes energy and strength, restores and preserves health, and infuses new life and vigor throughout the entire system."

Sabina smiled ironically as she passed by. The only thing Dr. Wallmann's tonic promoted was drunkenness, since its central ingredient, as was that of most such patent medicines, was alcohol.

The crowd of onlookers was largely composed of men; the women among them were for the most part prostitutes strolling in pairs and wearing flirtatious smiles, or the wives and lady friends of men too poor to afford the luxuries of the Cocktail Route. There were relatively few unescorted women, and those Sabina encountered were the wrong age or size or facial structure, or not outfitted in the sort of concealing hat and dress the pickpocket favored.

On a platform at the back of one of the wagons, a dancer draped in filmy veils was peforming. Unfortunately for her, during an awkward pirouette, the veils slipped and fell open to reveal her scarlet long johns—an accident that elicited howls of laughter from the watchers. At another wagon nearby, a salesman began expounding upon the virtues of Sydney's Celebrated Cough Killer, only to fall into a fit of coughing, which resulted in more derisive laughter. In the group that stood watching him was a lone woman in a rather large hat. Sabina moved close enough to determine that the face under the hat's brim was elderly, with age-fissured cheeks and gray hair. She moved on.

Wide-brimmed hat with bedraggled ostrich feathers: a badly scarred young woman whose affliction made Sabina flinch. Toque draped in fading tulle: red hair and freckles. Another feather-bedecked chapeau: porcine, with a double chin and heavily rouged cheeks

The proprietor of a small, tawdry freak exhibit urged Sabina to surrender five cents for the privilege of viewing a deformed infant preserved in formaldehyde. She declined—not at all pleasantly.

Extravagant hat with many layers of feathers and a stuffed bird's head protruding at the front: long blond hair and an unblemished chin.

A pair of temperance speakers warning of the evils of drink and painful death from diseased kidneys and handing out tracts to support their claims. No, thank you.

Yet another bird-themed hat. What *was* the fascination with wearing dead avian creatures on one's head? The woman beneath the brim looked not much healthier than the bird that had died to grace her headpiece.

Another pitchman tried to entice Sabina to buy a bottle of something called the Kickapoo Indians Tape-Worm Secret. An emphatic no to that, also.

In front of the next wagon, a single woman wearing rather baggy clothes and a green hat with a wide brim drawn down low on her forehead caught Sabina's eye. The woman seemed less interested in the miraculous electrified belt filled with cayenne pepper whose purveyor was claiming would cure any debilitation, than in the faces of the men grouped around her. Sabina's blood quickened. She moved closer—close enough to recognize the large blue glass Horner hatpin overlaid with gold that decorated the green hat.

The woman evidently found none of the men around her suitable prey. She moved on at a leisurely pace, her gaze roaming all the while. Sabina followed a few paces behind.

The pickpocket stopped to listen to the Salvation Army band. Paused again in front of a shill exalting the virtue of White's Female Complaint Cure. Accepted a flyer from a man hawking the Single Tax doctrine and pretended to read it by the light of a flickering torch. All the while her head and her eyes continued their restless search.

An elderly chap leaning on a cane, walking haltingly nearly ten yards away, struck Sabina as a likely candidate. But no, the dip passed him by. A well-attired man carrying a malaca walking stick. No. A tall blond gent dressed in a broadloom suit and gaudy vest. No.

More wandering. More pretended interest in the shows and wares. Sabina was careful to maintain a measured distance, with her small body shielded from the woman's view by those of the larger men.

In front of the bright red-and-yellow coach belonging to the purveyor of Dr. Wallmann's Nerve and Brain Tonic, the woman stopped again. Stood watching as a fat, middle-aged man wearing a plug hat and sporting a gold watch chain questioned the pitchman, then examined one of the brown bottles as if he were having difficulty making up his mind whether or not to buy it. Sabina sensed he was the dip's choice even before the woman sidled up next to him, stretching an arm up as she did so to snatch the Horner pin free from her hat.

Sabina elbowed in behind her, calling out a warning that was lost in the sudden shrieking of an organ grinder's monkey. The fat man suddenly twisted, clutching at his corporation, and the dip had his purse. She was turning away when Sabina reached her and caught hold of her right arm, bending it so that she dropped the purse, then pinning the arm behind her back. The pickpocket emitted a cry of pain, then a curse, and began struggling and trying to stab her captor with the hatpin she held in her other hand. Sabina pulled the arm higher, making her cry out again, while she clutched at the dangerously flailing wrist.

Men surged in around them, voices raised in alarmed query. Sabina cried, "Help me, she's a pickpocket!" to the man nearest her—a mistake, as it turned out. The man made a clumsy effort to assist, which earned him a puncture wound from the slashing pin. He yelled in pain and reeled into the two women, throwing Sabina off balance and allowing the dip to squirm out of her grasp. A hatpin thrust grazed Sabina's arm, then she felt a painful blow to her ribs—and the woman lunged away past the medicine pitchman's wagon, bowling him over when he tried to stop her.

Sabina gave chase, but to no avail. Once again her quarry managed to escape into the milling crowd.

As galling as this was, there was some small comfort in the fact that she now knew who she was after. She had had a clear look at the woman's face during their struggle, and was certain of her identity: Clara Wilds, who had evidently forsaken the extortion racket for the equally lucrative trade of cut-purse.

What made the identification even more provocative was the fact that Clara Wilds's last-known consort was Dodger Brown, the slippery yegg John suspected of being responsible for the recent string of home burglaries.

10

QUINCANNON

He was late reaching the agency on Thursday morning, through no fault of his own. The cable car he regularly rode to Market Street from his apartment building on Leavenworth failed to come by—some sort of mechanical problem, probably, as all too often happened with the cable and trolley lines. The distance was too far to walk; he hired a cab instead, with every intention of adding the cost to the Great Western expense account.

Sabina was present when he arrived, but about to depart. She was in the process of putting on her long coat over her shirtwaist and bell-bottomed skirt—a slender vision in no need of the tight corsetting most women favored. He held his scrutiny to a minimum; the tight set of her mouth plainly indicated that she was in no mood today for bandinage.

He shifted his gaze to his desktop, which was conspicuously bare. "No word yet from Ezra Bluefield," he said. Messages from the Scarlet Lady's owner sometimes came at night or in the early morning hours, in the form of an envelope slipped under the door. "Dodger Brown's hideout must be well concealed. Either that, or he's riding the rods for parts unknown."

"If he is still in the area," Sabina said, "I hope it's in the company of Clara Wilds."

"The extortionist? Why mention her name?"

"She has another trade now. Picking pockets. She's the dip who has been menacing customers at the Chutes and on the Cocktail Route."

"Ah. You crossed paths with her again."

"Last night at the bazaar opposite the Palace." Sabina's voice was bitter. "I caught her robbing another mark, but she got away from me again. She's as slippery as an eel."

"What happened?"

Sabina provided terse explanations, making no excuse for Clara Wilds having now twice eluded her. She was even more determined to locate and nab the woman, now that she knew Wilds's modus operandi had rendered her a murderess as well as a thief.

"Did she recognize you?" Quincannon asked.

"She may have. I'm not certain. In any case, the close call may keep her from plying her new trade for a time."

"Gone to ground with Dodger Brown, mayhap."

"There's no mention in her dossier that the pair ever cohabited, merely that they were known consorts."

"Do you have her last known address?"

"A rooming house on the edge of the Barbary Coast. The information is some months old, but perhaps someone there has knowledge of her current whereabouts. That's where I'm bound now."

Quincannon said, "I'd go with you, but I should keep myself available for a message from Bluefield. And I have an appointment with R. W. Jackson at one o'clock."

"I'm perfectly capable of pursuing Clara Wilds on my own."

"Of course you are—"

"I'll telephone or send word by messenger if I learn anything you should know."

When Sabina had gone, Quincannon spied the Wilds dossier on her desk and sat down to read it over. The information on the woman was scant. Born on a farm in the San Joaquin Valley twenty-eight years ago; orphaned at age ten and sent to live with an aunt in Carson City, Nevada, from whom she picked up some of her wicked habits—extortion primary among them. Expert at collecting damning information on individuals in positions of trust or power and then using her knowledge to extract cash or favors from them. Arrested and tried for attempted fraud in Nevada, but acquitted for lack of evidence. Moved to San Francisco four years ago and arrested twice here on similar charges, the second time last year—Sabina's initial encounter with her, the agency having been hired by the victim—but again escaped conviction as a result of police and judicial incompetence.

Since then, there was no record of any criminal activity. To the unschooled eye, Wilds might have been inactive during this period. At the extortion game, possibly, but not in her other criminal pursuit. She may have been picking pockets for years, and managed to avoid being caught, or she may have learned the game more recently and spent the past year or so perfecting it. Not surprising in either case; criminals of both sexes sometimes adopted new and more lucrative or less risky specialties.

If Wilds was still keeping company with Dodger Brown, Quincannon reflected, it would make his and Sabina's tasks much easier. Snaffle one, snaffle both. The difficulty lay in finding one or the other.

His first order of business was to write the letter of reference he'd promised Ezra Bluefield. When he left to keep his one o'clock appointment with R. W. Jackson, he would give the letter to the messenger service in the building next door. It would cost extra to have it delivered to the Barbary Coast, but that was a small price to pay for Bluefield's continued assistance.

Next he finished his report on the Jackson investigation, a chore he disliked even though it allowed him to do a certain amount of justifiable boasting; he was a man of action, not a sedentary wordsmith. The client, R. W. Jackson, was an investment broker who ought to have known better than to fall victim to a stock swindle, but instead had been gullible enough to lose five thousand dollars to a pair of confidence men known in the underworld as Lonesome Jack Vereen and the Nevada Kid. Quincannon had tracked down the thimbleriggers, who were in Redwood City running another of their con games, the gold-brick swindle, and not only pinched them but recovered the full amount of R. W. Jackson's loss. The five thousand dollars was being held in escrow for him, payable once he had in turn paid the agency's fee. Which he would do today upon receipt of the final report.

Still no word from Bluefield by the time Quincannon finished. He was about to put on his coat when the door opened to admit a frog-faced youth wearing a cap with a sewn decal proclaiming his employers to be Citywide Messenger Service. Quincannon's first thought was that old Ezra had taken to employing a legitimate service rather than sending a Coast runner as was his usual custom, but no such luck. Nor was the message from his partner. "For Mr. John Quincannon, Esquire," the youth said—a term neither Sabina nor the deadfall owner would ever have used.

He accepted the envelope, signed for it, and tore it open. The messenger, looking hopeful, remained standing in place. "Well?" Quincannon said to him. "You've done your duty, lad. Off with you!"

The command, accompanied by a scowl and a step forward, sent the youth into a hurried exit. If Sabina had been there, she would have insisted that he be tipped the customary nickel. But Sabina wasn't there and Quincannon didn't believe in tipping. As a matter of fact, he felt that he'd done the lad a good turn by *not* giving him a nickel; at his young age, he would only have spent it profligately.

The envelope contained a sheet of bond paper that bore the letterhead and signature of Andrew Costain, Attorney-at-Law. The curt message, written in a rather shaky hand, read:

I should like to discuss a business matter with you. If you will call on me at my offices at your earliest convenience, I am sure you will find it to your financial advantage.

A business matter, eh? It must have something to do with the burglaries; Costain had never before sought his professional assistance. The lawyer's name was one of the three left on Dodger Brown's target list, and the man had struck him as a Nervous Nelly.

Quincannon glanced again at the paper. The number of lawyers he liked and trusted could have danced together on the bowl of his pipe. The phrase "financial advantage," however, was too powerful a lure to be ignored.

"At your service, Mr. Costain," he said aloud. "For the right price."

11

SABINA

The boarding house the dossier had listed as Clara Wilds's last known address was on Washington Street south of Broadway, on the fringe of the Barbary Coast. Upper-class women were seldom seen in this neighborhood, and none would dare to walk the squalid and dangerous streets within the one-square-mile of gambling hells, cheapjack saloons, brothels, and opium dens nearby. Sabina's hack driver looked startled when she gave him the lodging house address. For a moment she thought he might try to dissuade her, but then he shrugged and urged his horse away along the cobbled streets.

The lodging house was a dilapidated wooden structure with cupolas at either end of its sagging roof, and a faded sign proclaiming HOUSEKEEPING ROOMS next to the front door. Trash clung to the foundation; its windows were speckled with dirt; a bundle of discarded newspapers lay on its front steps. The woman who answered Sabina's ring owned a coarse middle-aged face and gray stringy hair, and wore a stained and ill-fitting housedress; most of her front teeth were missing, and the few that were left were chipped and discolored.

Her surprise at finding a well-dressed young woman on her doorstep was evident. "What do you want?" she demanded.

Sabina neither presented her card nor otherwise identified herself as a detective. Such would gain her nothing but scorn and suspicion. Women such as this landlady would find it difficult to believe that one of their sex was a professional detective, and would be close-mouthed as a result.

She said only, "I am looking for a woman named Clara Wilds."

"Who?"

"Clara Wilds. She was one of your tenants eighteen months ago—"

"Eighteen months! How do you expect me to remember that far back? I can't remember half the 'ladies' I got living here now."

Sabina described Clara Wilds. The landlady started to shake her head, but then the light of remembrance came into her eyes. "Oh, her. A trollop and worse. She's long gone, and good riddance."

"When did she move out?"

"You mean when did I throw her out. Right after she got out of jail. The police come here and arrested her—just the kind of thing I don't need. Gives my place a bad name. My roomers ain't exactly the cream of society, but they're not criminals, either."

"Do you have any idea where she moved to?"

"No, and I don't care. What do you want her for, anyway?"

"A personal matter. Do you know a friend of Clara Wilds's named Dodger Brown?"

"Who?"

"Dodger Brown. A small man of about forty, with a fondness for wine. She was known to keep company with him."

"Not in my place, she didn't. I don't allow no men in my house, not even in the parlor. I wouldn't even let her uncle in if he come calling."

"Uncle? I didn't know Clara Wilds had an uncle."

"Well, he don't advertise the fact."

Likely he was an uncle by marriage, Sabina thought, which was why the information had escaped mention in the dossier. "Where does he reside?"

"How should I know? All I know is where he has his business."

"And where would that be?"

"The California Market. Sometimes when that trollop needed money she'd help Tony out in his fish stall."

"How do you know that?"

"He told me, that's how. Back when he knew she was lodging with me. I buy my fish and seafood from him."

"Has he said anything about his niece since you evicted her?"

The landlady frowned in thought. "Once, last year. They had some kinda falling out. She must of stole from him, that's the kind she is."

"Did he tell you that was the reason for the falling out?"

"No. You want to know, maybe he'll tell you. But I wouldn't count on it if I was you."

"What's his last name?"

The woman shrugged. "Tony's Fish Stand, that's all I know."

And with that, she shut the door in Sabina's face.

———

The open-air California Market, known far and wide as San Francisco's "entrepôt of foods," ran for an entire block from Pine to California streets between Montgomery and Kearney. Founded in 1867, when an Irishman nicknamed The Oyster King began selling oysters harvested from the bay tidelands near Burlingame, it was now a vast bazaar of stalls dispensing meat, fresh fish and shellfish, produce, and flowers to hotels and restaurants as well as private individuals.

Sabina had been there a number of times before, to shop and once with Callie to have a meal at another of the market's prominent features, Sam's Grill. It was an enticing place, filled with a tantalizing mixture of aromas stirred and carried by a breeze from the bay. As always, the aisles were crowded with women carrying shopping baskets, men pushing handcarts loaded with a variety of goods to and from the vendors.

She stopped one of the men to ask where Tony's Fish Stand was located. He informed her it was near Pine Street, midway within the marketplace. She made her way through the throng of shoppers, ignoring the entreaties of sellers hawking their wares. Poultry, lamb, beef, seafood. Pineapples, alligator pears, papayas from Hawaii, and great bunches of ripe bananas from Mexico. Locally grown fruits and vegetables. Freshly baked breads, cakes, pies. Freshly roasted coffee beans. And such appetizing cooked foods as grilled sausages, Indian kabobs, and fried calamari.

The aroma of cooking sausages reminded her that it was past lunchtime and she was hungry. And sausages, in her opinion, were one of man's greatest concoctions. The thought of a grilled bratwurst on rye bread made her mouth water. Her appetite, always healthy, had returned with a vengeance once she'd come to terms with Stephen's death. She never gained a pound, however, no matter how much she ate; her slender waist was the same as it had been on her wedding day. Sometimes she thought it unseemly to be so fond of food, but as John had said to her once, God would not have put so much of it on earth if it wasn't meant to be eaten. How could she do less than her part in obeying His will?

Tony's Fish Stand was a large and thriving enterprise, its ice bins displaying a wide array of fresh fish and seafood. The filets of smoked salmon looked particularly good; Sabina thought she would purchase a piece for her supper.

Three employees were serving customers and restocking bins. Sabina pushed up to the nearest of them. When she asked if he was Tony, he shook his head and called to a handsome, mustached man with graying black hair, "This lady wants you, Mr. Antonelli."

Tony Antonelli's eyes sparkled when he saw Sabina. But his examination was appreciative only, without either guile or leer. He filled a tiny paper cup and held it out to her. "Bay shrimp, *bella signora*," he said. "Best anywhere in the Market."

She smiled and took the cup. The shrimp were indeed fresh and succulent.

"You like to buy some for your supper?"

"I was thinking of a piece of smoked salmon. But yes, a quarter pound of the shrimp as well."

"Come right up."

He chose one of the best-looking fillets. As he began wrapping it and the shrimp, Sabina said, "Would you mind if I asked you a few questions, Mr. Antonelli?"

"Mr. Antonelli . . . pah. Tony the Fish Monger, that's what everybody calls me. Questions about my fish?"

"No. Your niece, Clara Wilds."

Tony's cheerful demeanor disappeared. He frowned, and one of his mustaches twitched. "Why you want to know about her?"

"I'm very anxious to find her."

"Why? What you want with her, *bella signora* like you?"

Sabina debated the wisdom of identifying herself, decided to take the chance, and presented him with her card.

His frown deepened as he studied it. "Lady detective," he said, but not in the way so many did, as if the concept was difficult to grasp. He hesitated, then motioned her off to an uncrowded side of the stall. In a low flat voice he asked, "Clara, she's in trouble again, hah?"

"I'm afraid so."

"What she do, steal money?"

"Yes. By picking pockets."

"*Dio mio!* You sure?"

"I'm afraid so."

"That Sally woman, that's where she learn that game. Sure."

"Sally?"

"Friend of Clara's aunt Bess," Tony said disgustedly. "Some friend—a thief. Used to be pickpocket when she's younger, before her hands go bad with *artrite*."

"Sally Tatum?"

"That's right. You know her?"

"I know of her." Dippin' Sal, one of the more famous cutpurses who had plied her trade in Virginia City in the early days of the Comstock Lode. She must be in her sixties now, and long retired if her hands had become crippled with arthritis. "Is she still living in Nevada?"

"No, she's come live down here now."

"Do you know where?"

"With her son Victor. Another crook, that one. Whole family of *truffatori*."

"What's Victor's last name?" Dippin' Sal had been married twice.

"Pope. He owns hardware store, but hammers and nails, they not all he buys and sells."

"Stolen property?"

Tony shrugged elaborately, then made a dismissive gesture. "I don't have nothing to do with crooks like him."

"Do you know where his hardware store is located? Or where he lives?"

"In the Mission district. I know because my niece say so when she works for me last year, before she . . ." He didn't finish the sentence. Instead he scowled and muttered something in Italian under his breath. "You think maybe that's where you find Clara?"

"It's possible."

"And then what? You arrest her?"

"If I don't, the police will."

He nodded. "*Cosi sia*. You tell her something for me, eh?"

"What's that?"

"Don't come to her uncle Tony for money to get out of jail. She's no longer *la familia,* you understand?"

"I understand, Mr. Antontelli."

"Tony. Tony the Fish Monger."

12

SABINA

The hansom clattered along bustling Mission Street, past shops and sidewalk stands and the oldest building in the city, Mission Dolores, the adobe church having been established by Father Junipero Serra the same year as the Declaration of Independence was signed.

A few blocks farther on, the driver turned off onto Twenty-second Street and urged his horse uphill. Victor Pope's house was on Jersey Street between Sanchez and Noe, a fact Sabina had learned by stopping off at the agency long enough to consult their office copy of the city directory. She had also gleaned the address of the hardware store Victor Pope operated, but it was much more likely that his mother would be at his home than at his place of business.

The small clapboard house was in the middle of a block lined with similar dwellings. Rosebushes bloomed in the front yard behind a white picket fence. Even among those who trespassed frequently across the boundaries of the law, the Popes were probably considered better-than-average citizens in a respectable working-class neighborhood such as this. The crime of buying and selling stolen property was a relatively inconsequential one in a city where many more serious felonies occurred on a daily basis, and if Victor Pope were accused of being a fenceman, he would no doubt claim he had no knowledge that the items he traded in were stolen property. As for Dippin' Sal, he would present her as an honest but poor elderly relative.

Sabina asked the hansom driver to wait for her, and mounted the front steps. There was no bell push, so she rapped on the door. Slow, shuffling sounds came from within, the door opened a few inches, and a wizened face peered out at her. The woman's eyes were cloudy with cataracts, and the hand that clutched the door's edge was knobbed and misshapen with arthritis.

"Mrs. Tatum?" Sabina asked.

"Who're you?"

"A friend of Clara Wilds."

"Clara don't have friends look like you, missy. What you want with me?"

"She mentioned your name to me once. I thought you might know where I can find her."

"If you're her friend, how come you don't know?"

"We've fallen out of touch."

"What you want with her?" the old woman asked suspiciously.

"A business matter. She did me a favor awhile ago and now I have a chance to return it."

"What kind of favor?"

"The money-making kind."

"Hah. What's your game, missy?"

"The same one you used to be in. The one you taught her." Sabina punctuated those statements by reaching up to finger her Charles Horner hatpin. "Only my territory is the Uptown Tenderloin."

There were several seconds of silence. Then Dippin' Sal nodded once, satisfied, and her crabbed fingers opened the door all the way. Past her Sabina had glimpses of a small front parlor with striped wallpaper and old, worn furniture decorated with antimacassars.

"I can't tell you where Clara's livin' now. She used to come around regular, now she don't. Can't be bothered anymore with an old woman taught her most every trick she knows."

"Including the hatpin diversion?"

"No, she thought that one up herself. Pretty smart. You're using it, too, eh?"

Sabina nodded. "Do you know anyone who can tell me where to find her?"

"Talk to my son. Likely he knows."

"Fencing for her, is he?"

"And laying her, too, likely, not that he'd ever admit it to me. My Victor's the same as his father was. Same as most men, come to that."

"Is Clara still keeping company with Dodger Brown?"

"The Dodger? Maybe she is, maybe she isn't. How would I know?" Dippin' Sal raised and dropped her crippled hands. She smacked her lips as if there was a bitter taste in her mouth. "I'm just an old woman nobody cares about no more. But I was good in my day—the best there was workin' the Comstock, smooth as silk. You better believe that, missy. The damn best there was, and I didn't need no hatpin, either."

Pope's Hardware Store stood on the corner of Twenty-third Street and Guerrero. Its wood floors were buckled with age, so that one had a sensation of walking on the deck of a ship at sea, and it smelled not unpleasantly of creosote and sawdust. A heavyset man with thick, black hair who was selling paintbrushes to a customer in work clothes concluded the transaction and rang up the sale on an ornate gold-filigree cash register. Sabina waited until the customer had left and there was no one else in sight before she approached the heavyset man.

"Are you Victor Pope?" she asked.

"At your service."

"I understand you know Clara Wilds."

The name made him wary. "Who told you that?"

"Your mother."

"Why would she—? Say, who are you?"

"Call me Lil. I need to get in touch with Clara. Dippin' Sal said you'd have her address."

"Old woman can't keep her mouth shut—" Pope blinked. "What name was that?"

"You heard me right. I'm in the same profession your mother used to be and Clara is now."

Pope glanced furtively toward the door, as if he were afraid someone might have crept in while he wasn't looking. He passed a hand over his coarse features. "How come you're looking for Clara?"

"I have a business proposition for her. One that'll fatten both our purses. And yours as well, if you're fencing for her."

"Doing what for her?"

"Pardon the pun, Mr. Pope, but let's not fence. We both know you've been disposing of the swag from Clara's robberies."

Pope decided there was no point in further denial. "My mother tell you that, too?"

"She didn't have to."

"But she did, didn't she? Old woman hates me. I took her in when she got all crippled up, and still she hates me. I don't know why."

He might not, but Sabina had a good idea of the reason.

"What else did the old lady say? That I've been seeing Clara on the sly? Well, it's a lie. A damn lie."

No, it wasn't. The lie was Pope's, not Dippin' Sal's. It was in his close-set brown eyes as well as on his lips.

"Has Clara brought you anything within the past few days?" Sabina asked.

"No. I haven't seen her in more than a week." Pope licked his lips, all but drooling his avarice when he asked, "What kind of business proposition?"

"For Clara's ears only. All you need to know is that there's plenty of money for you in the game. Where can I get in touch with her?"

Pope hesitated, but as usual with his type of petty crook, greed trumped caution. "She rooms in North Beach now. Brown-shingled lodging house on the corner of Union and Grant, north side. Ground floor rear."

"Does she live there alone?"

"Far as I know."

"But she is still seeing Dodger Brown?"

"If she is, she hasn't said anything to me about it. I haven't seen him in months. He don't bring any . . . goods to me to sell."

"Do you know who his fenceman is?"

"No. You and Clara won't use anybody but me?"

"Don't worry, Mr. Pope. You'll get what's coming to you."

The area known as North Beach was a misnomer. Though there had once been a beach there, Sabina had been told, the name derived from a nearby bayside resort called the North Beach. But in recent years the city had begun filling in the land to allow the building of fishing wharves, warehouses, and docks, and both beach and resort no longer existed. The heart of North Beach, Washington Square, was also a misnomer: it was not a square at all because Columbus Avenue sliced through one edge in a long diagonal. Just as ironic was the fact that the statue it was reportedly named for was not of George Washington, but Benjamin Franklin.

The neighborhood around the nonsquare was a lively one, originally settled by Italian fishermen because of its proximity to the waterfront where many plied their trade. Its relatively cheap rents, and nostalgia among the Italians because the newly made section of shoreline was said to resemble the Bay of Naples, added to the attraction. When Sabina emerged from the hack on the southeast corner of Union and Grant, the air was redolent with the mingled aromas of Italian cooking dispensed by vendors in pushcarts—garlic, basil, oregano, tomatoes. Why, she wondered, was her primary perception of places so often their food smells? Her overly healthy appetite was at work again, despite the grilled bratwurst she had treated herself to at the California Market.

She made her way uphill on Union and soon located the brown-shingled house. A small sign on the front gate identified it as PARSONS' ROOMING HOUSE. A narrow lane and a weed-choked vacant lot bordered its far side, and as she approached she could see that entrances to the lodging house opened off the lane. Ground floor rear, Victor Pope had said.

The immediate area was deserted. Sabina turned into the lane, walked along one of the ruts to the steps that led up to the rear side entrance. The door, she saw when she neared the top of the steps, was slightly ajar. This gave her pause. She stood for a moment to listen. No sounds came from within.

A sharp rap on the door produced no response. Neither did calling out Clara Wilds's name. After a few moments she pushed on the door until it creaked open all the way.

What she saw when she entered made her gasp and recoil. A female form clad in pale green linen lay sprawled on a rag rug before a small gas hearth. The woman's face was turned aside and partially covered by strands of long brown hair, but there was no mistaking her identity. Nor the fact that she was the victim of foul play.

The weapon that protruded from her throat, surrounded by a welter of bright crimson, was the same one she'd used in the commission of her crimes—the familiar Charles Horner hatpin.

Sabina had seen violent death before—the vision of Stephen's bullet-riddled body still haunted her dreams—but she had never become inured to it. Indeed, she questioned the veracity of those who claimed to be. Her legs were unsteady, her breath coming short, as she crossed the untidy parlor to kneel beside the dead woman.

The hatpin had been thrust deeply into the flesh just below the Adam's apple, and the blood that had spilled from the wound was dark and coagulating. Dead not much more than an hour.

As Sabina started to rise, one of the outflung hands caught her attention—a dark gleam of red on two of the fingertips. A closer look revealed it to be blood mixed with particles of skin and a few short hairs under the nails. Clara Wilds had clawed and marked her attacker.

Sabina peered at the hairs without touching them. Brunette and silky, perhaps a man's though she couldn't be sure. According to the dossier on Dodger Brown, his hair was the color of his surname, but whether or not it was fine and slightly curly hadn't been mentioned. John would know. But the Dodger was only one possible suspect; an extortionist and pickpocket made any number of enemies over the course of a long criminal career. If he *was* guilty, the telltale scratches and gouges from Wilds's nails would be evidence of it once John tracked him down.

Sabina rose, stepped back to lean against the wall while she steadied herself. The police must be notified, of course, but she shared John's distrust of the local constabulary, and did not want under any circumstances to be taken in and questioned by them. Better an anonymous call from the nearest telephone. But first . . .

She scanned the parlor. Her initial impression of untidiness had been false, she realized then. The room had been searched—not ransacked but gone through in a systematic way. An old horsehair sofa drawn out of position, a floor lamp tilted against it, drawers partially open in tables and sideboards. And in the bedroom, visible through an open doorway, the mattress pulled half off the bed. Someone looking for the loot from her pocket-picking exploits at the Chutes and elsewhere? And if so, had it been found?

Averting her eyes from the body, Sabina began a hurried search of her own. There was nothing for her to find in the parlor. In the bedroom she looked in the small nightstand next to the bed, then in a heavy armoire thick with a violet scent that emanated from a satin sachet bag on a hanger. The armoire was filled with clothing and an array of different styles of hats, some with veils—the costumes Wilds had worn on dipping excursions. These, too, had been searched by the murderer; there was nothing left to find.

Sabina spied a large trunk under the room's one window. Its top was hinged open, the tray askew on the floor, the contents of both piled nearby. A worn quilt; a child's rag doll, one eye missing; a dictionary whose main use apparently had been to press and dry flowers; an empty cut-glass perfume bottle; an old, cracked leather man's purse; a handbag beaded with what looked to be real pearls but probably weren't.

Sabina examined the purse, found it empty. The late Henry Holbrooke's billfold, judging from his widow's description. If so, the cash he'd carried had been removed and either spent or stashed elsewhere.

She set it aside and examined the beaded bag. Regular handbags were not fashionable these days, but small, decorative ones with a dainty strap that hung from the wrist were sometimes used in the evenings. This one was old and worn, but of good quality—a Corticelli manufactured in Florence, Italy, a type Sabina had long admired but could not justify the expense of purchasing. She flipped the little mother-of-pearl clasp and felt inside. Also empty.

When she turned from the bench, a thin sprinkling of dirt particles on the bottom window ledge caught her eye. The particles appeared to be moist, freshly strewn there. And were, she found when she picked one up between her thumb and forefinger. Likely it had come from a box of geraniums hanging on a hook outside.

She raised the sash and looked more closely at the box. One of the plants was tipped slightly against the other. She thrust her hand into the dirt between the two, felt roots and, toward the bottom, the object that Clara Wilds had hidden there—a small sack of dark blue velvet tied with a drawstring.

Sabina emptied the sack onto the bed. A diamond stickpin, two gold pocket watches, a large ivory watch fob, a hammered silver money clip with an intricate design, a handful of similarly valuable items, and a thick roll of greenbacks bound with a rubber band. Literally buried treasure. Clara Wilds's murderer had fled the scene of his crime empty-handed.

Or had he? There was no way of telling.

Sabina flipped through the greenbacks, found the total to be in excess of two hundred dollars. Then she gathered up all the items, returned them to the blue velvet sack, and tucked the sack into her reticule. After a moment's reflection, she added the cracked leather purse. There had been no question that she should confiscate everything herself; if she left the items for the police to find, they would never be returned to their rightful owners.

She had been here long enough. At the door she peered out to make sure the carriageway was still deserted, then stepped out and away.

13

QUINCANNON

Andrew Costain's offices were in a brick building on Geary Street that housed a dozen attorneys and half as many other professional men. The anteroom held a secretary's desk but no secretary; the bare desktop and dusty file cabinets behind it suggested that there hadn't been one in some while. A pair of neatly lettered and somewhat contradictory signs were affixed to one of two closed doors in the inside wall. The upper one proclaimed PRIVATE, the lower invited KNOCK FOR ADMITTANCE.

Quincannon knocked. There were a few seconds of silence before Costain's whiskey baritone called out, "Yes? Who is it?"

"John Quincannon."

Another few seconds vanished, as if the lawyer were finishing up business at hand before moving on to the business that required the services of a private investigative agency. Then, "Come in, Mr. Quincannon. Come in."

Costain was sitting behind a cluttered desk set before a wall covered with what appeared to be a full set of Blackstone, writing in a leather-bound notebook slightly larger than a billfold. More books and papers were scattered on dusty pieces of furniture. On another wall, next to a framed law degree, was a lithograph of John L. Sullivan in a typical fighting pose.

The lawyer motioned to Quincannon to wait while he finished whatever notations he was making. After a few moments he closed the notebook and consigned it to a desk drawer, then sat back with his fingers twiddling an elk's tooth attached to a thin gold watch chain.

His person was somewhat more tidy than his office, though not as tidy as he'd been in evening dress at the Axminster home. The successful image, however, was belied by the rumpled condition of his expensive tweed suit and striped vest, the frayed edges of his shirt cuffs and collar, his rum-blossom nose and flushed features, and the perfume of forty-rod whiskey that could be detected at ten paces or more. If Quincannon had been a prospective client, instead of it being the other way around, he would have thought twice about entrusting legal matters to Mr. Andrew Costain.

"Thank you for coming," Costain said. He seemed even more nervous today than he had last night; the fluttering tic on his cheek gave the false impression that he was winking and his hands continued to twitch over the elk's tooth fob. "You didn't stop by earlier, by any chance?"

"No, I had other business to attend to."

"Good, good. I asked because I had to leave the office for a short time—an urgent summons from a client."

More likely, Quincannon thought cynically, the "urgent summons" had involved a visit to whichever nearby saloon he frequented.

"Have a seat. Cigar? Drink?"

"Neither."

"I believe I'll have a small libation, if you don't mind. It has been something of a trying day."

"It's your office, Mr. Costain."

While Quincannon moved a heavy volume of Blackstone from the single client's chair and replaced it with his backside, Costain produced a bottle of rye whiskey and a none-too-clean glass from his desk drawer. His idea of a "small one" was three fingers of rye, half of which he tossed off at a gulp. The rum blossom glowed and the flush deepened, but the lawyer's hands continued their restless roaming.

"Your message mentioned a financial advantage. For what service?"

"That's rather obvious, isn't it, in light of recent events. Have you caught the burglar yet?"

"No, not yet."

"Identified him?"

"To my satisfaction. A man named Dodger Brown."

"I don't recognize the name."

"No reason you should as a civil attorney," Quincannon said. "It's only a matter of time until he's locked away in the city jail."

"How much time?"

"Within forty-eight hours, if all goes well."

"How do you plan to catch him? While in the act?"

"If not before."

"Don't be ambiguous, man. I have a right to know what you're up to."

"Indeed? My client is the Great Western Insurance Company. I need answer only to them."

Costain drained his glass, looked yearningly at the bottle,

wet his lips, and then with a steadfast effort returned both bottle and glass to the desk drawer and pushed it shut. "My name is on that list of potential victims, you said so last night. Naturally I'm concerned. Suppose this man Brown wasn't frightened off by his near capture at the Truesdales'? Suppose he's bold enough to try burgling *my* home next, even this very night? My wife and I can ill afford to have our house ransacked and our valuables stolen. The damned insurance companies never pay off at full value."

"A legitimate fear."

"I want you to see to it that we're not victimized. Hire you to keep watch on my home tonight and every night until you've caught this man Brown."

Quincannon said, "There are other alternatives, you know, which would cost you nothing."

"Yes, yes, I know. Move our valuables to a safe place and simply stay home nights until the threat is ended. But we have too many possessions to haul away willy-nilly and too little time to undertake the chore. Even if we did remove everything of value, Brown might still break in and if he found nothing worth stealing, vandalize the premises. That has been known to happen, hasn't it?"

"It has, though not very often."

"I don't like the idea of my home being invaded in any case," Costain said. "And it well could be since it's on that list of yours. My wife and I have separate appointments tonight and a joint one tomorrow evening that we're loath to cancel. The house will be empty and fair game from seven until midnight or later both nights."

"You have no servants?"

"None that live in. And it would be useless to ask for help from the city police without certain knowledge of a crime to be committed."

Quincannon nodded, considering. If Costain wanted to pay him for the same work he had been engaged to do by Great Western Insurance, there was neither conflict of interest nor any other reasonable argument against it. The notion of another night or two hiding in shrubbery and risking pneumonia had no appeal, but minor hardships were part and parcel of the detective game.

"You'll accept the job, then?"

"I will," Quincannon said blandly, "provided you're willing to pay the standard rate for my time plus an additional fee."

"What's that? Additional fee for what?"

"Surveillance on your home is a job for two men."

"Why? You were by yourself at the Truesdales'."

"The Truesdale house has front and side entrances that could be watched by one man alone. Yours has front and rear entrances, therefore requiring a second operative."

"How is it you know my house?"

"I tabbed it up, along with the others on the list, the day I was hired by Great Western."

"Tabbed it up?"

"Crook's argot. Paid visits and scrutinized the properties, the same as the housebreaker would have done to size up the lay."

Costain continued to twitch, but he didn't argue. "Very well," he said. "How much will it cost me?"

Quincannon named a per diem figure, only slightly higher than his usual for a two-detective operation. His dislike for the bibulous lawyer was not sufficient to warrant gouging him unduly.

The amount induced Costain to mutter, "That's damned close to extortion," then to reopen his desk drawer and help himself to another "small libation."

"Hardly."

"I suppose the figure is nonnegotiable?"

"I don't haggle," Quincannon said.

"All right. How much in advance?"

"One day's fee in full."

"For services not yet rendered? No, by God. Half, and not a penny more."

Quincannon shrugged. Half in advance was more than he usually requested from his clients.

"You'll take a check, I assume?"

"Of course." As long as it wasn't made of rubber.

"You had better not fail me, Quincannon," Costain said as he wrote out the check. "If there is a repeat of your bungling at the Truesdales', you'll regret it. I promise you that."

Quincannon bit back an oath, scowled his displeasure instead, and managed an even-toned reply. "I did not bungle at the Truesdales'. What happened two nights ago—"

"—wasn't your fault. Yes, yes, I know. And if anything similar happens it won't be your fault again, no doubt."

"You'll have your money's worth."

"I had better."

And I'll have my money's worth, and then some, Quincannon thought. He tucked the check into a waistcoat pocket and left Costain to stew in his alcoholic juices.

The Geary Street address was not far from his bank or the

agency offices. He went first to the Miner's Bank, where he made sure Costain had sufficient funds in his account before depositing the check. Then he set off for the agency at a brisk pace.

San Francisco was a fine city, he reflected as he walked, the more so on a nippy but sun-bright day such as this one. The fresh salt smell from the bay, the rumble and clang of cable cars on Market Street, the stately presence of the Ferry Building in the distance—he had yet to tire of any of it. It had been a banner day when he was reassigned here during his days with the United States Secret Service. The nation's capital had not been the same for him after his father succumbed to the assassin's bullet on the Baltimore waterfront; he had been ready for a change. His new home suited him as Washington, D.C., had suited Thomas Quincannon. The same was true of the business of private investigation, a much more lucrative and satisfying profession than that of an underpaid and overworked government operative.

When he arrived at the building that housed Carpenter and Quincannon, Professional Detective Services, he was in a cheerful mood. Temperance songs were among his favorite tunes, not because of his vow of sobriety but because he found them as exaggerated and amusing as temperance tracts; he whistled "Lips that Touch Liquor Will Never Touch Mine" as he climbed to the second floor and approached the agency's door. But he came to an abrupt halt when he saw that the door stood ajar by a few inches, and heard the voice that came from within.

"I consider that a man's brain originally is like a little empty attic," the voice was declaiming, "and you have to stock it with such furniture as you choose. A fool takes in all the lumber of every sort that he comes across, so that the knowledge which might be useful to him gets crowded out, or at best is jumbled up with a lot of other things, so that he has a difficulty in laying his hands upon it. Now the skillful workman is very careful indeed as to what he takes in to his brain attic. He will have nothing but the tools which may help him in doing his work, but of these he has a large assortment, and all in the most perfect order. It is a mistake to think that little room has elastic walls and can distend to any extent. There comes a time when for every addition of knowledge you forget something that you knew before. It is of the highest importance, therefore, not to have useless facts elbowing out the useful ones."

Quincannon's smile turned upside down as he elbowed inside. The voice belonged to the crackbrain masquerading as Sherlock Holmes.

14

The Englishman sat comfortably in the client's chair in front of her desk, a gray cape draped over his shoulders and a deerstalker cap pulled down over his ears. Even though she had opened both windows, the office was blue with smoke from the long, curved clay pipe he was smoking. The tobacco was worse than the shag John preferred, a mixture that might have been made from floor sweepings.

He had arrived at the agency twenty minutes earlier, shortly after her return. Sabina had had just enough time to transfer most of the valuables she'd gathered in Clara Wilds's rooms from her bag into the office safe before he strolled in. Paying a call, he said, for a look at the offices of Carpenter and Quincannon, Professional Detective Services, for he had a keen interest in learning how his American counterparts conducted their business.

Sabina, suspecting an ulterior motive, was none too welcoming, but the Englishman didn't appear to notice and made himself comfortable across from her. She was in no mood for his foolishness and anxious to confer with John about the death of

Clara Wilds, so tried to tell the probable impostor she was busy and send him on his way. But he was persistent without being offensive—courtly and charming, in fact, if something of a bore once he began expounding on such arcane topics as brain attics.

He may well have been the addlepate John and Ambrose Bierce believed him to be, but Sabina had to admit he seemed benign enough and extremely well educated, with knowledge of a variety of subjects. And his "parlor tricks," of which she'd had a sampling, were certainly impressive—so much so that she felt he must have exhaustively studied the deductive methods utilized by the London detective he pretended or believed himself to be. Nonetheless she had had just about enough of him, and soon would have gotten rid of him, if necessary at the point of the derringer she kept in her reticule if her partner hadn't finally returned.

John sized up the situation from Sabina's frustrated expression and was not gentle in closing the door, or gracious in his opening remark. He aimed one of his piratical scowls at their caller, and said to Sabina, "I seem to have walked in on a lecture."

A lecture was exactly what she had mentally termed it. If she'd wanted to hear one, she'd have sooner visited the Academy of Sciences or one of the city's excellent art museums.

The Englishman answered John before Sabina could. "Hardly that, sir. Hardly that. I was merely stating a portion of my methodology to the most engaging Mrs. Carpenter."

"And demonstrating your amazing powers of observation and deduction, no doubt."

Sabina waved away a plume of smoke from the clay pipe. "Oh, yes. He wasn't here three minutes before he knew about Adam."

"Adam?" John said suspiciously. "Who the deuce is Adam?"

"My roommate."

"Your . . . *what*?"

"You needn't look so horrified. Adam is a cat."

"A young cat, in point of fact," the Englishman said. "No older than six months."

"Cat? You never told me you had a cat."

The look she gave him reaffirmed the fact that there were many things about herself and her personal life she had never told him. "Adam only recently came to live with me."

Sherlock Holmes, for want of another name, puffed out another great cloud of acrid smoke. "Rather a curious mix of Abyssinian and long-haired Siamese," he announced.

"Mr. Holmes was able to deduce that from a few wisps of fur on the hem of my skirt. Adam's approximate age, as well."

"Remarkable fellow," John said sourly. "Have you written a monograph on breeds of cat as well as tobacco ash?"

"No, but perhaps one day I shall." The Englishman once again assumed his pontifical air. "Remarkable creatures, felines. As one of our more famous philosophers once wrote, 'God made the cat so that man could have the pleasure of caressing the tiger.' "

Sabina had to admit that was an apt assessment, but John was not impressed. He demanded of Holmes, "What brought you here, pray tell?"

"An abiding interest in the inner workings of an American private inquiry agency. As I told your charming associate, I occupied much of yesterday studying accounts of the various investigations you've conducted. Excellent detective work, sir and madam. Most commendable."

"You'll find no better anywhere."

"No better anywhere in America, perhaps."

John bristled at that, but made no comment.

Holmes adjusted his deerstalker at a rakish angle and leaned back comfortably in the chair. "May I ask how your investigation into the residential burglaries is progressing? Have you caught your pannyman yet?"

"What business is that of yours?"

"Now that I've finished my researches in your admirable city, I fear I've grown bored with conventional tourist activities. San Francisco is quite cosmopolitan for an American city in its infancy, but its geographical, cultural, and historical attractions have decidedly limited appeal in comparison to my native London."

"Bah. What researches?"

"They are of an esoteric nature, of no interest to the average person or even to fellow sleuths."

John's curled lip said he found that to be another addlepated statement. He shed his Chesterfield and went to sit glowering behind his desk.

"The time of my self-imposed exile has almost ended," Holmes was saying. "Soon I shall return to England and my former pursuits. Crime and the criminal mind challenge my intellect, give zest to my life. I've been away from the game too long."

"I can't imagine leaving it in the first place."

"I daresay there were mitigating factors."

"Not for *any* reason, with or without mitigating factors."

Their gazes locked, seemed to strike a spark or two. Sabina

sighed, and said, "If you'll excuse us now, Mr. Holmes, my partner and I have business to discuss."

"Pray, don't let my presence stop you. Perhaps I might be of some assistance."

"Not likely," John growled.

The Englishman ignored this. He remained seated, his eyes agleam, and said through another cloud of smoke, "Doctor Axminster provided a brief tour of your infamous Barbary Coast shortly after my arrival, but it was superficial and hardly enlightening. I should like to see it as I've seen Limehouse in London, from the perspective of a consulting detective. Foul dives, foul deeds! My blood races at the prospect."

John rolled his eyes and fluffed his beard.

"Would you permit me to join you on your next excursion? Introduce me to the district's hidden intrigues, some of its more colorful denizens—the dance-hall queen known as The Galloping Cow, Emperor Norton, the odd fellow who allows himself to be assaulted for money?"

"The Galloping Cow has slowed to a bovine walk. Emperor Norton is long dead, and Oofty Goofty soon will be if he allows one more thump on his cranium with a baseball bat. Besides, I'm a detective, not a tour guide."

"Tut, tut. It is knowledge I'm interested in, not sensation. In return, I offer the benefit of my experience in tracking down your pannyman and his ill-gotten gains."

"The only experience I need to call on is my own. I have no intention—"

John broke off abruptly, and Sabina saw his expression alter and a wicked light brighten his hazel eyes. She knew that look all too well. It meant a devious notion had come to him and his wily brain was busy concocting mischief.

He said through a wolfish smile, "I had a message from Andrew Costain this morning requesting a meeting. I've just come from his offices."

"Ah. A matter pertaining to the burglaries?"

"Yes. He's afraid of being the burglar's next victim and wants his home put under surveillance until the yegg is caught."

Sabina said, "You didn't accept?"

"I did, and why not? There is no conflict of interest in accepting payment from more than one client to perform the same task, as Costain himself pointed out."

"Still, it's not quite ethical. . . ."

"Ethics be damned. A fee is a fee for services rendered, and that includes providing peace of mind to nervous citizens. Eh, Holmes?"

"Indubitably."

"We're to begin tonight. Costain's home is near South Park, not as large a property as banker Truesdale's but nonetheless substantial, and with both front and rear entrances. I explained to the lawyer that proper surveillance will require two operatives, and he agreed to the extra fee."

Now Sabina understood the nature of the mischief he'd hatched. She said his name warningly, but he pretended not to hear. He continued to address the Englishman.

"There are a number of operatives I could call upon, but I wonder, given your interest in this case and your eagerness to return to the game, if you might be willing to join me at the task?"

Another noxious cloud erupted from Holmes's pipe. Sabina smothered a cough and turned her head toward the window for fresh air.

"Splendid suggestion!" Holmes said. "I would be honored. In return for my services, I ask only that you acquaint me with the Barbary Coast as you know it."

"Agreed. You'll see the Coast as few ever have."

Holmes smiled.

John smiled.

Sabina grimaced.

The two men made arrangements to meet at Hoolihan's Saloon at seven o'clock, after which Holmes finally departed. When she and John were alone, Sabina let her exasperation with his cavalier and less-than-scrupulous behavior bubble to the surface. "You've taken leave of your senses, John Quincannon. You're as daft as the Englishman."

"Daft? Sly as a fox, you mean. Now there's no need to pay another operative for the work of an evening or two. Andrew Costain's fees belong entirely to us."

"Holmes only believes himself to be a trained detective. He could do more harm than good on a night's surveillance."

"Poppycock. I'll see to it he doesn't interfere if Dodger Brown comes skulking again tonight."

"The way you didn't let him interfere two nights ago?"

John looked pained. "That won't happen again."

"Don't be too sure. Dodger Brown may be more dangerous than you think."

"A scrawny yegg like him? Faugh."

"Not only a yegg—possibly a murderer."

"What's that? Who would he have murdered?"

"Clara Wilds. I found her dead in her rooms earlier this afternoon. Stabbed in the throat with her hatpin."

Quickly she related her activities of the day, ending with her discovery of the hiding place of the pickpocket's spoils and her removal of them to the security of their office safe. John listened without interruption, tugging at his whiskers as he considered the news.

When she finished, he said, "Was there any evidence of who committed the deed?"

"None of a specific nature. But it could have been Dodger Brown."

"Did you find anything to suggest he had been visiting Wilds in her rooms?"

"No."

"None of the people you spoke to were able to verify whether or not she was still consorting with him?"

"Not willingly, at least."

"Then he's no more a suspect in her murder than anyone else."

"Except that he does have brown hair," Sabina said. "Do you recall if it's fine and on the curly side?"

"I believe it is. We'll know if he's guilty when he's found."

"I take it you failed to get a line on his whereabouts?"

"In my rounds today, yes, but it's only a matter of time. Ezra Bluefield agreed to put the word out on him."

"I hope for your sake that it produces rapid results."

John waved that away. "You were well advised to confiscate the swag from Clara Wilds's crimes before the blue coats could steal it. Have you notified Charles Ackerman yet?"

"No, but I will soon. I haven't had time to telephone for an appointment."

"You don't propose to tell him how and where you recovered the loot?"

"Of course not. I've no intention of mentioning Clara Wilds by name, or revealing the fact that she's dead."

"And the valuables?"

"I'll return them to their rightful owners personally. Assuming I can identify what belongs to whom. There are some that are not on the lists of stolen items from the Chutes and Wilds's other recent forays."

"Let's have a look."

Sabina opened the safe and removed the valuables, though she left the roll of greenbacks in the drawer where she'd tucked it. John examined the silver money clip with a covetous eye. But even if she weren't in the office with him, he would not have considered appropriating it; her partner sometimes walked the borderline between honesty and illegality, but a healthy contempt for crooks of all types was too strong for him to descend to their level. His greed, fortunately, was limited to money received for services rendered.

He sifted among the other items, then opened and looked inside Henry Holbrooke's purse, as she'd known he would. "Empty," he said. "Why did you bring the purse? It has no value."

"Perhaps it does."

"To the owner?"

"No. To the owner's widow. Let me worry about this matter, John. You'd do well to keep your mind on Dodger Brown."

15

SABINA

Before John left the office, she again argued against what he called his "evening's entertainment with Mr. Sherlock Holmes." To no avail. He could be infuriatingly stubborn when taken with one of his perverse notions, and this was such an instance. He simply refused to believe that using the Englishman as he was planning to do, for sport as well as for the saving of a few dollars, was both foolish and potentially dangerous.

She had learned ways to curb his more outrageous behavior, but they required considerable effort and guile and she reserved them for matters of greater importance than this. And yet, this was not necessarily a minor matter. If something went awry tonight, and serious mistakes were made and—God forbid—John or the Englishman or some innocent party were harmed, the agency's reputation would be severely damaged. Carpenter and Quincannon, Professional Detective Services, was known for conducting successful investigations with discretion and a minimum of trouble and publicity. Employing a man whose faculties were suspect was a risky undertaking; if their important clients were to hear of it, some or all might decide to patronize another agency.

But it was too late now to renew her efforts to change his mind. She had several other items of business to occupy her time and her concerns. She would just have to hope for the best where John and the poor deluded Englishman were concerned.

Clara Wilds's murder still troubled her. If Dodger Brown was the killer, he would bear the marks of Wilds's nails when he was found and captured and a confession would be wrung from him as a result. But she was not convinced that he was guilty; there was no evidence that he was still consorting with Wilds, and the circumstances of the pickpocket's death didn't seem to fit either his nature or his past crimes.

If he wasn't responsible, then the murder might well go unsolved and unpunished. The prospect didn't set well with Sabina. She disliked loose ends, and offenses, especially violent offenses after what had happened to Stephen, that had no resolution. But what could she do about it? Mounting an investigation of her own without benefit of a client wasn't justifiable, and there was little prospect of anyone hiring her on Clara Wilds's behalf. Certainly not the woman's uncle; even if Tony the Fish Monger had cared for his niece, it was unlikely that he could afford the agency's fees. The only person Sabina had met who might have cared enough was Dippin' Sal, and she too lacked the necessary funds. . . .

Sabina put these thoughts aside and turned her attention to the valuables she had recovered from the pickpocket's rooms, which were still spread out on her desk. She checked each item against the list of Chutes victims' losses Lester Sweeney had given her, and the information she'd obtained from Wilds's victims on the Cocktail Route and at the Market Street bazaar. The items she was able to identify went into manila envelopes with the individual's name written on each, then into her reticule.

When she was done, several pieces were still unaccounted for. All but one of these bore no identifying marks of any kind, so the only thing she could do was to check reports of stolen mechandise filed with police and insurance companies—a task that, with her busy schedule, would have to be done catch-as-catch-can. The one exception was the hammered silver money clip with the name of the silversmith who had made it etched into the metal.

In the city directory she found a listing for W. Reilly & Sons, Silversmiths—a shop that was large enough and modern enough to be a subscriber to the telephone exchange. Her call was answered by a deep-voiced man who gave his name as Wendell Reilly, the owner. Sabina identified herself and made her request, giving it weight by saying that the money clip had been stolen from its owner and would be returned once she knew to whom it belonged.

"If the clip is one of ours," Reilly said, "I may be able to identify the customer. Many of our pieces are made to special order and this sounds as if it might be one of them. But I'll have to see it to be sure."

"Of course. I should be able to stop by later today. What are your hours?"

"The shop is open until five thirty, but I'm usually here until seven."

Sabina thanked him and rang off.

There was one more task to be done before she was ready to

leave. She removed two hundred dollars from the roll of confiscated greenbacks and added it to the single note remaining in the worn leather billfold. John wouldn't approve if he knew—his view was that they were entitled to unverifiable cash sums recovered from crooks' clutches—but she had no intention of telling him. Henry Holbrooke deserved a proper burial marker, and his widow needed whatever was left far more than Carpenter and Quincannon, Professional Detective Services.

The offices of Mr. Charles Ackerman, owner of the Chutes and attorney for the Southern Pacific Railroad and the Market Street and Sutter Street railway lines, were in the Montgomery Block, a favored location for upper-echelon lawyers, physicians, and businessmen. The building, the first fireproof edifice constructed in the city, was known affectionately as the Monkey Block, but its stern gray masonry belied the nickname.

The suite belonging to Charles Ackerman & Associates was on the top floor, the fourth—an impressively appointed group of rooms that testified to the financial success of his many ventures. Sabina presented her card to a clerk in the outer office, who took it away with him. He returned in short order to usher her into Mr. Ackerman's private sanctum.

Their client was a tall, broad-shouldered man with an ample corporation, impeccably dressed in black broadcloth. His mane of hair shone silver in the light slanting in through a pair of windows that offered views of the city and the bay. He took Sabina's hand, bowed in a courtly fashion, then gestured for her to be seated across the polished expanse of his desk.

"Your investigation has produced rapid results, has it, Mrs. Carpenter?" he said without preamble.

"Yes, fortunately." She withdrew the manila envelopes from her reticule, opened two of them, and placed the contents on the desk blotter for Mr. Ackerman's brief inspection.

"You've recovered all the stolen items?"

"All those on the list Mr. Sweeney provided."

"Excellent. You'll return them immediately, I trust?"

"Beginning as soon as our interview is concluded."

"And what of the person responsible?"

"I can guarantee," Sabina said, "that the pickpocket will never again menace patrons at the Chutes or elsewhere."

This satisfied Ackerman—a good thing because she had no intention of elaborating and would have employed evasive measures if he had pressed her. He produced a ledger, wrote out a check for the agreed-upon fee, rose to shake her hand a second time, and congratulated her on a job well done. "If ever I or any of my acquaintances should require your services again, I will not hesitate to recommend the Carpenter and Quincannon agency."

To John, the best part of any successful transaction such as this was the amount of money collected. To her, the goodwill of a man of Charles Ackerman's stature was of greater value.

Jessie Street seemed even shabbier today than it had on her previous visit. The cobblestones along its length were in serious need of repair. A trash bin had been overturned in the tiny yard of the home next door to the Holbrooke residence, and garbage was strewn across the weedy ground. No one was outdoors in the vicinity except for a pair of young boys playing a game that involved bashing a picket fence with sticks.

A FOR SALE sign now stood next to the Holbrookes' gate. Financial straits, loneliness now that her husband was gone, or a combination of both had evidently convinced the widow to give up the property. This made Sabina even more certain that she was doing the right thing. As did the look of poor Mrs. Holbrooke when the old woman opened the door to Sabina's knock. Her deeply lined face and sorrowful eyes, the tremors radiating around her mouth, were painful to behold.

"You remember me, Mrs. Holbrooke? Sabina Carpenter."

"Yes. Have you something else to ask about what happened to my husband?"

"Not this time." Sabina withdrew the old leather billfold from her reticule. "Is this your husband's purse?"

The old woman took it, squinting, and ran her fingers over the beaded leather. "Why . . . why, yes, it is. Where did you find it? And so quickly?"

"A bit of good luck."

"The woman who stole it . . . will she be punished?"

"She already has been."

"I'm glad. I'm not a vengeful woman, but after what she did to Henry . . ."

"I understand."

"But I don't suppose . . . Henry's money . . ."

"Look inside, Mrs. Holbrooke."

The old woman opened the billfold, and when her eyes beheld the fold of greenbacks she gasped her surprise.

"Two hundred dollars," Sabina said, "the full amount. I know it can't begin to make up for your loss, but perhaps it will help."

"Oh! Oh, yes! Now I can afford the headstone for Henry's grave. And with what's left over, I'll have enough to buy my own train ticket to Antioch. My sister and her family have invited me to live with them now that I've decided to sell the house. They've been so kind. *You've* been so kind." She took Sabina's hand, pressed it tightly between hers. "Bless you, Mrs. Carpenter. Bless you!"

Sabina had a warm feeling of satisfaction when she left the widow Holbrooke. The old woman's gratitude was worth even more than Charles Ackerman's goodwill.

Her next planned stop was the home of George Davis near Washington Square. The route her hack driver chose to take her there passed near the shop of Wendell Reilly & Sons, Silversmiths, on Battery Street near the U.S. Customs House. This being the case, Sabina made up her mind to stop there first.

The shop was a modest one-story frame building sandwiched between two taller structures, with dark green–shuttered windows on either side of an equally dark green door. A sign on the door bade customers to enter.

Inside Sabina found a large room containing a brick forge that took up one entire wall. The fire in it was banked, but she could feel its residual warmth. Across from the forge were a row of grinding wheels and a long workbench covered with various tools and molds of different sizes and shapes. A man with a fringe of curly gray hair circling a shiny bald pate was placing an ornate silver tea service on one of a series of shelves holding other pieces, among them a display of intricately adorned stacker rings.

At the sound of the door closing the man turned. He had a ruddy face in the center of which was a long blade of a nose. When he smiled at Sabina, his blue eyes twinkled.

"May I help you?"

"Are you Mr. Wendell Reilly?"

"At your service."

"I'm Sabina Carpenter." She presented one of her cards to verify the fact. "We spoke on the telephone earlier."

"Oh, yes. Well, I must say you've come at the right time, Mrs. Carpenter. The forge has been banked for the night, so the premises aren't as heated as they are during the day."

They still seemed overly warm to Sabina, but she supposed those in the trade were used to working in high-temperature surroundings.

"A money clip, I believe you said. You brought it with you?"

Sabina nodded and produced the article. The silversmith examined it carefully through a jeweler's loupe. Then he, too, nodded.

"It's one of my design and manufacture, yes. As I recall— and this, mind you, was three or four years ago—the gent who ordered it was very particular about the detailing. This border, you see"—his finger traced a design of curving lines—"had to be just so far apart and extend and interweave in this exact way. Fussy, he was."

"Do you recall the man's name?"

"Not offhand. But we keep careful records. It shouldn't take me long to find it." He disappeared through a flowered curtain into a back room.

While she waited, Sabina moved about the room studying the displays of the smith's wares. Cutlery and utensils, candle-holders, intricately designed belt buckles, an antique-style coffee urn. A glass-topped case containing an array of women's and men's jewelry held her attention briefly, though she seldom wore any herself except for her plain gold wedding ring and a string of pearls Stephen had given her upon the occasion of their first wedding anniversary. Her collection of hatpins, beautiful and carefully chosen as they were, she considered a necessity because the winds often blew hard in this city by the bay and hats of the type she preferred were too expensive to risk losing.

Mr. Reilly returned carrying a slip of paper. "I remember the gent now," he said as he handed it to her. "He bought this and other pieces from us several years ago, though he hasn't been back in recent memory. I've noted his address as well."

Sabina's eyes widened when she read the name of the man who owned the stolen money clip.

Andrew Costain.

16

QUINCANNON

In his drinking days, Quincannon's favorite watering hole was Hoolihan's Saloon on Second Street. It was there that he had sought for two long years to drown his conscience after the incident in Virginia City, Nevada, when a woman named Katherine Bennett, eight months pregnant, had perished with a bullet from his pistol in her breast.

The shooting had been a tragic accident. It had happened during a gunfight that erupted when he and a team of local law enforcement officers had attempted the arrest of a pair of brothers who were counterfeiting United States government currency. In the skirmish behind their print shop, one of the brothers had wounded a deputy and then attempted to flee through the backyards of a row of houses. Quincannon had shot him, to avoid being shot himself; but one of his bullets had gone wild and found Katherine Bennett, who was outside hanging up her washing.

He had not been able to bear the burden of responsibility for the loss of two innocent lives. Guilt and remorse had eaten away at him; he had taken so heavily to drink over the next two

years that he'd been in danger of losing his position with the
Secret Service, perhaps even ending his days as another lost
and sodden patron of Jack Foyles' wine dump. Two things had
saved him: the first was another counterfeiting case, in the
Owyhee Mountains of Idaho; the second was meeting Sabina
there and eventually entering into his partnership with her.
Not a drop of alcohol had passed his lips since his return from
Silver City, and never would again. He had made peace with
himself. Demon rum was no longer even a minor temptation,
despite the occasional nightmares that still plagued his sleep.

Nevertheless, he continued to frequent Hoolihan's because
he felt comfortable among its clientele of small merchants, office workers, tradesmen, drummers, and a somewhat rougher
element up from the waterfront. No city leaders came there on
their nightly rounds, as they did to the Palace Hotel bar, Pop
Sullivan's Hoffman Café, and the other first-class saloons along
the Cocktail Route; no judges, politicians, bankers—Samuel
Truesdale had likely never set foot through its swinging
doors—or gay young blades in their striped trousers, fine cra-
vats, and brocaded waistcoats.

Hoolihan's had no crystal chandeliers, fancy mirrors, expensive oil paintings, white-coated barmen, or elaborate free
lunch. It was dark and bare by comparison, sawdust thickly
scattered on the floor and a back room containing pool and
billiard tables on which Quincannon often played. The only
glitter and sparkle came from the shine of its old-style gas-
lights on the ranks of bottles along the backbar, and its hungry
drinkers dined not on crab legs and oysters on the half shell
but on corned beef, strong cheese, rye bread, and tubs of
briny pickles.

Quincannon had first gravitated there because the saloon was a short cable-car ride from his rooms and because staff and clientele both respected the solitary drinker's desire for privacy. Even after taking the pledge, it remained his refuge—an honest place, made for those who sought neither bombast nor trouble. Far fewer lies were told in Hoolihan's than in the rarefied atmosphere of the Palace bar, he suspected, and far fewer dark deeds were hatched.

It was a few minutes shy of seven o'clock when he arrived at Hoolihan's and claimed a place at the bar near the entrance. Ben Joyce, the head barman, greeted him in his mildly profane fashion. "What'll it be tonight, you bloody Scotsman? Coffee or fresh clam juice?"

"Clam juice, and leave out the arsenic this time."

"Hah. As if I'd waste good ratsbane on the likes of you."

Ben brought him a steaming mug of Hoolihan's special broth. Quincannon sipped, smoked a pipeful of tobacco, and listened to the ebb and flow of conversation around him. Men came in, singly and in pairs; men drifted out. The hands on the massive Seth Thomas clock over the backboard moved forward to seven. And seven-oh-five. And seven-ten . . .

Annoyance nibbled at him. Where the devil was that dingbat Holmes? He'd considered himself a sly fox for his conscription of the Englishman, but Sabina might have been right in reproaching him for an error in judgment; for once he may have outsmarted himself. If the fellow was untrustworthy as well as unbalanced . . .

Someone moved in next to him, jostling his arm. A gruff Cockney voice said, "Yer standing in me way, mate."

Quincannon turned to glare at the voice's owner. Tall, thin

ragamuffin dressed in patched trousers and a threadbare sailor's pea jacket, a cap pulled down low on his forehead. He opened his mouth to make a sharp retort, then snapped it shut again and took a closer look at the man. Little surprised him anymore, but he was a bit taken aback by what he saw.

"Holmes?" he said.

"At yer service, mate."

"What's the purpose of that outlandish getup?"

"It seemed appropriate for the night's mission," the Englishman said in his normal voice. His eyes, peering up from under the brim of his cap, were as bright as oil lamps. "Disguise has served me well during my career, and the opportunity for some has not presented itself in some time. I must say I enjoy playacting. It has been said, perhaps truly, that the stage lost a consummate actor when I decided to become a detective."

Daft as a church mouse, Quincannon thought.

Quickly he ushered Holmes outside and into a hansom waiting nearby. The crackbrain had no more to say on the subject of disguises, but as the hack rattled along the cobblestones to Mission Street and on toward Rincon Hill, he put forth a slew of questions on the night's venture, the "pannyman" responsible for the burglaries, and the various methods employed by American burglars in general. The man was obsessed with details on every conceivable topic.

For the most part Quincannon answered in monosyllables in the hope that Holmes would wind down and be quiet. This was not to be. The Englishman kept up a running colloquy on a variety of esoteric subjects from the remarkable explorations of a Norwegian named Sigerson to the latest advances in chemistry and other sciences to the inner workings and possible improvements of horseless carriages. He even knew somehow that an ex-housebreaker living in Warsaw, Illinois, manufactured burglar tools, advertised them as novelties in the *National Police Gazette,* and sold them mail-order for ten dollars for the set—a declaration that came as no surprise to Quincannon since the lock picks he carried for emergencies had come from just such a set liberated from an East Bay scruff.

Holmes's monologue ceased, mercifully, when they departed the hack two blocks from Andrew Costain's home. It was another night made for the prowling of footpads and yeggs, restless streams of cloud playing peekaboo games with stars and the scythe-blade moon. The neighborhood, the first of San Francisco's fashionable residential districts, was built around an oval-shaped park that was an exact copy of London's Berkeley Square—a fact the Englishman naturally chose to comment on. It had begun to fall into disfavor in 1869, when Second Street was carved through the west edge of Rincon Hill to connect downtown with the southern waterfront. Now its grandeur, along with that of Rincon Hill, was fading. Most of the powerful millionaires and their families had moved to more fashionable venues such as Nob Hill. Now it was on the shabby genteel side, though far from the "new slum, a place of solitary ancient houses and butt ends of streets," as it had been unfairly dubbed by that insolent fellow Scotsman, Robert Louis Stevenson.

Many of the houses they passed showed light, but the Costain home, near South Park, was dark except for an electric porch globe. It was not as large as the Truesdale pile, but its front and rear yards were spacious and contained almost as many plants, trees, and shadowy hiding places.

Holmes peered intently through the row of iron pickets into the front yard as they strolled by. "Which of us will be stationed here?" he asked.

"You will. I've a spot picked out at the rear."

"Splendid. The *mucronulatum,* perhaps. Or . . . ah, yes, even better. A *Juniperus chinensis 'corymbosa variegata,'* I do believe."

"What are you prattling on about?"

"Shrubbery."

"Eh?"

"*Mucronulatum* is the species more commonly known as rhododendron. Quite a healthy specimen there by that garden bench."

"And what the devil is *Jupiter chinchin thrombosa?*"

"*Juniperus chinensis 'corymbosa variegata,'*" the Englishman corrected. "One of the more handsome and sturdy varieties of juniper shrub. Its flowers are a variegated creamy yellow and its growth regular, without twisted branches, and generally of no more than ten feet in height. I thought at first that it might be a *chinensis corymbosa,* a close cousin, but the *chinensis corymbosa* grows to a greater height, often above fifteen feet."

Quincannon had nothing to say to that.

"I've decided the *corymbosa variegata* will afford the best concealment," Holmes said. "Without obstructing vision, of course. But I should like to see the rear of the property as well, if you have no objection. So that I may have a more complete knowledge of the . . . ah . . . lay. That is the American term, lay?"

"It is."

"I find your idiom fascinating," Holmes said. "One day I shall make a study of American slang."

"And write a monograph about it, no doubt."

"Or an article for one of the London popular journals."

They reached the end of the block and circled around into a deserted carriageway. When they drew near the carriage barn at the rear of the Costain property, Holmes stopped and peered through the fence as intently as he had in front. After which he asked where Quincannon would station himself.

"That tree there on your left," Quincannon lied. "I don't happen to know its Latin or its English name—"

"Taxus brevifolia," Holmes said promptly, "the Pacific yew."

Quincannon ground his teeth. The prospect of a cold night in the Englishman's company, not to mention a day trip to the low dives of the Barbary Coast, was as appealing as having one of his molars pulled without benefit of nitrous oxide.

He said, "If you've tabbed up enough, we'll take our positions now."

" 'I see you stand like greyhound in the slips, straining upon the start. The game's afoot.' "

"What's that you're blathering now?"

"Not blather, my good man. A quote from the immortal Bard—*King Henry the Fifth*. Aptly applied, eh?"

"Bah."

The confounded fellow rubbed his hands together briskly and winked. "A long low whistle if our man should appear, and we'll then join forces at the fountain in the side yard. Agreed?"

"Your memory is as keen as your conversation," Quincannon said sardonically.

Holmes seemed not to notice the sarcasm. He said, "Indeed," and hurried on his way.

Quincannon returned to the gate that gave access to a small carriage barn inside the Costain property. He made sure he was still alone and unobserved, then unlatched the gate and made his way carefully through the shadows alongside the barn. The surveillance spot he had picked out on his earlier tabbing was a shed set at an angle midway between barn and house. Not only did the shed provide a viewpoint of the rear-yard part of the side yard, but also afforded some shelter from the wind and the night's chill. The thought of the bughouse Sherlock shivering among the *chinensis whosis* in front would warm him even more.

He crossed to the shed, eased the door open and himself inside. The interior was cramped with stacks of cordwood and a jumble of gardening implements. By careful feel with his gloved hands he found that the stack nearest the door was low enough and sturdy enough to afford a seat, if he were careful not to move about too much. He lowered himself onto the wood. Even with the door wide open, he was in such darkness that he couldn't be seen from outside. Yet his range of vision was mostly unimpeded and aided by star shine and patchy moonlight.

He judged that it was well after seven by now. Andrew Costain had told him that his wife was due home no later than ten thirty, and that he himself would return by midnight. Even if Dodger Brown failed to appear, three and a half hours was little enough discomfort in exchange for a double fee.

His wait, however, lasted less than two hours. He was on his feet, flexing his limbs to ease them of cold and cramp, when he spied the interloper. A shadow among shadows, moving crosswise from his left—the same silent, flitting approach he had observed on the banker's property two nights ago. Dodger Brown was evidently bolder and more greedy than experience had taught him.

Quincannon rubbed his gloved hands together in anticipation, watching the shadow's progress toward the rear of the house. Pause, drift, pause again at the rear end of the porch. Up and over the railing there, briefly silhouetted: the same small figure dressed in dark cap and clothing. Across to the door, and at work there for just a few seconds. The door opened, closed again behind the burglar.

Quincannon spent several seconds readying his dark lantern, just in case. When one of the wind-herded clouds blotted the moon, he stepped out of the shed and hurried laterally to the bole of a tree a dozen rods from the house. He was about to give the signal whistle when a low ululation came from the front yard.

What the devil? He answered in kind, paused and whistled again. In a matter of moments he spied Holmes approaching. The Englishman seemed to have an uncanny sense of direction in the dark; he came in an unerring line straight to where Quincannon stood.

"Why did you whistle?" Quincannon demanded in a fierce whisper. "You couldn't have seen—"

"Andrew Costain is here."

"What?"

"Arrived not three minutes ago, alone in a trap."

"Blasted fool! He couldn't have chosen a worse time. You didn't stop him from going inside?"

"He seemed in a great hurry and I saw no purpose in revealing myself. The pannyman is also here, I presume?"

"Already inside through the rear door, not four minutes ago."

"Inside with us, too, Quincannon!" Holmes said urgently. "We've not a moment to lose!"

But it was already too late. In that instant a sharp report came from the house, muffled but unmistakable.

Holmes said, "Pistol shot."

Quincannon said, "Hell and damn!"

Both men broke into a run.

17

QUINCANNON

Quincannon had no need to order the Englishman to cover the front door; Holmes immediately veered off in that direction. The Navy Colt and the dark lantern were both at the ready when Quincannon reached the rear porch. Somewhere inside, another door slammed. He ran up the steps to the rear entrance, thumbed open the lantern's bull's-eye lens, and shouldered his way through.

The thin beam showed him a utility porch, then an opening into a broad kitchen. His foot struck something as he started ahead; the light revealed it to be a wooden wedge, of the sort used to prop open doors. He shut the door and toed the wedge tightly between the bottom and the frame—a safeguard against swift escape that took only a clutch of seconds.

Two or three additional sounds reached his ears as he plunged ahead, none distinguishable or close by. The beam picked out an electric switch on the kitchen wall; he turned it to flood the room with light. Empty. Likewise an adjoining dining room.

His twitching nose picked up the acrid tang of burnt gunpowder. The odor led him into a central hallway, which he flooded with more electric light. Then he eased past two closed doors to a third at the far end, where another hallway intersected this one. The powder smell was strongest there.

Quincannon paused to listen.

Thick, crackling silence.

He moved ahead to where he could see along the intersecting hall, found it deserted, and stepped to the third door to try the latch. Locked from within. There was no key on this side.

He rapped sharply on the panel, called out, "Mr. Costain?"

No response.

"John Quincannon here. It's safe for you to come out now."

Again, no response.

More sounds came from the front of the house—a heavy dragging noise, as of a piece of furniture being moved.

"Costain?" Louder this time.

Silence from behind the door.

Movement at the corner of his eye swung Quincannon around and brought the Navy to bear on the intersecting hallway. The Englishman was but a short distance away, approaching as noiselessly as a cat stalking prey.

Quincannon lowered his weapon and extinguished the lantern. "A sign of either man?" he said as Holmes hurried up.

"None."

"One or both must be on the other side of this door. It's locked on the inside."

"If the intruder is elsewhere and attempts to leave by the front door, he'll first have to move a heavy oak chair. We'll hear him."

"I wedged the rear door shut for the same reason."

Quincannon holstered the Navy, then backed off two steps

and flung the full weight of his body against the door panel. This rash action succeeded only in bruising flesh, jarring bone and teeth. Holmes, who was standing with his head cocked in a listening attitude, made no remark. If he had, he would have gotten his ears blistered.

Grumbling to himself, Quincannon again backed off and then drove the flat of his booted foot against the panel above the latch. Two more kicks were necessary to splinter the wood, tear the locking mechanism loose, and send the door wobbling inward.

Only a few scant inches inward, however, before it bound up against something bulky and inert on the floor.

Quincannon shoved hard against the panel until he was able to widen the opening enough to wedge his body through. The room was dark except for faint patches that marked uncurtained windows at the far end. He swept his hand along the wall, located a switch, turned it. The pale burst of electric light revealed what lay on the floor just inside the door—Andrew Costain in a facedown sprawl, both arms outflung, the one visible eye staring blankly.

Dead, and no mistake. Blood stained the back of his cheviot coat, the sleeve of his left forearm. Scorch marks blackened the sleeve as well.

The room, evidently the lawyer's study, was otherwise empty. Two drawers in a rolltop desk stood open; another had been yanked out and upended on the desktop. Papers littered the surface and the floor around the desk. Also on the floor, between the dead man and the desk, were two other items: a new-looking revolver, and a brassbound valuables case that appeared to have been pried open and was now plainly empty.

Holmes crowded in and swept the room with a keen gaze while Quincannon crossed to examine the windows. Both were of the casement type, with hook latches firmly in place; Dodger Brown hadn't gotten out that way. Still hiding somewhere in the house, upstairs or down. Or possibly gone by now through another window.

When Quincannon turned, he found himself looking at the bughouse Sherlock down on one knee, hunched over the corpse and peering through a large magnifying glass at the wound in Costain's back. Under the ridiculous cap, his lean hawk's face was darkly flushed, his brows warped into two hard black lines. A small smile appeared as he lifted his head. His eyes showed a glitter that was steely, mad, or both.

"Interesting," he said. "Quite."

"What is?"

"Andrew Costain was stabbed to death."

"Stabbed?"

"He was also shot."

"What!"

"Two separate and distinct wounds," Holmes said. "The superficial one in his forearm was made by a bullet. The fatal wound was the result of a single thrust with an instrument at least eight inches in length and quite sharp. A stiletto, I should say. The blow was struck by a right-handed person approximately five and a half feet tall, at an upward angle of perhaps fifteen degrees."

Quincannon gawped at him. "How the devil can you judge that from one quick study?"

The Englishman flashed his enigmatic smile and said nothing.

It took only a few seconds to locate the lead pellet that had passed through Costain's arm; it was in the cushion of an armchair near the desk. While Holmes commenced studying it through his blasted glass, Quincannon picked up the revolver. It was a Forehand & Wadsworth .38 caliber, its nickel-plated finish and wooden grips free of marks of any kind. He sniffed the barrel to confirm that it had been recently fired, then opened the breech for a squint inside. All of the chambers were empty. A few seconds after he returned the weapon to the place where it had lain, Holmes was down on his knees examining it under magnification as he had the bullet.

Glowering, Quincannon left the study to comb the premises. Not long afterward, the Englishman joined in the search. The results were rather astonishing.

They found no sign of Dodger Brown, and yet every window, upstairs and down, was firmly latched. Furthermore, the wedge Quincannon had kicked under the back door was still in place, as was the heavy chair Holmes had dragged over to block the front door. Those were the only two doors that provided an exit from the house.

"How the deuce could he have gotten out?" Quincannon wondered aloud. "Even the cellar door in the kitchen is locked tight. And there wasn't enough time for him to have slippped away *before* we entered."

"Dear me, no," Holmes agreed. "You or I would have seen him."

"Well, he managed it somehow."

"So it would seem. A miraculous double escape, in fact."

"Double escape?"

"From a locked room, and then from a sealed house." The

Englishman punctuated this statement with another of his dauncy little smiles. "According to Dr. Axminster, you are adept at solving seemingly impossible crimes. How then did the pannyman manage a double escape? Why was Andrew Costain shot as well as stabbed? Why was the pistol left in the locked study and the bloody stiletto taken away? And why was the study door bolted in the first place? A pretty puzzle, eh, Quincannon? One to challenge the deductive skills of even the cleverest sleuth."

Quincannon muttered five short, colorful words, none of them remotely of a deductive nature.

As much as Quincannon disliked and mistrusted the city police, the circumstances of this crime were such that notifying them was unavoidable. He telephoned the Hall of Justice on the instrument in Costain's study. After that he paced and cogitated, to no reasonable conclusion.

The Englishman, meanwhile, examined the corpse a second time, paying particular attention, it seemed, to a pale smear on the coat near the fatal knife wound. He then proceeded to squint through the glass at the carpet in both the study and the hallway, crawling to and fro on his hands and knees, and at any number of other things after that. Now and then he muttered aloud to himself: "More data! I can't make bricks without clay!" and "Hallo! That's more like it!" and "Ah, plain as a pikestaff!"

Neither man had anything more to say to the other. It was as if a gauntlet had been thrown down, a tacit challenge issued—which the bughouse Sherlock seemed to think was the case. Two bloodhounds on the scent, no longer working in consort, but as competitors in an undeclared contest of wills. Quincannon would have none of that nonsense. As far as he was concerned, there was only one detective at work here, only one sane man qualified and capable of answering the challenge.

The blue coats arrived in less than half an hour, what for them was swift dispatch. They were half a dozen in number, accompanied by a handful of reporters representing Fremont Older's *Call,* the *Daily Alta,* and San Francisco's other newspapers, who were made to wait outside—half as many of both breeds as there would have been if the murder of a prominent attorney had happened on Nob Hill.

The inspector in charge was a beefy, red-faced Prussian named Kleinhoffer, whom Quincannon knew slightly and condoned not in the slightest. Inspector Kleinhoffer was both stupid and corrupt, a lethal combination, and a political toady besides. His opinion of flycops was on par with Quincannon's opinion of him.

His first comment was, "Involved in another killing, eh, Quincannon? What's your excuse this time?"

Quincannon explained, briefly, the reason he was there. He omitted mention of Dodger Brown by name, using the phrase "unknown burglar" instead and catching the Englishman's eye as he spoke so the lunatic would say nothing to contradict him. He was not about to chance losing a fee—small chance though it was, the police being such a generally inept bunch—by providing information that might allow them to stumble across the Dodger ahead of him.

Kleinhoffer sneered. "Some fancy flycop. You're sure he's not still somewhere in the house?"

"Sure enough."

"We'll see about that." He gestured to a burly red-faced sergeant, who stepped forward. "Mahoney, you and your men search the premises top to bottom."

"Yes, sir."

Kleinhoffer's beady gaze settled on the Englishman, ran over his face and his ridiculous disguise. "Who're you?" he demanded.

"S. Holmes, of London, England. A temporary associate of Mr. Quincannon's private inquiry agency."

Quincannon was none too pleased at the last statement, but he offered no disclaimer. Better that false assertion than a rambling monologue on what a masterful detective Holmes fancied himself to be.

"A limey, eh?" Kleinhoffer said. Then, to Quincannon, "Picking your operatives off the docks these days, are you?"

"If I am, it's no concern of yours."

"None of your guff. Where's the stiff?"

"In the study."

Kleinhoffer gave Andrew Costain's remains a cursory examination. "Shot and stabbed both," he said wonderingly. "You didn't tell me that. What the hell happened here tonight?"

Quincannon's account, given in detail, heightened the inspector's apoplectic color and narrowed his beady eyes to slits. Any crime more complicated than a Barbary Coast stabbing or coshing invariably confused him, and the evident facts in this case threatened to tie a permanent knot in his cranial lobes.

He shook his head, as if trying to shake loose cobwebs, and snapped, "None of that makes a damned bit of sense."

"Sense or not, that is exactly what took place."

"You there, limey. He leave anything out?"

"Tut, tut," Holmes said with dignity. "I am an Englishman, sir, a British subject . . . not a 'limey.'"

"I don't care if you're the president of England—"

"There is no president of England. My country is a monarchy."

Kleinhoffer gnashed his yellowed teeth. "Never mind that. Did Quincannon leave anything out or didn't he?"

"He did not. His re-creation of events was precise in every detail."

"So you say. I say it couldn't have happened the way you two tell it."

"Nonetheless, it did, though what seems to have transpired is not necessarily what actually took place. What we are dealing with here is illusion and obfuscation."

The inspector wrapped an obscene noun in a casing of disgust. After which he stooped to pick up the Forehand & Wadsworth revolver. He sniffed the barrel, broke it open to check the chambers as Quincannon had done, then dropped the weapon into his coat pocket. He was squinting at the empty valuables case when Sergeant Mahoney entered the room.

"No sign of anybody in the house," he reported.

"Back door still wedged shut?"

"Yes, sir."

"Then he must've managed to slip out the front while these two flycops weren't looking."

"I beg to differ," Holmes said. He mentioned the heavy chair. "It was not moved until your arrival, Inspector, by Mr. Quincannon and myself. Even if it had been, I would surely have heard the scraping and dragging sounds. My hearing is preternaturally acute."

Kleinhoffer said the rude word again.

Mahoney said, "Mrs. Costain is here."

"What's that?"

"The dead man's wife. Mrs. Penelope Costain. She just come home."

"Well, why didn't you say so? Bring her in here."

The sergeant did as directed. Penelope Costain was stylishly garbed in a high-collared blouse, flounced skirt, and fur-trimmed cloak, her brunette curls tucked under a hat adorned with an ostrich plume. She took one look at her husband's remains, shuddered violently, and began to sway as if about to faint. Mahoney caught one arm to steady her. Quincannon took hold of the other and together they helped her to one of the chairs.

She drew several deep breaths, fanned herself with one hand. "I . . . I'm all right," she said after a few moments. Her gaze touched the body again and immediately away. "Poor Andrew. He was a brave man. . . . He must have fought terribly for his life."

"We'll get the man who did it," Kleinhoffer promised foolishly.

"Can't you . . . cover him with something?"

"Mahoney. Find a cloth."

"Yes, sir."

Penelope Costain nibbled at a torn fingernail, her head tilted to one side as she peered up at the faces ringed above her. "Is that you, Mr. Holmes? What are you doing here, dressed in such outlandish clothing?"

"He was working with me," Quincannon said.

"With you? Two detectives in tandem failed to prevent this . . . this outrage?"

"None of what happened was our fault."

She said bitterly, "That is the same statement you made two nights ago. Nothing, no tragedy, is ever your fault, evidently."

Kleinhoffer was still holding the empty valuables case. He extended it to the widow, saying, "This was on the floor, Mrs. Costain."

"Yes. My husband kept it in his desk."

"What was in it?"

"Twenty-dollar gold pieces, a dozen or so. And the more expensive pieces among my jewelery . . . a diamond brooch, a pair of diamond earrings, a pearl necklace."

"Worth how much, would you say?"

"I don't know . . . several thousand dollars, I should think." She looked again at Quincannon, this time with open hostility.

Kleinhoffer did the same. He said, "You and the limey were here the entire time, and still you let that yegg murder Mr. Costain and get away with the swag . . . right under your noses. Well? What've you got to say for yourselves?"

Quincannon had nothing to say.

Neither did the bughouse Sherlock.

18

QUINCANNON

It was well past midnight when Quincannon finally trudged wearily up the stairs to his rooms. After Kleinhoffer had finished with him, the newspapermen had descended—on him but not on the Englishman, who managed to slip away unnoticed. Quincannon had taken pains to keep Holmes well in the background; in his comments to the reporters, he referred to him as a "temporary operative" and an "underling."

He donned his nightshirt and crawled into bed, but the night's jumbled events plagued his mind and refused to let him sleep. At length he lit his bedside lamp, picked up a copy of Walt Whitman's *Sea-Drift*. Usually Whitman, or Emily Dickinson or James Lowell, freed his brain of clutter and allowed him to relax, but not tonight. He switched reading matter to *Drunkards and Curs: The Truth About Demon Rum*. He and Sabina had once been hired by the True Christian Temperance Society to catch an embezzler, and this had led him to his second collecting interest: temperance tracts, whose highly inflammatory rhetoric he found amusing.

Drunkards and Curs did the trick. Before the end of one turgid chapter he was sound asleep.

He awoke not long past seven, allowed himself a hasty breakfast, and within an hour was at the agency offices. For once he was the first to arrive. And when he unlocked the door and stepped inside, he was pleased to find an envelope that had been slipped under the door. It contained a single sheet of paper, on which was written in Ezra Bluefield's backhand scrawl:

> Duff's Curio Shop. He knows.
> E.B.

A wolf's smile split Quincannon's freebooter's whiskers. Ezra Bluefield, true to his word as always, had finally come through, and the morning was now considerably brighter.

He went to coax steam heat from the radiator; on mornings such as this, the offices were as damp and chill as a cave. While he was so engaged, Sabina arrived.

"Up bright and early this morning, I see," she said. Then, as she removed her straw boater, "But not bushy-tailed. Another sleepless night?"

"For the most part."

"Did something happen at the Costain home?"

"Unfortunately, yes."

"Dodger Brown struck again?"

"Struck, and committed another cold-blooded murder."

"Murder? Who was killed? Not that man Holmes—"

"No. More's the pity."

"Who, then?"

"Andrew Costain. Stabbed and shot in bizarre circumstances." He went on to outline the evening's events.

Sabina's only reaction was the high lift of her eyebrows as he unfolded the tale. "It all seems fantastic. How could Dodger Brown possibly have escaped both the locked study and the house?"

"How indeed. A pretty puzzle, the crackbrain called it. His only worthwhile remark the entire night."

"You have no one to blame for his presence but yourself," she reminded him.

Quincannon ignored the remark. "You should have seen him, crawling around on hands and knees, peering through his magnifying glass. Ludicrous. Why, he even seems to think there's to be a contest between us to see who can solve the riddle. As if he could manage it by aping methods used by the real Sherlock Holmes!"

"Perhaps he can."

"Balderdash. There's only one man clever enough to get to the bottom of a crime such as this."

Sabina fixed him with one of her analytical looks. "You wouldn't be feeling a touch threatened by him, would you?"

"Threatened? By a lunatic? Faugh!"

"Well and good, then. Have you any theories yet?"

"No, but it's only a matter of time and a bit more legwork."

"You know, John, this business may be more complicated than you realize."

"Why do you say that?"

"You recall the silver money clip I found in Clara Wilds's rooms? It belonged to Costain."

"Costain? You're sure of that?"

"Yesterday I took it to the silversmith who made it. He made a positive identification."

Quincannon loaded and fired his briar while he pondered this. "So then Costain must have been one of the dip's victims. And a recent one, if what I took to be gastric discomfort at our first meeting was in fact pain from a wound caused by one of Wilds's hatpin thrusts."

"Coincidence, do you think?"

"I don't see how it could be anything else," he said when he had the pipe drawing. "And yet . . ."

"Yes, 'and yet.' Clara Wilds was murdered two days ago, Andrew Costain was murdered last night. And both, conceivably, by the same person. That would seem to be stretching coincidence to the breaking point."

"So it would."

"There's something else that bothers me," Sabina said, "if we assume Dodger Brown is guilty of both crimes. His criminal record."

"What about it?"

"His felonies have always been nonviolent. Why, all of a sudden, would he commit two bloody homicides in two days?"

"Greed. Fear of capture. He is known to carry a pistol."

"But never to have used it."

"True."

"Is it likely he'd also carry a weapon such as a stiletto?"

"Not from what we know about him, but his habits might have changed for some reason." Quincannon ruminated again. "It may also be that either or both weapons used belonged to Costain. The revolver bought by him for protection, a purchase he neglected to tell his wife about. The lethal weapon an object from his desk, such as a letter opener. In any case, the murder would seem to be the result of a brief but fierce struggle."

"That seems plausible," Sabina said. "But why would Dodger Brown carry a bloody stiletto or letter opener away with him and leave the pistol behind?"

"Panic. A man who has just taken another man's life doesn't always act rationally. Whatever happened in Costain's study, we'll find out when I've yaffled the Dodger. And that won't be long now."

"You said that yesterday. He's still at large."

"But now we have a lead," Quincannon told her, "courtesy of Ezra Bluefield." He showed her the message that had been slipped under the office door.

"Our old friend Luther Duff."

"One of the easier eggs to crack in the city. For our purposes, Dodger Brown couldn't have picked a better fenceman."

"Assuming Duff knows his whereabouts. With at least one murder on his conscience, he may have already gone on the lammas."

"If he has," Quincannon said darkly, "I'll track him down no matter where he goes. But I have a feeling he's still in the area. If he is and he's planning to run, he'll need cash and Duff drives a hard bargain. Luther should know where to find him if anyone does."

"Let's hope so. John, have you informed Jackson Pollard of last night's events?"

"No, not yet."

"Don't you think you should?"

Quincannon grimaced at the prospect. "Likely he'll lay the blame on me and I'm in no mood for one of his rants."

"If you'd rather I telephoned him . . ."

"No, the duty's mine. I'll stop in at Great Western after I've seen Luther Duff."

"Before would be better."

"But afterward I expect to have favorable news to sweeten his temper." Quincannon reached for his derby, tipped it onto his head. "And with a smile from lady luck, before the end of the day I'll have Dodger Brown."

19

SABINA

Despite her misgivings about investigating Clara Wilds's murder, Sabina found herself doing just that when she left the home of the last of the pickpocket's victims. She had no other pressing business, and she was still not convinced Dodger Brown was the guilty party. Whether it was Brown or someone else who had stabbed Wilds, the culprit might have been seen entering or leaving her rooms. The police operated on the theory that the deaths of felons, male or female, violent or otherwise, were a benefit to society and so expended little effort in such cases. They would not have bothered with any but a routine investigation.

Wilds had been a wicked woman whose extortion schemes and dipping forays had harmed numerous individuals, but she had also been a human being. In Sabina's view, murder should never be condoned no matter who the victim. Besides, there were curious elements in the woman's sudden demise—the silver money clip belonging to a second murder victim, Andrew Costain, for one—that aroused Sabina's sleuthing instincts.

She spent the rest of the morning in the vicinity of Wilds's rooms, asking carefully phrased questions of residents, passersby, and wandering street vendors. The pickpocket's murder seemed to have aroused only mild interest in the neighborhood, and only two individuals acknowledged knowing her by sight. But neither knew or would say anything about Wilds's comings and goings or any regular male visitors she might have had.

Sabina's perseverance finally produced results at two o'clock, when she knocked on the door of a home across the carriageway that ran behind Wilds's boarding house.

The woman who answered the door seemed more inquisitive than any of the other neighbors. When she admitted to having seen Wilds on several occasions and to being shocked by the murder, Sabina decided that the best way to gain her confidence was to identify herself—something she had avoided doing elsewhere in the neighborhood. She presented her card, and explained her interest in Clara Wilds in vague terms, saying that Wilds was "the subject of an investigation for an important client." The neighbor, whose name was Mrs. Anthony Marcus, seemed thrilled to be in the presence of a lady detective; she invited Sabina into a tidy parlor free of the usual gimcracks for further conversation.

Mrs. Marcus was a large individual of some forty years who wore her age and weight well. Her graying hair was dressed close to the head with curled fringe at the forehead and fairly high buns on top, her rather plain face open and eager, her eyes bright as a bird's. Not exactly a busybody or a gossip, Sabina thought, but nonetheless a woman who took a much keener interest in her surroundings than most.

"Ever since that woman moved in across the way," Mrs. Marcus said, "I've thought there was something . . . well, furtive about her. The circumstances of her death certainly seem to confirm it."

"In what ways did you think her furtive?"

"Her comings and goings were extremely irregular. Early mornings to very late nights, and as often as not she would approach her rooms along the carriageway below. Her dress was . . . how shall I put it . . . eccentric and varied greatly, as if she were trying to disguise her real person."

Sabina nodded. "Please, go on."

"Not that I'm the sort to spy on my neighbors, you understand. It's just that my kitchen windows overlook the end corner of the boarding house where she had her rooms. My husband claims I spend too much time in the kitchen, day and night, but I believe in cleanliness and careful preparation of meals—"

"Is there anything else you can tell me about her? Did she have many visitors?"

"Well, the times I saw her leave and return she was alone. Except one evening, that is, when she was accompanied by a man who entered her rooms with her. That dreadful Barbary Coast isn't far from here. I wouldn't be surprised to hear that she spent much of her time there. She wasn't a . . . soiled dove, was she?"

"No."

"Something just as wicked, though?"

"I'm not at liberty to say. Did you have a clear look at the man?"

"Yes, fairly clear." Mrs. Marcus sniffed. "It was still light and they came strolling up the carriageway arm in arm."

Sabina described Dodger Brown. "Is he the one?"

"Oh, no. The man was . . . let me see . . . in his forties, stocky. Bushy black hair. And rather well-dressed."

Victor Pope.

"How long ago was it that you saw them together, Mrs. Marcus?"

"Just last week."

"Did you happen to see Clara Wilds yesterday?"

"No. No, the last time was the day before."

"Or anyone else in the vicinity of her rooms?"

"The person who took her life? No. If I had, I would certainly have informed the police."

It was fortunate that Mrs. Marcus hadn't been at her kitchen window when Sabina arrived or when she'd left a short time later. Not that she was particularly well known by sight to the city detectives, but Mrs. Marcus was an observer with a sharp eye for detail. A description of Sabina might have led to a certain amount of unpleasant questioning about her presence in the murdered pickpocket's rooms.

"Oh, but there is one thing I did see yesterday, Mrs. Carpenter. I don't know if it means anything or not, but it did seem a bit odd at the time."

"And what would that be?"

"There was a buggy parked in the alley below, behind the boarding house. A rather nice one that I've never seen before or since. That's why I noticed it—buggies like that are uncommon in this neighborhood."

"What time was this?"

"Midafternoon, shortly before I left to do my marketing. It was gone when I returned . . . Oh! You don't suppose . . . ?"

"Possibly. In which direction was it facing?"

"Toward Columbus Avenue."

"Was there any sign of the driver?"

"No, none."

"Can you describe the buggy?"

"Well, it was black, with its top up."

"Distinctive trim of any sort?"

"No . . . Wait, yes. The wheel spokes were a faded gold color."

"Faded. The rig wasn't new, then?"

"No, I don't believe it was."

"Did you recognize the manufacturer?"

Mrs. Marcus shook her head. "I'm afraid I know nothing at all about equipages."

"One horse or two?"

"One. A brown one."

"Bay, sorrel, chestnut?"

"I really couldn't say. Brown is brown to me."

Sabina thanked the woman and rose to leave. At the door Mrs. Marcus asked if she should notify the police about the buggy. Sabina said no, that wasn't necessary, she would attend to the matter herself, and asked that her visit and investigation be kept in the strictest confidence as well. The less her confidante had to do with the blue coats, the better.

Outside again, she made her way to the carriageway that bisected the block. At the approximate place behind Wilds's boarding house where the horse and buggy had been parked, she briefly examined the ground in the small hope of finding a footprint or some other clue. But there was nothing in the matted-down grass and weeds except meaningless bits of litter and unidentifiable wheel marks. After a time she continued on down the carriageway to where it intersected with Columbus Avenue across from Washington Square.

A flower seller's stand occupied the corner of the square directly opposite: a great showy splash of red and green, yellow and blue, pink and purple. A young man with a flowing mane of blond hair was urging a bouquet of multicolored carnations upon an older man, who finally succumbed and departed, looking dubiously at his purchase. Sabina took his place at the stand.

"Roses for you, miss?" the vendor asked. "Pink, to match your lovely complexion?"

A pink rose for the former Pink Rose. Well, why not? "I'll buy one in exchange for some information."

"Only one?"

"Only one."

"A half dozen is a much better value."

She was in no mood to haggle. "A half dozen, then."

As he set about choosing and wrapping them, she described the buggy and the approximate time it had been parked and asked if he had happened to see it entering or leaving the carriageway. He handed her the cone-shaped package, rubbed his chin in thought, and then nodded.

"I did see a rig like that come by around that time. Black one—Concord, I think it was. Big old bay in the traces. Reason I noticed it, it almost collided with a brewer's dray just up the block."

"Did you have a clear look at the driver?"

"Fair look. Small fellow, wore dark clothes and a cloth cap."

Dodger Brown, Sabina thought. But what would a common yegg like the Dodger be doing driving an expensive Concord buggy, even an old one?

"Can you describe his features?" she asked.

"Afraid not. Had his cap pulled down and coat collar up." The flower seller grinned crookedly, exposing stained yellow teeth. "Drove worse than a woman, he did."

"Why do you say that?"

"Almost caused the accident. In a big hurry, swerving all over the road, not paying attention the way women—" At Sabina's sharp look, he broke off and then added hastily, "No offense, miss."

"None taken," she lied, dropped coins into his hand, and turned away thinking that it would require a great deal of education to bring men like him into the era of the New Woman.

A quick canvass of the other vendors in the area revealed nothing further about the buggy or its driver. Sabina crossed Washington Square and went on down to a hack stand opposite the Saints Peter and Paul church at the corner of Filbert and Grant. By the time she entered one of the cabs, she'd decided on her next destination: the Jersey Street home of Victor Pope.

Evidently Pope had been Clara Wilds's lover as well as her greed-driven fenceman. It was just possible he was her murderer as well, though one factor mitigated against it: the time element. Sabina had gone directly to Washington Square after leaving Pope's hardware store. True, her cabbie had been in no hurry, but even if Pope had left immediately afterward and driven swiftly and directly to Clara Wilds's lodging house, there would have been precious little time for him to kill his paramour, conduct his search, and vanish before Sabina's arrival.

In order for this to have happened, the murder would have

to have been premeditated; there simply wasn't enough time for a falling out of some sort, a sudden homicidal rage. And why would he have wanted Wilds dead badly enough to commit the deed in broad daylight? Besides, he'd seemed calm enough during Sabina's meeting with him, and had snatched eagerly at the bait for greater riches that she'd dangled in front of him.

No, it wasn't likely that he was the guilty party. But she wouldn't be satisfied of the fact until she learned whether or not Pope owned a black Concord buggy and a bay horse.

Confronting him again would have necessitated more lies and perhaps put her at risk. Guilty or innocent, his suspicions would be aroused. His mother, however, might not yet know of Wilds's demise; Pope wouldn't have told her in any case, and the deaths of common criminals were seldom reported in the newspapers. She could find out what she needed to know, she reasoned, from Dippin' Sal.

The crippled old woman was home and if not happy to see her, not hostile, either. "Well, missy, back again. Did you find Clara?"

"No. Not yet."

"Victor wouldn't tell you where she's livin', eh? Close-mouthed rascal, same as his father. But it's no use askin' me again. Like I told you the other day, that ungrateful bitch don't come around to see me no more."

The thought occurred to Sabina that Dippin' Sal might be lying. That she'd known all along where Clara Wilds was residing, that she might have harbored a deadly grudge against her protégée and coveted her spoils, and that she might be the murderer. But as quickly as the notion came, Sabina dismissed it. No one as old as this woman, with those misshapen, arthritic hands, could have driven a buggy a long distance or overpowered one as young and strong as Wilds.

Victor Pope was not guilty, either. She was convinced of that moments later when in a roundabout way she brought up the subject of Victor Pope's transportation.

"He don't own a buggy," Dippin' Sal said, "and he don't own a horse. How does he get around? Trolleys and cable cars, that's how. Too cheap to hire cabs. He don't take me anywhere, neither. Can't be bothered with an old woman like me, just lets me sit here in this house and listening to my arteries harden and my bones creak." She added bitterly, "I done some things in my time that I ain't proud of, but the worst I ever done was give birth to that damn no-account son of mine."

Dippin' Sal had been a hellion in her day, but Sabina couldn't help feeling a touch sorry for her as she was now. She still carried the half-dozen roses she'd bought from the vendor at Washington Square; on impulse she handed the packet to the old woman, who blinked her surprise.

"What're these for?"

"I thought you might like a bit of color to brighten your day, Mrs. Tatum."

"Pink roses." The rheumy eyes glistened. "Why . . . that's real nice of you, missy. Nobody give me flowers in so long, I can't remember the last time."

Nor ever would again, Sabina thought as she returned to the waiting hansom, likely not even when Dippin' Sal went to her final resting place.

———

The cobbled street in front of the Costain house near South Park was deserted, though Sabina imagined that it had been teeming with vehicles and curious neighbors and bystanders last night and perhaps earlier today. In her experience, citizens in neighborhoods such as the one where Clara Wilds had died were generally indifferent to scenes of violent crime, but those in residential neighborhoods like this one always drew a crowd. The lower classes were used to violence in their midst and had learned to live with it; those in the upper classes were not and had not.

This would be her last stop before returning to the agency, she thought as she alighted from the cab. She disliked intruding on Andrew Costain's widow so soon after his demise, but she had no other avenues left to explore. Until Dodger Brown was caught and examined, the possibility existed that someone else had stabbed the pickpocket and driven the buggy from the scene of the crime. If that were true, then it was also possible the two cases were connected in a way as yet undetermined. Penelope Costain might conceivably know something that would provide her with a new lead.

Sabina opened the gate and walked up a path that wound through an unkempt front yard dominated by lilac shrubs. The house was on the unkempt side as well, in need of fresh paint and gingerbread repair. On the front door, a large funeral wreath hung slightly askew from a brass knocker speckled with verdigris. No, not askew—the door was open a few inches as if it hadn't been properly latched and the light afternoon breeze had pushed it inward. As she drew nearer she heard the sound of voices rise from within, the first a woman's quivering with anger, the second a man's calm and controlled.

"How dare you lurk about spying on me, then break into my home!"

"My dear Mrs. Costain, I neither lurked nor spied on you. I knew from Dr. Axminster when you would be leaving for your appointment with him and so seized the opportunity for further investigation. Nor did I break and enter. The police left a rear window unlatched. I merely stepped over the sill."

"You're still trespassing. You have no right to be here!"

"Ah, but I believe I do. Inasmuch as I was present during last night's unfortunate tragedy, as a temporary employee of the agency hired by your husband, I am duty bound to continue my inquiries."

Penelope Costain. And Sherlock Holmes.

20

QUINCANNON

Duff's Curio Shop was crowded among similar establishments in the second block of McAllister Street west of Van Ness. It contained, according to its proprietor, "bric-a-brac and curios of every type and description, from every culture and every nation . . . the new, the old, the mild, the exotic." In short, it was full of junk.

This was Quincannon's fourth visit to the place, once in his capacity as a Secret Service operative on a case involving the counterfeiting of 1840s eagles and half eagles, three times as private investigator, and he had yet to see a single customer. It may have been that Luther Duff sold some of his wares now and then, but if so, it was by accident and with little or no effort on his part. Where he had procured his inventory was a mystery; all that anyone knew for certain was that he had it and seldom if ever added new items to the dusty, moldering stock.

Duff's primary profession was receiver and disburser of stolen goods. Burglars, box men, pickpockets, footpads, and other felons far and wide beat a steady path to his door. Like other fencemen, he professed to offer his fellow thieves a square deal: half of what he expected to realize on the resale of any particular item. In fact, his notion of fifty-fifty was akin to putting a lead dollar on a Salvation Army tambourine and asking for fifty cents change.

He took a 75 percent cut of most profits, an even higher percentage from the more gullible and desperate among his suppliers. Stolen weapons of all types were his specialty— often enough at an 80 or 90 percent profit. A Tenderloin hockshop might offer a thief more cash, but hockshop owners put their marks on pistols, shotguns, and the like—marks that had been known to lead police agencies straight to the source. Hockshop proprietors were thus considered hangman's handmaidens, and crooks generally stayed shy of them, preferring smaller but safer returns from men like Luther Duff.

Despite being well known in the trade, Duff had somehow managed to avoid prosecution. This was both a strong advertisement and his Achilles' heel. He had a horror of arrest and imprisonment and was subject to intimidation as a result. Quincannon was of the opinion that Duff would sell his mother, if he had one, and his entire line of relatives rather than spend a single night at the mercy of a city prison guard.

A bell above the door jingled unmusically as Quincannon entered the shop. On the instant, the combined smells of dust, mildew, and slow decay pinched his nostrils. He made his way slowly through the dimly lighted interior, around and through an amazing hodgepodge of furniture that included a Chinese wardrobe festooned with fire-breathing dragons, a Tyrolean pine coffer, a saber-scarred Spanish refectory table, a brass-bound "pirate treasure" chest from Madagascar, and a damascened suit of armor. He passed shelves of worm-ridden books, an assortment of corpses that had once been clocks, a stuffed and molting weasel, an artillery bugle, a ship's sextant, a broken marble tombstone with the name HORSE-SHY HALLORAN chiseled into its face, and a yellow-varnished portrait of a fat nude woman who would have looked more aesthetic, he thought, with her clothes on.

When he neared the long counter at the rear, a set of musty damask drapes parted and Luther Duff emerged grinning. He was short, round, balding, fiftyish, and about as appetizing as a tainted oyster. He wore shyness and venality as openly as the garters on his sleeves and the moneylender's eyeshade across his forehead. The grin and the suddenness of his appearance made Quincannon think, as always, of a balky-eyed troll jumping out from under a bridge in front of an unwary traveler.

"Hello, hello, hello," the troll said. "What can I do for . . . awk!"

The strangled-chicken noise was the result of his having recognized his visitor. The grin vanished in a wash of nervous terror. He stood stiffly and darted looks everywhere but across the counter into Quincannon's eyes.

"How are you, Luther?" Quincannon asked pleasantly.

"Ah . . . well and good, well and good."

"No health problems, I trust?"

"No, no, none, fit as a fiddle."

"Sound of body, pure of heart?"

"Ah, well, ah . . ."

"But it's a harsh and uncertain world we live in, eh, Luther? Illness can strike any time. Accidents, likewise."

"Accidents?"

"Terrible, crippling accidents. Requiring a long stay in the hospital."

It was cold in the shop, but Duff's face was already damp. He produced a dark-flecked handkerchief, twitchily began to mop his brow.

"Of course, there are worse things even than illness and accident," Quincannon said. "Worse for some, that is. Such as those who suffer from claustrophobia."

"Claustro . . . what?"

"The awful fear of being trapped in small enclosed spaces. A prison cell, for instance."

"Gahh," the troll said. A shudder passed through him.

"Such a man would suffer greatly under those circumstances. I would hate to see it happen to someone like you, the more so when it could be easily avoided."

"Ah . . ."

Quincannon simulated a tolerant smile. "Well, no more of that, eh? We'll move along to my reason for calling this morning. I'm after a bit of information I believe you can supply."

"Ah . . ."

"It happens that I have urgent business with a lad named Dodger Brown. However, he seems to have dropped from sight."

"Dodger Brown?"

"The same. Wine dump habitue, gambler, and burglar by trade. You've had recent dealings with him, I understand."

"Recent dealings? No, you're mistaken."

"Now, now, Luther. Remember what I said about prison cells? Cold, unpleasant—and very, very small."

Duff fidgeted and perspired. "What . . . ah . . . what business do you have with Dodger Brown?"

"Mine and none of yours. All you need do is tell me where I can find him."

"Ah . . ."

"You must have some idea of where he's holed up." Quincannon let the smile slip away, his voice harden. "It wouldn't be in your best interest to tax my patience."

"Oh . . . ah . . . I wouldn't, I won't," Duff said. The tip of his tongue flicked over thin lips. "An idea, perhaps. A possibility. You won't say where you heard?"

"No one need know of our little talk but us."

"Well . . . ah . . . he has a cousin, a fisherman known as Salty Jim."

"Does he now." This was news to Quincannon; there was nothing in the Dodger's dossier about a living relative.

Duff said, "Dodger Brown bunks with him from time to time on his boat. So . . . ah . . . so I've heard on the earie."

"Where does this Salty Jim keep his boat?"

"Across the bay . . . the Oakland City Wharf. He . . . ah . . . he's involved in the oyster trade."

"The name of his craft?"

"Something with 'oyster' in it. That's all I can tell you."

"Is it? Cudgel that cunning brain of yours, Luther, and see if you can recall the exact name."

Duff cudgeled. To no avail. At length he shook his head so miserably that it seemed his memory really had failed him.

"Good enough," Quincannon said. "Now we'll move along to other matters. Did you sell the Dodger a revolver recently?"

"Revolver?"

"Specifically, a brand-new Forehand and Wadsworth thirty-eight-caliber."

"No. No, absolutely not."

"That had better be the truth."

"It is! I swear I sold him no weapon of any kind."

"When did you last see him?"

"I . . . ah . . . don't remember . . ."

"Luther."

". . . Yesterday. Yesterday morning."

"And you paid him cash for whatever goods he brought. What were they, and how much?"

"I don't, ah, know what you mean. He came to see me, yes, but it was only to discuss selling certain property . . ."

Quincannon drew his Navy Colt, laid the weapon on the countertop between them. "You were saying?"

"Awk."

"No, that wasn't it. You were about to identify the items and how much you paid Dodger Brown for them. In fact, in the spirit of cooperation and good fellowship between us, you were about to show me these items. And don't tell me you don't still have them all. I know how you operate."

The troll swallowed in a way that was remarkably similar to a cow swallowing its cud. He twitched, looked at the pistol, nibbled at his lower lip like a rat nibbling cheese.

Quincannon picked up the Navy and held it loosely in his hand, the barrel aimed in the general direction of Duff's right eye. "My time is valuable, Luther," he said. "And yours is fast running out."

The troll turned abruptly and stepped through the drapery. Quincannon vaulted the counter, followed him into an incredibly cluttered office lighted by an oil lamp. A farrago of items covered the surface of a battered rolltop desk; boxes and wrappings littered the floor; piles of curios teetered precariously on a pair of claw-foot tables. In one corner was a large and fairly new Mosler safe. Duff glanced back, noted Quincannon's expression, and reluctantly proceeded to open the safe. He tried to shield the interior with his body, but Quincannon loomed up behind to peer over the troll's shoulder as his hands sifted through the contents.

"If I find out you've withheld so much as a collar stay," Quincannon warned him, "I'll pay you a return visit that won't be half so pleasant as this one."

Duff shuddered again and brought forth a chamois pouch, which he handed over with even greater reluctance. Quincannon holstered the Navy, shook the contents of the pouch into his palm. One sapphire brooch, two pairs of sapphire earrings, and a large gold-nugget watch fob.

"This is only a small portion of the Dodger's recent acquisitions. Where's the rest?"

"I swear this is all he brought me yesterday!"

"Then he's planning to return with the rest. When? Today?"

"I don't know. He didn't say."

"The truth now."

"That is the truth, I swear it."

"How much did you give him for these baubles?"

"Two hundred dollars. He . . . ah . . . seemed to think they were worth more, but he took the cash. He seemed in a hurry."

"Yes? Frightened, was he?"

"No. Eager, excited about something. All in a lather."

"Did he give you an idea of what had raised his blood pressure?"

"No. None."

"Or happen to mention Clara Wilds?"

"Who? I don't . . ."

"Luther."

"No. No, we only discussed business."

"But he is still consorting with her, isn't he?"

"I have no idea. He's never brought her here, never spoken of her to me. Someone else . . . ah . . ."

"Fences her ill-gotten gains. Yes, I know."

Quincannon was satisfied that Duff hadn't withheld anything important to his investigation. He returned the items of jewelry to the pouch and tucked the pouch into his coat pocket.

"Here, now!" the troll cried. "You can't . . . that's my property!"

"No, it isn't. Not yours and not Dodger Brown's. These sparklers belong to Judge Adam Winthrop and his wife, two of the Dodger's recent victims. Don't worry, I'll make certain they're returned to their rightful owners safe and sound, with your compliments."

Duff looked as if he were about to burst into tears.

"Gahh," he said.

21

QUINCANNON

A trolley car delivered Quincannon to the Ferry Building at the foot of Market Street. Ferries for the East Bay left every twenty to thirty minutes, and he arrived just in time to catch one of the Southern Pacific boats. A chilly half hour later, he disembarked with the other passengers and made his way up the Estuary to the Oakland City Wharf.

The place was an amalgam of the colorful and the squalid. Arctic whalers, Chinese junks, Greek fishing boats, Yankee sailing ships, disreputable freighters, scows, sloops, shrimpers, oyster boats, houseboats; long rows of warehouses crowded here and there by shacks fashioned from bits and pieces of wreckage or from dismantled ships; long barren sandpits.

He approached three men in turn to ask the whereabouts of an oysterman named Salty Jim, owner of a boat with "oyster" in the name. The first two either didn't know or wouldn't say, but the third, a crusty old sailor with a Tam-o'-Shanter pulled down over his ears, who sat propped against an iron cleat with a half-mended fishnet across his lap, knew Salty Jim well enough. And clearly didn't like him.

"Salty Jim O'Bannon," he said, "ain't no oysterman."

"No? What is he?"

The oldster screwed up his face and spat off the wharf side. "A damn pirate, that's what."

Involved in the oyster trade, indeed, Quincannon thought sardonically. He'd had a run-in with oyster pirates once and did not relish a repeat performance. They were a scurvy lot, the dregs of the coastal waters—worse by far than Chinese shrimp raiders or Greek salmon poachers. At the first flood tide in June, an entire fleet of them would head down the bay to Asparagus Island to set up raiding parties on the beds. And much of the harvest would be stolen despite the efforts of the Fish Patrol and privately hired agencies such as Carpenter and Quincannon, Professional Detective Services. The only thing that kept the pirates from taking complete control of the bay waters was their own vicious behavior. Regular consumption of alcohol and opium combined with general cussedness had led to many a cutting or shooting scrape and many a corpse in the sandpits.

"How come you're lookin' for the likes of Salty Jim O'Bannon?" the old sailor asked. "Not fixin' to join up with him, are you?"

"No chance of that. It's not him I'm after."

"Who, then?"

"A cousin of his, Dodger Brown. Know the lad?"

"Can't say I do. Don't want to know him, if he's as black-hearted a cuss as Salty Jim."

"He may be, at that."

"What's his dodge? Not another pirate, is he?"

"Housebreaker."

"And what're you? You've got the look and questions of a nabber."

"Policeman?" Quincannon was mildly offended. "Manhunter on the scent is more like it. Where does Salty Jim O'Bannon keep his boat? Hereabouts?"

"Hell. He wouldn't dare." The oldster spat again for emphasis. "He anchors off Davis Wharf. Don't tie up for fear of one of his pirate pals slippin' on board at night and murderin' him in his sleep."

"What's her name?"

"*Oyster Catcher.* Now ain't that a laugh."

"He lives aboard, does he?"

"He does. Might find him there now—I ain't seen nor heard of him puttin' out into the bay yet today. If you're fixin' to go out and see him, I hope you're carryin' a weapon and ain't shy about usin' it. Salty Jim ain't exactly sociable to strangers."

Meaningfully Quincannon patted the holster where his Navy Colt rested. The old sailor's rheumy eyes brightened at the gesture. "Why, then, I hope you find that son of a bitch, mate. I purely hope you do."

He provided directions to Davis Wharf. When Quincannon arrived there, he saw that sloops and schooners were anchored in the bay nearby, so many that he wasted no time in trying to pick out the *Oyster Catcher.* A ragged youth who was fishing with a hand line off the wharf side made the identification for him. The youth also agreed to rent out his own patched skiff beached in the tidal mud fifty rods distant. The boy seemed impressed that Quincannon was intent on visiting Salty Jim, the oyster pirate, but not for the same reason as the old sailor; the shine of hero worship was in his eyes.

Quincannon repressed the urge to shake some sense into the lad. You couldn't hope to make everyone walk the straight and narrow. Besides, a new generation of crooks meant continued prosperity for Carpenter and Quincannon, Professional Detective Services, well into his and Sabina's dotage.

He stowed his grip in the skiff, rowed out to the *Oyster Catcher*. She was a good-size sloop with a small cabin amidships, her mainsail furled, her hull in need of paint, but otherwise in reasonably good repair. No one was on deck, but from inside the cabin he could hear the discordant strumming of a banjo—an instrument for which he held an active dislike. He shipped his oars until he was able to draw in next to a disreputable rowboat tied to a portside Jacob's ladder. He tied the skiff's painter to another rung, drew his Navy, and climbed quickly on board.

The cabin's occupant heard or felt his presence; the banjo twanged and went silent, and a moment later the cabin door burst open and a bear of a man, naked to the waist, stepped out with a belaying pin clenched in one hand.

Quincannon snapped, "Stand fast!" and brought the pistol to bear. The scruff pulled up short, blinking and glowering. He was thirtyish, sported a patchy beard and hair that hung in matted ropes. The cold bay wind blew smells of "four-bit micky" and body odor off him in such a ripe wave that Quincannon's nostrils pinched in self-defense.

"Who in foggy hell're you?"

"My name is of no matter to you. Drop your weapon."

"Huh?"

"The belaying pin. Drop it, O'Bannon."

"Like hell I will."

"There'll be hell to pay if you don't."

Salty Jim gaped at him, rubbing at his scraggly beard with his free hand, his mouth open at least two inches—a fair approximation of a drooling idiot. "What's the idee comin' on my boat? You ain't the goddamn fish patrol."

"It's your cousin I want, not you."

"Cousin?"

"Dodger Brown."

"Huh? What you want with him?"

"That's none of your concern," Quincannon said. "If he's here, call him out. If he's not, tell me where I can find him."

"I ain't gonna tell you nothin'."

"You will, or you'll find a lead pellet nestling in your hide."

The oyster pirate's mean little eyes narrowed to slits. He took a step forward and said with drunken belligerence, "By gar, nobody's gonna shoot me on my own boat."

"I'm warning you, O'Bannon. Drop your weapon and hold hard, or—"

Salty Jim was too witless and too much taken with drink to be either scared or intimidated. He growled deeply in his throat, hoisted the belaying pin aloft, and mounted a lumbering charge.

Quincannon had no desire to commit mayhem if it could be avoided. He took two swift steps forward, jabbed the Navy's muzzle hard and straight into the rough bird's sternum.

Salty Jim said an explosive, "Uff!" and rounded at the middle like an archer's bow. The blow took the force out of his downsweeping arm; the belaying pin caromed more or less harmlessly off the meaty part of Quincannon's shoulder. Another jab with the Colt, followed by a quick reverse flip of the weapon, and then with the butt end he fetched O'Bannon a solid thump on the crown of his empty cranium. There was another satisfying "Uff!" after which Salty Jim stretched out on the scaly deck for a nap. Rather amazingly he even commenced to make snoring noises.

The brief skirmish brought no one else out of the cabin. Nor were there any sounds from within to indicate another's presence on board. Quincannon holstered the Navy, prodded the pirate with the toe of his boot; the nap and the snores continued unabated. A frisk of O'Bannon's apparently never-washed trousers and shirt netted him nothing except a sack of Bull Durham, some papers to go with the tobacco, and a greasy French postcard of no artistic merit whatsoever.

Quincannon picked up the belaying pin, tossed it overboard. After a moment's hesitation he sent the French postcard sailing after it. A frayed belt that held up the pirate's filthy trousers served to tie his hands behind his back. Quincannon then stepped over the unconscious man and entered the cabin.

He had been in hobo jungles and opium dens that were tidier and less aromatic. Breathing through his mouth, he searched the confines. It was evident from the first that two men lived here recently. Verminous blankets were wadded on each of two bunks, and there were empty bottles of Salty Jim's tipple, the cheap and potent white-line whiskey also known as four-bit micky and Dr. Hall, and empty flasks of the foot juice favored by Dodger Brown. The galley table, however, bore remnants of a single meal of oyster stew and sourdough bread, one tin coffee mug, one dirty glass, and one half-empty jug of Dr. Hall.

Under one of the bunks was a pasteboard suitcase. Quincannon drew it out, laid it on the blankets, snapped the cheap lock with the blade of his pocketknife, and sifted through the contents. Cheap John clothing of a size much too small to fit Salty Jim. An oilskin pouch that contained an array of lock picks and other burglar tools. An old Smith & Wesson revolver wrapped in cloth, unloaded, no cartridges in evidence. And a larger, felt-lined sack that rattled provocatively as he lifted it out.

When he upended the sack onto the blanket, out tumbled a variety of jewelry, timepieces, small silver and gold gewgaws. Pay dirt! A quick accounting told him that he was now in possession of the remaining stolen goods from Dodger Brown's first three robberies.

There was one other item of interest in the suitcase, which he'd missed on his first look. It lay on the bottom, facedown, caught under a torn corner. He fished it out, flipped it over. A business card, creased and thumb-marked, but not of the sort he himself carried. He had seen such discreet advertisements before; they had grown more common in the Uptown Tenderloin, handed out by the more enterprising businesswomen in the district. This one read:

FIDDLE DEE DEE
Miss Lettie Carew Presents
Bountiful Beauties from Exotic Lands
Maison de Joie
244 O'Farrell Street

Well, now. Such a relatively refined establishment as the Fiddle Dee Dee was hardly the type of bawdy house Salty Jim would want or be permitted to patronize. The card, therefore, must belong to Dodger Brown. Quincannon was certain of it when he turned the card over and found pencil-scrawled on the back: *Chinee girls!!*

He considered. Was it possible that the Dodger wasn't in quite as much hurry to flee the Bay Area as it had seemed from his visit to Luther Duff yesterday? That a different urge had prompted his eagerness for cash, and was the reason why the rest of his ill-gotten gains were still stashed here and he hadn't spent last night on this scabrous tub?

A likely prospect. As was the Dodger's eventual return. But when would that be? Salty Jim might know, but he was bound to be even more uncommunicative when he awoke from his nap. And the prospect of a long and possibly fruitless vigil in the pirate's company held no appeal. After a few moments of reflection, Quincannon decided to follow his hunch and pay a call on Miss Lettie Carew in her *maison de joie.*

He returned the swag to its felt-lined nest and added the sack to the one he'd pocketed in Duff's Curio Shop, after which he stepped onto the deck with Dodger Brown's revolver in hand. Salty Jim was still *non compos,* but now starting to stir a bit. Quincannon left him bound where he lay, dropped the pistol into the bay, and further coppered his bet by untying and setting the pirate's rowboat adrift. Then, whistling "The Brewers Big Horses Can't Run Over Me," one of his favorite temperance songs, he climbed down into the rented skiff and rowed briskly back to the wharf.

22

SABINA

Inside the house Penelope Costain's voice said angrily, "And just what did you expect to find in my home, Mr. Holmes? The police went over every inch of the premises last night."

"Clues to the unfortunate events that took place here."

"And you found none that the police overlooked, I'm sure. If you've disturbed or taken anything, I'll have you arrested."

"Tut, tut. Nothing has been disturbed or removed."

"I should have you arrested for trespassing anyway, but I won't if you leave at once."

"As you wish, madam. *Au revoir.*"

Footsteps sounded inside. Sabina had just enough time to back down onto the path before the door opened and the cape-and-deerstalker Englishman emerged, his blackthorn walking stick in hand. He hesitated when he spied her, and glanced behind him. The door remained closed, Mrs. Costain still inside.

Holmes bowed as he joined Sabina. There was a smudge of dirt on one of his cheeks, as if he had spent part of his time inside crawling around in dark corners or a dusty attic. "My dear

Mrs. Carpenter. An unexpected pleasure. May I ask what brings you here?"

"I've come to extend my condolences to the widow."

"Detective business as well, perchance?"

"Perhaps. Though not of the same sort you've been indulging in."

"Ah, you overheard my conversation with Mrs. Costain."

"Part of it. I'll thank you to cease claiming to be what you're not—an authorized employee of the Carpenter and Quincannon agency."

"My apologies, dear lady, for the small deception. But it was in a good cause, I assure you."

"Yes? Did you learn something my partner and I should know?"

Holmes's smile was crafty. Instead of answering her question, he said, "It's almost teatime. On my way here I noticed a tea shop around the corner on Federal Street. Would you do me the honor of joining me there after you've finished speaking to Mrs. Costain?"

"I have no time for social niceties, Mr. Holmes."

"You might find it worthwhile nonetheless," he said. He bowed again and sauntered off, the ferrule of his stick tapping rhythmically.

Sabina watched after him for a few seconds, then returned to her former place at the front door. She had to move the funeral wreath aside in order to lift the heavy brass knocker.

The door opened abruptly and there appeared a pale, wrathful face under a black hat with a drawn-up veil, her prominent chin outthrust. "Now what do you—? Oh. I thought you were someone else." The woman's expression modulated into a frown. "I don't know you. What do you want?"

"A few minutes of your time. My name is Sabina Carpenter."

"Carpenter? Of the detective agency?"

"Yes."

Penelope Costain hesitated. "I shouldn't be speaking to you at all. If your partner and that fool Holmes had done their jobs properly, my husband would still be alive."

"Please don't blame Mr. Quincannon for what happened to your husband. If it had been humanly possible for him to have prevented it, he would have done so."

"So you say."

"May I come in?"

"I've just returned from making funeral arrangements. I'm really quite tired."

"I won't keep you long."

". . . Oh, very well."

The widow's mourning attire was a rather inappropriate black taffeta dress that rustled and crackled from static electricity as she ushered Sabina into an underheated and overdecorated parlor. Flowers and ruffles, statues of shepherds and shepherdesses, a hideous ormolu clock on the mantel. Antimacassars, Fabergé eggs, ornately painted plates on a wall rail. Life-size china dogs beside every chair, multicolored glass baskets holding mints and candies. An empty gilt canary cage. And over it all, a patina of dust as if the room hadn't had a proper cleaning in some while. There was even a spiderweb between two of the ornate plates.

A gauche display of wealth that had been neglected—and

plundered a bit, judging from the spaces where more of the ostentatious clutter had once been displayed. How could people live in such surroundings?

Mrs. Costain stood stiffly, her head cocked to one side in an oddly birdlike fashion, her short dark hair touching the high collar of her dress. Eyes like the points of arrowheads jabbed at Sabina as she said, "Well, Mrs. Carpenter? Why are you here?"

"First, to offer my condolences."

"Thank you."

"And I have something of your husband's that I thought you might wish to have."

"Of Andrew's? What might that be?"

Sabina produced and handed over the silver money clip. Penelope Costain turned it over in her hand. As her fingers traced the intricate design, she winced slightly as if struck by a painful memory.

"Where did you get this?"

"From a pickpocket I was hired to apprehend."

"A pickpocket. I see. And did you apprehend him?"

"Her."

"A woman? Well, I suppose I shouldn't be surprised."

"She was killed yesterday by an unknown assailant."

"Deservedly, I'm sure. You'll pardon my callousness, but I have no sympathy for such creatures. I would not be unhappy to hear that the man who shot my husband has also been killed."

"Understandably so. You did know that the money clip was stolen from your husband?"

"He mentioned the fact, yes."

"When and where did it happen?"

"A few days ago, I believe. Near the Palace Hotel after Andrew left his office."

Another of Clara Wilds's random victims, then, on her prowls along the Cocktail Route?

"Did he say how much cash he carried in the clip?"

"A few banknotes, no more than thirty dollars. He was more upset at losing the clip than the money. That, and the fact that the pickpocket jabbed him with a sharp object just before she struck."

Sabina saw no need to reveal what the object was. "Was anything else stolen besides the clip and banknotes?"

"No."

"You're sure?"

"Andrew would have mentioned it if there had been. Why are you asking all these questions, Mrs. Carpenter? The pocket-picking incident is no longer of any importance. My husband has been cruelly murdered. Finding the man responsible is all that matters now."

"Of course. My partner is engaged in that very activity. In fact, he may already have accomplished it."

"He knows the identity of the burglar?"

"He believes so."

"But he's not sure?"

"He won't be until the man is in custody."

"Have the police been informed?"

"They may have been by now. You needn't worry, Mrs. Costain. Your husband's murderer will not escape punishment, whether he's the man Mr. Quincannon is pursuing or not."

"That is of little comfort to me at the moment," Penelope Costain said. Her head still cocked in that birdlike way, she made discomfited movements that caused the black taffeta to rustle and crackle again; her patience seemed to have worn thin. "Is there anything else?"

"Not at present, no."

"Then I trust you will be good enough to leave me alone to grieve in private."

"The history of teatime," Sherlock Holmes said sententiously, "extends back to the seventeenth century, when Queen Elizabeth granted the East India Company the right to establish worldwide trade routes. Originally the routes were used for the transport of spices, but by the time Charles the Second claimed the throne, tea had become the beverage of choice for English society. Now the custom has spread to your country, although of course it is not yet either properly refined or highly regarded here."

Sabina sipped her jasmine tea and wished the Englishman would cease pontificating and get to the point of this meeting. The tea shop on Federal Street was small and maintained a pretense of gentility despite the fact that the South Park neighborhood was no longer fashionable among the city's gentry. She and Holmes were seated at a window table. She was not overly fond of tea, preferring coffee or John's favorite beverage, warm clam juice, but she could appreciate a national tradition that supported eating well and often. Or she could if she weren't being bombarded with far more details of British habits and tastes than she cared to hear about.

"Naturally there are several variations on the tea service: cream tea, with scones, jam, and clotted cream; light tea, with scones and sweets; and full tea, with savories, scones, sweets, and dessert." Holmes motioned with mild distaste at the plate of scones and strawberry jam on the table between them. "This fare wouldn't do in England, you know. No, not at all. The scones and elderberry preserves served in the London shop near my rooms on Baker Street are far superior."

Sabina thought the scones and jam tasted just fine, but she didn't say so. It would only have encouraged him. Not that he needed any encouragement to continue his lecture on the subject of tea. He seemed oblivious to her impatience.

"Few people," he prattled on, "realize how many different varieties of tea there are from all over the globe. Assam, chamomile, Lapsang souchong, chai, jasmine—though the variety served in this establishment is rather poor. Oolong from the Far East, Darjeeling from India. Ali shan, Ti kuan yin, Formosa. Oh, yes, many, many different varieties. Perhaps one day I shall write a monograph on tea. Yes, I believe I will. Of course other studies have already been done, but I would adopt a much more scholarly approach—"

"Mr. Holmes," Sabina said. Her voice was tart; she had had enough tea, literally and figuratively.

"Yes, dear lady?"

"Why did you ask me to meet you here? Surely not to regale me with your esoteric knowledge."

"Nor merely to socialize, I confess. Did your interview with Mrs. Costain prove illuminating?"

What she had or hadn't learned from the widow was no concern of his. "Interview isn't the proper term. As I told you earlier, my purpose in visiting her was to offer my condolences."

"You also intimated a professional reason."

"Yes, as a matter of fact, there was another. The return of an item that had been stolen from her husband."

"Ah. And what would that item be?"

"A silver money clip."

"Not one of the items taken last evening, surely?"

"No. Andrew Costain was the victim of a pickpocket a few days ago."

"Was he indeed? And how did you come into possession of the money clip, pray tell?"

"I would rather not say."

Holmes shrugged. "As you wish."

Sabina said, "Now I'll ask you a question. Did you learn anything from your snoop inside her home?"

"Snoop? I must say I find your quaint American vulgarisms amusing, though that one is not quite applicable."

"What would you call unlawful entry into a private residence?"

"A continuance of my investigations, as you heard me tell Mrs. Costain."

"You're not authorized to investigate, as you heard me tell you."

"Not officially, perhaps," Holmes admitted, "but a bloodhound cannot be easily deterred when he has the scent. Particularly not when he has sighted his quarry."

"And just what does that mean?"

His eyes gleamed—rather madly, it seemed to Sabina. *"Le cas est resolu,"* he said.

"I beg your pardon?"

"The case is solved."

"Oh, it is?"

"Indubitably. I have deduced how Andrew Costain came to be murdered in his locked study, and how his assailant appeared to vanish from the premises after the crime was committed."

"How clever of you. Explain, please."

"You'll pardon me, but not just yet. I prefer to make my discoveries known in the presence of the various concerned parties, including you and Mr. Quincannon, and I require time to properly prepare. I confess to a propensity, you see, for the dramatic presentation. If I had not chosen to become a detective, I might well have sought a career on the stage."

Nonsense, Sabina thought. The man was a daft fraud, after all; the real, and now deceased, Sherlock Holmes would have been all too eager to trumpet his triumphs. Or would he? John was usually eager to trumpet *his* triumphs, but he, too, had been known to keep his deductions to himself until he was ready to unveil them in front of an audience.

She said, "When and where do you intend to make this presentation of yours?"

"Soon. As early as tomorrow morning, if arrangements can be made."

Lord, he was infuriating! No wonder John disliked him so intensely, though it was John's fault the fellow was involved. "Surely you understand that you have no right to withhold information in a robbery and homicide case."

"From you and your partner? As you took pains to point out, I am no longer even marginally in your employ."

"I meant from all concerned individuals. A man's life has been cruelly snuffed out and his widow left grieving. Violent death is not a matter to be taken lightly."

"I do not take it lightly," he said. "On the other hand, I do not regard death in quite as serious a light as you Americans. We British prefer to face its inevitability in a matter-of-fact fashion, without undue emotion, and I might say less euphemism and pretense as well."

Sabina said with temper, "There is no such thing as a national approach to either death or bereavement."

"If that is your belief, I shan't argue. However, there are many differences between our nations. We British . . ."

And he was off again on another monologue. Solidarity of British society despite problems with the Cornish, the Welsh, the Irish, the Scots, and the rebellious nature of the Empire's colonies; traditions passed down over multiple generations; the lessons taught and learned through the long and glorious history of the British Isles.

Sabina thought she might shriek if he didn't shut up. She forestalled the necessity by deliberately rattling her cup and saucer loudly enough to turn the head of the shop's elderly proprietress.

Holmes blinked at her.

"You seem to have invited me here in order to pontificate and gloat," she said. "I have better things to do with my time than to be subjected to either."

"You misunderstand me, dear lady. My one and only purpose was to inform you that I have solved the case, thus saving you and your estimable partner the need to continue your investigations."

"I'll believe that when you've proven it to me."

"And so I will—tomorrow."

"When and where tomorrow?"

"The time and place have yet to be determined."

Sabina had had enough of his sly, arrogant manner. She pushed her chair back and stood. "Thank you for the tea—and good-bye."

The Englishman also stood. "The pleasure was all mine," he said, and offered up another of his bows. "I shall let you know as soon as the necessary arrangements have been made. I guarantee neither you nor Mr. Quincannon will be disappointed."

Sabina knew what John would have said to that, but she was too much a lady to ever use "Bah!" as an exit line. She took her leave in dignified, if bristling, silence.

23

QUINCANNON

The district known as the Uptown Tenderloin was a pocket of sin more genteel and circumspect than the Barbary Coast, catering to the more playful among the city's respectable citizenry. It was located on the streets—Turk, Eddy, Ellis, O'Farrell—that slanted diagonally off Market. Some of San Francisco's better restaurants, saloons, variety-show theaters, and the Tivoli Opera House flourished here at the western end of the Cocktail Route that nightly drew the silk-hatted gentry.

Smartly dressed young women paraded along Market during the evening hours, not a few of them wearing violets pinned to their jackets and bright-colored feather boas around their necks that announced them to those in the know as uptown sporting ladies. Men of all ages lounged in front of cigar stores and saloons, engaged in the pastime that Quincannon himself had followed on occasion, known as "stacking the mash": ogling and flirting with parading ladies of both easy and well-guarded virtue.

Parlor houses also flourished here, so openly that the city's reform element had begun to mount a serious cleanup cam-

paign. The most notorious of these houses was the one operated by Miss Bessie Hall, the "Queen of O'Farrell Street," all
of whose girls were said to be blond and possessed of rare talents in the practice of their trade. Lettie Carew and her Fiddle
Dee Dee were among the second-rank of Bessie's rivals, spe-
cializing in nymphets of different cultures and hues.

The evening parade had yet to begin when Quincannon
alighted from the Market Street trolley at O'Farrell Street, his
pockets empty now of the stolen loot; he had stopped off at
the agency to lock it away in the office safe. Above him, as he
strolled along the wooden sidewalk, sundry flounced undergar-
ments clung to telephone wires, another form of advertisement
tossed out by the inhabitants of the shuttered houses lining the
route. This, too, had scandalized and provoked the blue-nose
reformers.

Midway in the third block, he paused before a plain shuttered building that bore the numerals 244 on its front door. A
small, discreet sign on the vestibule wall said FIDDLE DEE DEE
in gilt letters.

A smiling colored maid opened the door in answer to his
ring and escorted him into an ornately furnished parlor, where
he declined the offer of refreshment and requested an audience
with Miss Lettie Carew. When he was alone he perched on a
red plush chair, closed his nostrils to the mingled scent of incense and patchouli, and glanced around the room with professional interest.

Patterned lace curtains and red velvet drapes at the blinded
windows. Several red plush chairs and settees, rococo tables,
ruby-shaded lamps, gilt-framed mirrors, oil paintings of exoti-
cally voluptuous nudes. There was also a handful of framed

mottoes, one of which Quincannon could read from where he sat: *If every man was as true to his country as he is to his wife . . . God help the U.S.A.* In all, the parlor was similar to Bessie Hall's, doubtless by design, although it was neither as lavish nor as stylish. None could match "the woman who licked John L. Sullivan" when it came to extravagance.

At the end of five minutes, Lettie Carew swept into the room. Quincannon blinked and managed not to let his jaw unhinge. Miss Lettie had been described to him on more than one occasion, but this was his first glimpse of her in the flesh. And a great deal of flesh there was. She resembled nothing so much as a giant blond-haired cherub, pink and puffed and painted, dressed in pinkish white silk and trailing rose-colored feather boas and a cloud of sweet perfume that threatened to finish off what oxygen had been left undamaged by the patchouli and incense.

Even before she reached him she launched her into a practiced spiel: "Welcome, sir, welcome to the Fiddle Dee Dee, home of an array of bountiful beauties from exotic lands. I am the proprietress, Miss Lettie Carew."

Quincannon blinked again. The madam's voice was small and shrill, not much louder than a mouse squeak. The fact that it emanated from such a mountainous woman made it all the more startling.

"What can I do for you, sir? Don't be shy . . . ask and ye shall receive. Every gentleman's pleasure is my command."

"How many Chinese girls are employed here?"

"Ah, you have a taste for the mysterious East. Only one at present, Ming Toy, from far-off Shanghai. And most popular she is, sir, most popular. However, she is currently engaged."

"How long has she been engaged?"

"I beg your pardon?"

"Only a short while? Or for a longer period? It is possible to engage the services of one of your ladies by day as well as by hour, I'm sure."

"Oh, yes. For as long as a gentleman requires. Ming Toy has been entertaining since yesterday and may continue to do so for the rest of today. Would you like to make a reservation?"

"What I'd like," Quincannon said, "is to know if the lad she's entertaining is young, slight, with thinning brown hair and a fondness for red wine?"

Lettie Carew raised one artfully plucked eyebrow. "And why would you want to know that?"

"Answer my question, please."

"Our customers are entitled to privacy—"

"Balderdash." Quincannon hardened his voice and his expression. "Is Ming Toy's customer the gent I described?"

"And if he is? What's your interest in him?"

"Professional. The lad's a wanted felon."

Lettie Carew's subservient pose evaporated. "Oh, lordy, don't tell me you're a copper."

He allowed his stern expression to convince her that he was. Identifying himself would have served no purpose; parlor house madams were terrified of the police, but not of detectives who had no official standing.

"Bloody hell!" she said.

"How long has he been here, Lettie?"

"Since yesterday afternoon."

"But he did leave for a time in the evening?"

"He may have, I don't know. Ask him or Ming Toy."

"He's here now, is he?"

"Upstairs. Will you let me roust him out so you can make your arrest outside? I have other customers. I run a quiet house and I paid my graft this week, same as always. . . ."

"No. Which room is Ming Toy's?"

The madam muttered a naughty word. "There won't be any shooting, will there?"

"Not if it can be avoided."

"Well, if there's any damage, the city will pay for it or I'll sue. That includes bloodstains on the carpet, bedding, and furniture."

"Which room, Lettie?"

She impaled him with a long smoky glare before she squeaked, "Nine," and turned and flounced out of the room.

In the front hallway, a long carpeted staircase led to the second floor. Quincannon mounted it with his hand on the Navy Colt under his coat. The odd-numbered rooms were to the left of the stairs; in front of the door bearing a gilt-edged 9, he stopped to listen. No discernible sounds issued from within. He drew his revolver, depressed the latch, and stepped into a room decorated in an ostentatious Chinese-dragon style, dimly lighted by rice-paper lanterns and choked with incense and wine vapors.

He had no need for the Navy. Dodger Brown was sprawled supine on the near side of the four-poster bed, dressed in a pair of soiled long johns, flatulent snoring sounds emanating from his open mouth.

The girl who sat beside him was no more than twenty, delicate-featured, her comeliness marred by dark eyes already as old as Eve in the garden. She hopped off the bed, pulling a loose silk wrapper around her thin body, and hurried to where Quincannon stood. If she were aware of his weapon, it made no apparent impression on her.

"Busy," she said in a singsong voice, "busy, busy."

"Not anymore, Ming Toy. It's the lad there I'm after, not you."

"So?" The young-old eyes blinked several times. "Finished?" she asked hopefully.

"Finished," he agreed. "He'll spend this night in jail."

She bobbed her head as if the prospect pleased her, then aimed a disgusted look at the snoring Dodger. "Wine," she said.

"He won't be drinking anything but water from now on."

"Good-bye, Ming Toy?"

"Not until you answer my questions. What time did he leave last night?"

"Leave?"

"Yes, and what time did he return?"

"Not leave. Here all day, all night."

"He never left at all? You're sure he didn't slip out while you were asleep?"

"I not sleep, he sleep. Drink, hump, sleep, snore. Drink, hump, sleep, snore. All day, all night." Ming Toy wrinkled her nose. "Phooey," she said.

"All right. Good-bye now."

She went, vanishing as swiftly and silently as a wraith.

Quincannon padded to the bedside. Four rough shakes, and Dodger Brown stopped snoring and his eyes popped open. For several seconds he lay inert, peering up blearily at the face looming above him. Recognition came an instant before he levered himself off the bed in a single convulsive lunge.

The movement was so sudden, so swift, Quincannon had

205

no time to straighten or set himself. Or to avoid the lowered head that thudded into his midsection and sent him staggering backward into a bamboo screen. The screen folded up with a clatter and he went down on top of it. Before he could untangle himself, Dodger Brown had the door open and was stumbling out into the hallway.

Quincannon shoved furiously to his feet. The damned scruff had gotten away from him once, but not this time. No, by Godfrey, not this time! He unholstered the Navy again as he charged into the hallway.

Brown was running for the stairs, and when Quincannon spied him he loosed a bellow that shook the walls, brought startled noises from behind closed doors. The little burglar's head jerked around and his stride faltered, which caused one bare foot to slide and bind up in a carpet fold, which in turn caused him to stumble past the staircase into the newel post on its far side. He spun off with arms flailing, lurched sideways across the hallway, and thumped into the wall with such force that he bounced backward, somehow managing to remain upright as he did so. He threw a terrified glance at his fire-breathing pursuer, who was now almost to the stairs, and commenced a splay-footed run toward the end of the hall.

There was a street-front window there, but it was closed and covered with a red shade; the yegg's only chance for escape, or so he thought, was through one of the rooms. He clawed at the latch on the nearest one, yanked it open, and plunged inside to the sound of alarmed cries from the occupants.

Quincannon got there in time to prevent the back-flung door from slamming in his face. He shouldered it wide and barreled through. A naked fat man and an equally naked, equally fat Mexican girl were in the process of scrambling off a rumpled bed in a confusion of arms and legs, while Dodger Brown sprinted past to an airshaft window on the opposite side. He was frantically trying to open the window far enough to squeeze his scrawny body through when Quincannon reached him, caught hold of the collar of his long johns, lifted him off his feet, and yanked him around.

Brown fought him with body twists, fisted hands, and a shin kick, but this time Quincannon was ready for his sly tricks. He slammed the burglar backward into the wall next to the window, deftly avoiding another attempted shin kick. Held him there with a cocked hip and poked the bore of the Navy squarely between his bloodshot eyeballs.

"You're pinched, lad," he panted. "Resign yourself to it if you want to keep on breathing."

The Dodger, staring cross-eyed at the Colt, was neither brave nor stupid; he knew the game was up. All the struggle and sand left him at once and he sagged quiescently in Quincannon's grip.

"Here . . . what's the meaning of this . . . this outrage!"

The spluttering voice came from the fat man, who was crouched on the far side of the bed with some, though not all, of his nakedness now swaddled in bedclothes. He seemed to be trying to hide his face as well, but enough of it remained visible for Quincannon to recognize him. There was no sign of the Mexican girl; she was either cowering under the bed or had managed to flee during the skirmish.

Quincannon holstered his revolver as he hauled Dodger

Brown toward the door. On the way he used his free hand to doff his derby, which had miraculously managed to remain in place, at the fat man.

"Apologies for the interruption, Senator," he said. "Carry on as you were."

The last sound he heard before shutting the door behind himself and the Dodger was a mournful quacking cry like that of a ruptured duck.

Eyes followed the two of them back down the hallway, two of the brightest belonging to Lettie Carew, who had climbed puffing to the top of the stairs. When Quincannon assured her in passing that there would no more commotion, she said, "Well, at least there wasn't any shooting," sighed heavily, and headed back down to her lair.

In Ming Toy's room, Quincannon dumped Dodger Brown on the mussed bed and used the handcuffs he carried to circle both thin wrists. The little housebreaker offered no resistance; his vulpine features were now arranged in an expression of painful self-recrimination.

"It's my own fault," he said in tones almost as mournful as the state senator's. "After you near nabbed me the other night, I knew I should've staightaway hopped a rattler in the Oakland yards. Gone on the lammas instead of comin' over here."

"Aye, and let it be a lesson to you." Quincannon grinned and added sagely, "The best-laid plans aren't always the best-planned lays."

"Murder? *Me?*" Dodger Brown looked and sounded appalled at the notion. He squirmed on the rumpled bed, his manacled hands clutched together behind his scrawny back. "I never killed nobody in my life. Never! It wasn't me who broke into the Costain joint and bumped him off. I was here last night, all night—I never left for a minute. Ask Ming Toy, she'll tell you."

"I already asked her."

"Well, then? You know I done the other burglaries, okay, I admit it. But no more after you almost nabbed me at the banker's. I ain't been near the Costain place, not even to tab it up."

"What make of pistol do you carry these days, Dodger?"

"None. I give that up—too dangerous, even unloaded like I always carried mine. Look in my clothes over there, you won't even find a Barlow knife."

"We both know that's because Lettie Carew doesn't allow customers to bring their weapons upstairs," Quincannon said. "Will I find one downstairs in the lockbox with your name on it?"

The little burglar opened his mouth to lie again, changed his mind, and sighed instead. "Pocket pistol. Twenty-five caliber. But it's empty and you won't find any cartridges for it. I ain't loaded it once since I bought it and that's the plain truth."

"I thought your preference was a larger-caliber weapon. A Forehand and Wadsworth thirty-eight, for instance."

"Is that what plugged the lawyer? Well, I never owned a piece like that. Never. You can't put the frame on me for no killing."

"Clara Wilds," Quincannon said.

"Huh?" Dodger Brown blinked at the sudden shift of subjects. "What about Clara?"

"Still keeping company with her?"

"No. Not anymore. We busted up awhile back."

"Why?"

"She was two-timing me."

"While you remained faithful except for your regular parlor house visits. Who was her new lover?"

"Some no-account named Pope."

"Her fenceman, Victor Pope?"

"Yeah. How'd you know that?"

"When did you see Clara last?"

"Four, five months ago. Why all these questions about her?"

"She's dead. Murdered."

The Dodger's eyes bulged. "Clara? Bumped off? When? Where?"

"In her rooms yesterday afternoon."

"Who done it?"

Quincannon cocked an eyebrow.

"Say! You ain't tryin' to make out it was me?" Outrage replaced the scruff's real or feigned shock. The handcuffs rattled again noisily. "I told you, I never carried a loaded weapon and I never shot nobody—"

"Clara wasn't shot."

"Then how—?"

"Stabbed with her own hatpin. And her rooms ransacked afterward."

"Hatpin. Jesus."

"You knew about her new dodge, I'll wager."

"Doin' the dip? Yeah, she learned the game from old Sal Tatum. She must've made a big score and some bastard found out about it and was after the swag."

Quincannon cocked his eyebrow again.

"Not me! I got plenty from my own scores. Listen, you got to believe me, I never—"

"Scoot around and lie facedown on the bed."

". . . What?"

"You heard me."

Dodger Brown stared at him for three or four seconds, licked his lips, then twisted and flung himself flat across the bed. He squawked and began struggling when Quincannon caught hold of the collar of his unbuttoned long johns and dragged the top down over his shoulders. "Hey! What's the idea? What you gonna do?"

"Nothing, if you keep quiet and hold still."

No gouge or scratch marks had been visible on the yegg's face and neck; there were none on the upper back, shoulders, or upper arms. Quincannon rolled him over and pulled up first one sleeve, then the other. More unbroken skin. The Dodger made another squawking protest when Quincannon yanked the drawers down over his scrawny flanks long enough to determine that his belly and thighs were likewise free of injury.

The little housebreaker called him several colorful names, which Quincannon chose to ignore. He'd been feeling rather pleased with himself when he snapped the cuffs on Dodger Brown, for it had seemed then that one if not two cases of theft and foul play were nearing their conclusion. Now his mood had soured somewhat. Part of the burglary investigation for Great Western Insurance had been satisfactorily resolved, but as for the rest of it . . .

Dodger Brown was clearly not guilty of either his former paramour's murder nor Costain's. So who the devil was? Clara

Wilds's new paramour or one of her victims? A copycat burglar who had adopted the Dodger's modus operandi? Two separate cases, or were they somehow intertwined? Two murderers—or one?

Hell and damn! What had seemed a simple and easily resolved matter had turned out to be anything but. It was annoying and frustrating enough, though he hated to admit it, to tie the brain of even the most wily detective into temporary knots.

24

SABINA

Sabina seemed to be spending much of her time lately prowling about residential carriageways. Just one of the many exciting and glamorous aspects of detective work. Another being afternoon tea with a candidate for a mental institution.

The carriageway that bisected the block behind the Costain home was completely deserted. This genteel South Park neighborhood had seemed almost slumbrous as she made her way back to it from the tea shop. None of the few people abroad had paid any attention to her, and no one had been about when she entered the carriageway. Trees and shrubbery flanked the passage, making it unlikely that prying eyes such as those of Clara Wilds's neighbor, Mrs. Marcus, would follow her progress along its grassy expanse. Nonetheless she made her way slowly, as if she were a resident out for a casual late-afternoon stroll.

When she neared the halfway point in the block, the rear fence and outbuildings of the Costain property took shape ahead. Vegetation was her ally here, too, a pair of gnarled old walnut trees screening the roadbed from the house. John had mentioned the carriage barn at the rear, which meant the

Costains owned equipage and an animal to draw it. It seemed probable that Penelope Costain had driven herself to the funeral parlor, and since there'd been no sign of a rig on the street after her return home, it was also probable that she'd put it and the horse away.

The barn was of the small, utilitarian type painted a peeling white, adequate for the housing of a single carriage and the supplies necessary for its maintenance. A narrow shed-like attachment and a small, empty corral stretched along one side.

The double-sided gate that gave access to both the property and the barn was closed and latched, but it hadn't been locked last night, John had told her, and it wasn't locked now. Sabina paused with her hand on the latch to satisfy herself that she was still alone and unobserved, then opened one half of the gate and slipped inside, closing it again behind her.

The barn was set a few feet beyond the gate. She hurried across to the closed double doors, which also proved to be unlocked. The half she opened creaked and squeaked, but not loudly enough for the sounds to carry. It also bound up slightly at the bottom so that she had to tug and lift to open it.

Semidarkness redolent with the odors of hay and manure folded around her as she stepped inside. She left the door half ajar and took out the old flint lighter she carried for such occasions as this. When she snapped it alight, its pale flame showed her the buggy that filled most of the interior, and the horse munching hay in a side stall.

The rig's body, traces, and calash folding top were all black, showing signs of wear and neglect. But on closer inspection she saw that it was a Studebaker and that its wheel spokes were unpainted. The horse placidly munching hay in its stall was a chestnut roan.

Drat!

Sabina hesitated, then on impulse leaned inside the buggy. There was nothing on or under the wide leather seat, or on the floorboards. She ran her fingers into the crack between the two seat cushions, felt a thin piece of metal wedged there. At first she thought it was a coin, but the lighter flame revealed it to be made of brass—a token of some sort. Slot-machine token? Slot machines proliferated in San Francisco, and while tokens had not yet come into widespread use, there was a move afoot by the city fathers to disallow legal tender in the machines.

But no, this wasn't a slot-machine token. Nor the kind that had such phrases as "good for one drink" or "good for 5c in trade" etched into the metal. One side bore a triangle with HofC in its center; the other side was blank. The initials were unfamiliar to her. A meaningless discovery, probably, but Sabina slipped it into her pocket anyway. John might know what it signified and from where it had come.

Sabina returned to the door half, doused her light before opening it and stepping out. At the outer gate, she peered into the carriageway to make sure it was still empty before going through, closing up, and resuming her saunter to the end of the block.

So much for the notion that the buggy parked behind Clara Wilds's rooming house had belonged to and been driven by Andrew Costain, and that Costain was her murderer. It had been a stab in the dark in the first place. What motive could Costain have had for killing the pickpocket? Surely not the recovery of the silver money clip.

Now Sabina was back to where she'd been before, with no leads except for Dodger Brown.

Or was she?

The door was locked when she arrived at the agency. She was in the process of using her key when footsteps sounded on the stairs behind her and a somewhat breathless voice called out, "Mrs. Carpenter—finally."

The voice belonged to Jackson Pollard, Great Western Insurance's chief claims adjustor. It was after five o'clock and he had apparently just left his office for the day; he wore a greatcoat and top hat, carried his gold lion's head cane, and approached her in a cloud of the bay rum he liberally applied for his evenings' excursions along the Cocktail Route. Either that, or as John had once surmised, Pollard had a wife or mistress who liked her man to smell as if dunked in a vat of the stuff.

Nonetheless, his stop-off here was a mild surprise. Usually he conducted his business with Carpenter and Quincannon, Professional Detective Services, by telephone or summons to his office. One look at his frowning visage and pinched mouth told Sabina he was not the bearer of good tidings. Pollard confirmed it in irritable tones as soon as they were inside.

"I thought it was you I saw entering the building just now," he said. "I was beginning to think you had closed for business today."

"Why would you think that?"

"Why indeed. I expected a report, in person or at least by telephone of last night's catastrophe, and I've had neither. I telephoned three times."

"I've been out all day," Sabina said. "John didn't come by to see you? He told me he intended to."

"Well, he didn't."

"Then he must have a good reason." Which wasn't necessarily true; he might have simply avoided the inevitable unpleasantness—a mistake in judgment, if that was the case.

"He had better have a good reason." Pollard had been to the agency before, but he looked about the office now with an air of disapproval, as if seeing it for the first time and finding it lacking in some way. He was a fussy, sometimes crusty little man with sparse sandy hair and sideburns that resembled miniature tumbleweeds. His faded blue eyes, magnified by thick-lensed spectacles, seemed about to pop from their sockets when he was as upset as he was now. "When did you see him last?"

"Early this morning."

"And you haven't seen him since?"

"No." Nor had John returned to the office in her absence. If he had, he would have left a message, as was their long-established practice when investigations were in progress. The top of her desk was bare of any such note.

"And where was he bound when he left, if not to Great Western?" Pollard asked.

"To continue his investigation into the burglaries, naturally."

"Still proceeding blind, I suppose."

"As a matter of fact, John believes he knows the identity of the burglar and expects to have him in custody shortly."

The little claims adjustor was neither mollified nor reassured. "He expected to have the man in custody at the Truesdales', and should have but didn't."

"Through no fault of his."

"And I suppose what happened at the Costain home was no fault of his, either?"

"It was not. If the newspapers implied it was, they're quite wrong."

"I did not find out about it from the newspapers, any more than from you or your partner. Do you realize how embarrassing it can be to be caught completely unawares by news such as this?"

"Yes, and you have my apologies. It wasn't the police who told you?"

"Mrs. Penelope Costain. She came to see me this afternoon."

Sabina raised an eyebrow. "For what reason, so soon after her husband's death?"

"For what reason do you suppose? To file a pair of claims, one of which we'll have to honor even if the burglar is caught and the stolen valuables recovered."

"I assume one is for the assessed value of her stolen jewelry. And the other?"

"Life insurance policy. Double indemnity. Fifty thousand dollars."

Sabina managed to conceal a wince.

"According to Mrs. Costain," Pollard said, "Quincannon and a British detective named Holmes were at her home last night supposedly guarding it against invasion. The widow said this man Holmes was in the employ of your agency. I didn't authorize any such extra expense."

"And none will be charged to you." Fortunately Pollard seemed not to have read any of the real Holmes's investigations as recorded by Dr. Watson, or Ambrose Bierce's diatribe in the *Examiner.* If he had, he'd be even more up in arms. "Andrew

Costain also retained John to guard his home, a task which required a second man for the surveillance."

"Two detectives, and neither able to prevent blatant murder and robbery."

"It happened under peculiar and still unexplained circumstances no detective could have foreseen."

"So you say. Mrs. Costain seems to think otherwise."

"Mrs. Costain is hardly an impartial witness."

"Perhaps not. But if I find out she's correct, your agency will get no more business from Great Western Insurance."

"You needn't threaten me, Mr. Pollard. John and I have always maintained cordial relations with you, and we've never yet failed to carry out an assignment to mutual satisfaction."

"Never before has so much been at stake. Don't forget, Mrs. Carpenter—even if Quincannon recovers most or all of the stolen goods, which is by no means a certainty, Great Western is still liable for the fifty-thousand-dollar life insurance claim."

He wished her a gruff good day and departed.

Sabina opened the window behind her desk, letting in fresh air to dissipate the too-sweet odor Pollard had left behind him. The clock on the office wall read 5:20. John might or might not return to the office at this late hour; she decided she would wait until six o'clock before closing up. There was much to be discussed with him, not the least of which was the would-be Sherlock's claim to have solved the Costain mystery.

Fanciful nonsense, of course . . . wasn't it? John would surely think so, but she couldn't quite make up her mind whether the Englishman was a buffoon or in fact had some of the same ratiocinative brilliance as the genuine Baker Street sleuth.

25

QUINCANNON

The city prison, in the basement of the Hall of Justice at Kearney and Washington streets, was a busy place that testified to the amount of crime afoot in San Francisco. And to Quincannon's experienced eye, there were just as many crooks on the outside of the foul-smelling cells as on the inside. Corrupt policemen, seedy lawyers haggling at the desk about releases for prisoners, rapacious fixers, deceitful bail bondsmen . . . more of those, in fact, than honest officers and men charged with felonies or with vagracy, public drunkenness, and other misdemeanors.

Quincannon delivered a sullen Dodger Brown there, and spent the better part of an unpleasant hour in conversation with a plainclothesman he knew slightly and a booking sergeant he neither knew nor wanted to know. He made no mention of Andrew Costain in his statement; it would only have complicated matters and subjected himself and Dodger Brown to the questioning of that lummox, Kleinhoffer, an ordeal to be avoided at all costs in the present circumstances.

He signed a complaint on behalf of the Great Western Insurance Company, and before leaving, made sure that the Dodger would remain locked in one of the cells until Jackson Pollard and Great Western officially formalized the charge. He knew better than to turn over any of the stolen goods, did not even mention that they were in his possession.

His first stop after leaving the Hall's gray-stone pile was the insurance company's offices on Merchant Street just east of the Montgomery Block, his intention being to report his success to Jackson Pollard. The claims adjustor, however, was not there. He had vacated the premises a short while before and was not expected to return.

Quincannon's mood was still on the dour side when he entered the agency office. Sabina, seated at her desk, regarded him with her usual sharp eye. "Bad news, John?"

"Some bad, some good."

"Mine as well. Dodger Brown?"

"Yaffled and in police custody. That's the good news." He sketched the day's events for her, embellishing a bit on his brief skirmishes with Salty Jim O'Bannon on the oyster boat and the Dodger at Lettie Carew's.

"You take too many risks, John," she admonished him. "One of these days you'll pay dearly for such recklessness—just as your father and my husband did."

He waved that away. "I intend to die in bed at the age of ninety," he said. "And not alone."

"I wouldn't be surprised if either boast turned out to be true." Her generous mouth quirked slightly at the corners. "You had no difficulty finding your way around the Fiddle Dee Dee, I'm sure."

"Meaning what?"

"Don't tell me you've never been in a parlor house before."

"Only in the performance of my duties," he lied.

"If that's so, I pity the city's maidens."

"I have no designs on the virtue of young virgins." He added with a wink, "Young and handsome widows are another matter."

"Then you're fated to live out your years as celibate as a monk. Did you wring a confession from Dodger Brown?"

"Of the first three burglaries, yes."

"But not the one of the Costain home?"

"That's the bad news. The Dodger was cozied up at the Fiddle Dee Dee all of last night with bottles of wine and a Chinese strumpet named Ming Toy. She and Lettie Carew vouch for the fact."

"They could have been paid to lie."

"Could have been, but weren't. Whoever broke into the Costain home and shot our client, it wasn't Dodger Brown."

"A copycat burglar?"

"A possibility."

"Do you put much stock in it?"

"No. I can't abide another coincidence."

"Nor can I. I don't suppose Dodger Brown is guilty of Clara Wilds's murder any more than that of Andrew Costain?"

"Evidently not," Quincannon said. "He claims he hasn't seen her in months, since they parted company over her involvement with Victor Pope. And he has no claw marks anywhere on his person, as I had the distasteful task of confirming."

"I was afraid of that."

"Could Pope have stabbed the pickpocket?"

"No," Sabina said. "He had neither the time nor the means.

You may find this far-fetched, John, but for a time today I had the notion her murderer might have been Andrew Costain."

Quincannon paused in the process of charging his pipe with tobacco. "Yes? Why would you think that?"

"Grasping at straws, perhaps."

Sabina went on to explain about the buggy that had been parked in the carriageway behind Clara Wilds's rooming house, and her investigation of the carriage barn on the Costain property. While she spoke, she removed a circlet of brass from her skirt pocket and handed it to him, saying, "I found this wedged between the buggy's seat cushions. Do you recognize it?"

He turned it over in his fingers. "Yes. A gambling token from Charles Riley's House of Chance, a high-toned establishment on Polk Street. Good for one dollar in play. Riley gives them to favored customers."

"Andrew Costain being one?"

Quincannon said thoughtfully, "Perhaps. If it belonged to him. I'll just keep it, if you don't mind." He pocketed the token when Sabina nodded her consent. "Did you find anything else in the buggy?"

"No."

"Do you still consider Costain a suspect in Clara Wilds's murder?"

"I don't know," Sabina admitted. "He doesn't seem to have had any plausible motive. Nor any way to have identified Wilds as the woman who robbed him."

"It's also unlikely that he would have had time to change into old clothing, drive from his office to her lodging house, commit the crime, and then return to Geary Street, change back into his business attire, and be waiting when I arrived. If that was his plan, he wouldn't have sent his message to me when he did. Or admitted, as he did, to being away from the office at all."

Sabina nodded. "I'm sure you're right. But I do still believe the two cases are connected somehow. Don't you?"

"Possibly. Though at the moment I don't see how."

"Nor do I." Sabina paused to tuck away a stray wisp of her dark hair before saying, "There are some other things you should know, John."

"Yes?"

"For one, Jackson Pollard was here not long before you returned, all in a dither. And not just because of what happened last night. Two more claims, he said, have taxed his patience to the limit."

"Two more?"

"Both filed today by Mrs. Costain. One for the assessed value of her missing jewelry."

"And the other?"

"The Costains also have a joint life insurance policy with Great Western, for the double indemnity sum of fifty thousand dollars."

"So the widow wasted little time, did she," Quincannon said. "What did you say to Pollard?"

"That you knew the identity of the burglar, and expected to have him in custody and the stolen goods recovered soon. He should be somewhat mollified when he hears that you've accomplished that part of your mission."

"But not completely until the Costain matter is cleared up."

"No. And if that isn't done soon to his satisfaction, we may well lose one of our best clients. He threatened as much."

"It'll be done, never fear."

"Is that bluster, John? Or do you have some idea of the explanation for the Costain puzzle?"

"I never bluster," Quincannon said, which earned him one of Sabina's raised-eyebrow looks. "Of course I have some idea. No muddle, no matter how mysterious it might seem, has ever baffled me for long."

"Not even the one of how Andrew Costain was murdered and his assailant managed to escape from a locked room and then a sealed house under close observation?"

"Pshaw. I know how that was done." Which wasn't true. Glimmerings of the truth, yes, now that Dodger Brown had been exonerated of the crime, but the exact details were still unclear. Soon, however. Soon.

"Do you, now?" Sabina said in tones that he chose not to construe as dubious. "And how was it done, pray tell?"

"All in good time, my dear. All in good time."

"You may not have as much time as you think. You're not the only one investigating the Costain murder."

"If you mean that dolt Kleinhoffer—"

"No. I mean our 'employee,' thanks to you."

"Employee? The bughouse Sherlock? I thought we were rid of him."

"Not hardly. While Mrs. Costain was out making funeral arrangements today, he entered the house illegally. She caught him prowling around when she returned, and was in the process of evicting him when I arrived."

"What the devil was he looking for?"

"He wouldn't tell me when I met him outside," Sabina said, "or when I suffered through his invitation to tea a short while later. But he seemed very pleased with his search." Sabina paused again before continuing. "Now don't get upset, John, but I over-heard him tell Mrs. Costain that he was acting on our behalf."

"Damn the man!"

"Mrs. Costain was beside herself, but I think I managed to unruffle her feathers. I don't believe she'll press charges."

"If she does," Quincannon said darkly, "he'll be the one to suffer the consequences."

"I told him as much. I also told him he's to cease and desist pretending to be affiliated with this agency. He said he wouldn't because it was no longer necessary."

"What did he mean by that?"

"That's the other thing you should know. He alluded to having solved the mystery of Andrew Costain's death."

"Alluded?"

"The phrase he used was *'le cas est resolu.'* French for 'the case is solved.'"

"Humbug! That addlepate couldn't solve the riddle of how to fasten a pair of gaiters."

"I'm not so sure about that, John."

"Bah." Quincannon began to restlessly pace the office. "The mystery will be solved shortly, yes, but not by that blasted Englishman."

"Don't be too cocksure. He may be a bit daft, but he's canny nonetheless and he may well have found out something important, by accident if not by design. I think it would be a good idea if you spoke with him about it. As soon as possible."

"Consult with that pompous buffoon? A waste of valuable time."

"There's another reason you should see him."

"Yes? And what would that be?"

"He's so certain of himself that he plans to arrange a meeting of the principals in the case, at which he'll reveal what he knows or believes he knows."

"*What!*"

A favorite expression of Quincannon's father when taken with sudden fury had been that "his blood ran hot as boiling tar and just as dark." Such was an apt description of his own blood at this news. Snarling and muttering invective, he stomped the floor hard enough to produce tremors in the office furniture. From Sabina's expression, she had expected his furious reaction. She maintained a prudent silence.

"Make false claims and try to steal my thunder, will he?" Quincannon said when he had a reign on his anger. "By Godfrey, he won't get away with it!"

"Then you'll see him tonight?"

"As soon as I can find the rank dingbat. Still encroaching on Dr. Axminster's hospitality, is he?"

"He didn't say."

"I'll start there." Quincannon jammed his derby down so hard on his head that the brim blocked his vision momentarily. When he adjusted it upward, he saw that Sabina was putting on her hat as well.

"I'm going with you," she said.

"No, you're not—"

"Yes, I am. To forestall any mayhem you may be contemplating, if for no other reason."

An owl-eyed housekeeper opened the front door of Dr. Caleb Axminster's Russian Hill home and announced that the doctor had not yet returned from his surgery. From behind her, somewhere inside, Quincannon could hear the cheerful, somewhat fantastic plucking of violin strings—no melody he had ever heard before or wanted to hear again. It only served to start his blood boiling again.

He said, "It's that blasted . . . it's Sherlock Holmes we've come to see." He handed the housekeeper his card, and she carried it and his and Sabina's names away with her. Soon the violin grew silent, and shortly after that the housekeeper returned to usher them into a sitting room off the main parlor.

The Englishman, sprawled comfortably in an armchair, his violin and bow now on a table beside him, greeted them effusively. "Well, my esteemed colleagues, I must say I'm glad you've come. I intended to call on you at your rooms later this evening, Quincannon. Now you've saved me the trouble."

"How do you know where I live?"

Holmes smiled his enigmatic smile. "To what do I owe the pleasure of this visit? You have news? Located your pannyman, perchance?"

Quincannon glowered at him in silence. Sabina said, "Located and arrested Dodger Brown, yes. And recovered the burglary loot."

"My dear Quincannon, you surpass yourself!" Holmes assumed a sly expression. "And did he confess to the murder of Andrew Costain?"

Sabina shook her head. "No, because he's not guilty of it. It was someone else who broke into the house and fired the shot."

"Yes, I know."

Quincannon growled, "You know, do you?"

"Oh, yes. Broke in, rifled the fellow's strongbox, shot him, and then apparently vanished into thin air."

"And you claim to know how that was accomplished, and the name of the guilty party."

"Of course. Surely you do, too?"

"For some time now," Quincannon lied.

"Splendid. Elementary, wasn't it?"

Elementary. Quincannon's basilisk gaze left the Englishman's, slid down to his scrawny neck—a sight that made his fingers twitch. "Let's have your theory, if you're so all-fired sure of yourself."

"I shall be delighted—though it's not a theory, but certain fact. I expect you've arrived at the identical solution. By utilizing the same deductive methods, I wonder, or ones slightly different? It will be most interesting to compare notes, eh? Most interesting indeed."

"The devil it will. Mrs. Carpenter tells me you plan to arrange a meeting to reveal what you claim to know."

"Yes. Tomorrow, perhaps at the Hall of Justice. I deduce from your expression that you don't approve?"

"I not only disapprove, I demand that you scrap the notion."

"But why, my good fellow?" Holmes asked. "Surely you wish to have the matter resolved as quickly as possible. Mrs. Carpenter indicated as much during our talk earlier."

"Yes, but by us as the consulting detectives, not by you. You have no right to arrange anything. You no longer work for our agency. You are nothing but a confounded—"

Sabina nudged him sharply with her elbow.

"—interloper. When arrangements are ready to be made, I'll make them. Is that understood?"

"My intentions all along have been to aid, not hinder, your investigations. After all, I, too, am a skilled detective, if temporarily retired from the profession."

Quincannon growled, "You'll be permanently retired if you don't do as I say."

The Englishman essayed a languid shrug. "As you wish. With one caveat—that I am permitted to attend the gathering whenever and wherever it takes place."

"Oh, you'll be invited, never fear. I wouldn't have it any other way."

Sabina nudged him again. "*We* wouldn't have it any other way."

"Excellent. I look forward to the, ah, unveiling with great anticipation." He beamed at her, at Quincannon, and then reached for his violin and bow. "Now if you'll excuse me," he said, "I feel the need to resume playing. Mendelssohn's violin concerto in E minor helps to relax me after a strenuous day, though I must confess I prefer the effects of a seven percent solution. Dr. Axminster, however, has rather uncharitably asked that I not indulge my harmless habit while a guest in his home."

The bughouse Sherlock picked up the instrument and began sawing on it. Quincannon caught hold of Sabina's elbow and ushered her quickly out of the room; if he'd tarried, he might have given in to the impulse to create a collision between the violin and the Englishman's skull.

26

In the hack as it rattled away from the Axminster home, Sabina said, "Well, John?"

"Well what?"

"Is what you told Holmes the truth? *Do* you know the who, why, and how of the Costain homicide?"

"Do you believe *he* does?" John countered.

"At the least, he has a viable theory. He wouldn't have suggested a meeting of the principals if he didn't."

"Bah. He's mad as a barn owl."

"You haven't answered my question."

"Of course I know the who, why, and how," John said testily, but without quite meeting her eye. "Even if that pompous, preening, presumptuous popinjay has a glimmering of the truth, do you suppose I'll allow him to outshine me in front of our client?"

"Then tell me what you suspect. Who killed Costain and how was the escape from the sealed house managed? And in what way is Clara Wilds's murder connected?"

"All will become clear tomorrow."

"You're being as evasive as Holmes."

He made grumbling noises in his beard and lapsed into a brooding silence.

Sabina sighed. There were times when her partner was a heavy cross to bear. If he would trust in her, and in turn listen to her suspicions, of which she had more than a few, they could work together to clarify the details of the affair. But no, his pride and his conceit were too great, as was his passion for drama; he was as much a glory hound as the Englishman professed to be. He did not have all the answers now, she was sure of that, but expected to by morning and without any assistance from her. Perhaps he would succeed—he had before. He had also failed before, and if that happened in this case, he would bluster and make excuses and do whatever else he deemed necessary to save face.

Well, she could play the same closemouthed game herself. If the fancied Mr. Holmes had in fact arrived at the truth through observation and deduction, and if John expected to by morning, then there was no reason why she couldn't do the same.

The coach clattered along the cobblestones, heading downtown. Sabina hadn't heard the directions John had given the driver, and she broke the silence by asking, "Where are we bound?"

"You're going home. I have an errand to attend to."

"What sort of errand?"

"For the nonce that's my concern."

The remark roused her ire. She stamped her foot, and said sharply, "I will *not* be treated like a minion! You refuse to confide in me—very well, that's your privilege, but only up to a point. I'm as deeply involved as you are, and that means I have a right to know what you're up to if it's pertinent. Is it?"

". . . Perhaps."

"Your errand, then?"

"If you must know, a visit to Geary Street."

"Andrew Costain's law offices?"

"Yes."

"In search of what?"

"Proof to support my deductions."

Or to stimulate them. "The offices will surely be locked. Do you intend to break and enter?"

He patted his waistcoat pocket. "Not exactly."

"The use of lock picks still constitutes unlawful entry."

"You needn't explain the law to me, my dear. Besides, that bloody Englishman committed the same crime at the Costain home this afternoon, didn't he?"

"Yes, but he has a few screws loose and you don't. Ostensibly."

He said, "Hmpf," and busied himself with his pipe and tobacco pouch.

Sabina said, "I'm coming with you."

"What's that? No, you're not."

"Yes, I am. If we're caught, then we'll both suffer the consequences."

He glowered at her.

She glowered back. "I can be just as stubborn as you can," she said. "More so, if needs be."

"Of that I have no doubt."

"It's settled then. We'll break the law together."

———

They had no difficulty entering the Geary Street building that housed Andrew Costain's law offices. There was no nightwatchman, and lamplight glowed in the window of an office on the floor above—one of the other attorneys evidently working late.

The first floor hallway was deserted. The door to Costain's offices was locked, of course, but John's deft use of his lock picks had it open in less than a minute. He entered first, located a wall switch, and turned it to bring on a pale ceiling globe. John led the way across a neglected anteroom to the closed but unlocked door to Costain's private office. The mingled odors of dust and the stale residue of cigar smoke and alcohol assailed Sabina as she stepped inside. The whole place wanted a good airing. And a thorough cleaning as well. The amount of dust and dead flies on the floor, furniture, law books, and the helter-skelter of papers strewn about was considerable.

"Not very tidy, was he," she said.

"Nor as successful as he pretended to be."

Sabina eyed a nearly empty bottle of rye whiskey standing in plain sight on the desktop. "A fondness for alcohol being one of the reasons."

"No doubt. I'll start with the desk."

She nodded and stepped over to the file cabinets. They were no less neatly kept than the rest of the office. Client files, briefs, court records, correspondence, bills, receipts, and miscellaneous items were all jumbled together, some in labeled and unlabeled folders, others in manila envelopes. Andrew Costain had evidently had packrat tendencies: the dates on some of the accumulation ranged back ten years or more. A few of the names in the client files were familiar to Sabina, but none had any apparent relationship to the murders of Costain or Clara Wilds.

The correspondence was likewise worthless. A folder containing bills and invoices, however, appeared more promising.

Behind her at the desk, John exclaimed softly, "Just as I suspected."

Sabina turned. "What have you found?"

"Costain's bank book. As I suspected, he was in financial difficulty. Until fifteen months ago he maintained a substantial bank balance of five to six thousand dollars. Since then he made only a few small deposits, none in the past month, and steady withdrawals of a hundred here, two hundred there. His balance as of two days ago, after he wrote his check to me, was one thousand and fifty dollars. As of yesterday, there was only fifty left."

"Another check or a cash withdrawal?"

"Cash. Now why would a lawyer on the brink of insolvency want that much in greenbacks?"

"Yes," Sabina said musingly, "why would he?"

John tucked the bank book into his jacket pocket and resumed his rummaging through the desk drawers. Sabina did likewise among the files. She plucked out an unlabeled manila envelope, undid the string clasp. Inside were a sheaf of unpaid bills for both home and office—mortgage, rent, electricity, water, other services. Some were current, others past due and stamped as such. Andrew Costain hadn't just been insolvent, he'd been teetering on the brink of bankruptcy.

She opened the bottom file drawer. Inside was a stack of very old case files—and bound together by a rubber band at the back, a dozen small pocket notebooks the size of a billfold. She paged through one, then a second and a third. Each was filled with writing in Andrew Costain's somewhat crabbed hand. The man had not only been an alcoholic and a packrat, he'd been a compulsive recorder of bits and pieces of his life. The books contained a hodgepodge of jottings—calendar dates, brief chronicles of activities both social and professional, notes concerning clients and points of law, accounts of trips taken and trips planned, comments on sporting and social events, lists of figures in what appeared to be some kind of personal code, doodlings, even fragments of poorly conceived poetry.

John said, "What's that you have there?" He had finished with the desk and come over to stand behind her.

She showed him the most recent book, which spanned the period from January through August of the current year. He flipped through it until he reached the coded list of figures. Those pages he studied carefully, a small smile lifting the corners of his mouth.

"The figures mean something to you?" she asked.

"A list of gambling wagers, unless I miss my guess, at such establishments as the House of Chance. With far more losses noted than winnings."

"One of the reasons Costain was in financial straits, then."

"Yes. The final piece of the puzzle, by Godfrey."

"Well?"

But he just smiled his well-fed wolf's smile and refused to elaborate. Instead he ushered her out of the offices, relocking the door behind him. They left the building without incident, and soon parted company at a nearby hack stand.

Her partner's cryptic behavior would have irritated her more than it did if not for the fact that the search had also provided her with the final pieces of the Clara Wilds puzzle. If John chose to keep his conclusions secret until he deemed it suitable to announce them, then she would do the same with hers.

Sabina let herself into her furnished Russian Hill flat and for a moment leaned wearily against the closed door. A long day, and a productive one, but she was glad to be back in this comfortable nest she'd created for herself. Adam twined around her ankles, making soft burbling sounds that she knew were a plea for food.

"Yes, I know you're hungry. I am, too."

She removed her cloak and hung it on the oak hall tree. In the small parlor with its Morris chair and rather ugly Beauchamp settee, she lighted the gas heater to relieve the evening chill, then went into the tiny kitchen. She took chopped chicken livers from the icebox under the sink and served them to the kitten on one of the few remaining pieces of her grandmother's Sevres china, a delicate floral pattern that had not stood up well to her several moves.

Her larder was not well stocked; she had been too busy to do marketing this week. But the piece of smoked salmon and the bay shrimp she'd purchased from Tony the Fish Monger would be more than enough for her dinner. To go with them she heated a cup of clam broth on the cumbersome black-iron stove, set out crackers to go with the seafood.

Solitary meals did not displease her. She and Stephen had often had differing schedules and frequently ate alone. What she missed was the notes they'd left for each other: little lovers' missives, often jokingly worded in a fashion calculated to produce smiles and chuckles. Stephen had left one for her the night before he died, its exact wording forever etched in her memory.

My dearest helpmeet,

There is dust on my bureau. If you persist in ignoring your housewifely duties, I will divorce you and marry a fat Cuban lady.

The case I am on being neither a difficult, protracted, nor dangerous one, I look forward to seeing you and my well-dusted bureau tomorrow evening.

Your exasperated but loving husband,
Stephen

She had laughed heartily, with not an inkling that it would be the last laughter to come from her for many months. For when she read the note, her loving husband was already lying dead in a Denver alleyway.

Sighing, she cleared the table and washed the dishes. Usually she spent her post-prandial hours in the parlor writing personal letters or reading *Harper's Bazaar, The Cosmopolitan,* and a magazine that most proper ladies of the day avoided as shocking fare, the *National Police Gazette.* This evening she sat with pad and paper and carefully set down all the information she'd gleaned during her investigation and the conclusions she drew from them. She often did this when a case was nearing its closure. Hers was an orderly mind, unlike her partner's; creating a careful written outline of facts, observations, and suppositions satisfied her that she hadn't overlooked anything important and had events detailed in their proper sequence.

The last thing John had said to her before their parting earlier was, "There will be a public unveiling of the facts tomorrow, my dear, just as that blasted Englishman wants. Only I'll be the one to arrange it. And I'll be the one to take the credit."

Given his flair for the dramatic, Sabina thought, he would no doubt put on quite a performance. But he wouldn't be alone on whatever stage he set, and for once he wouldn't receive all the applause.

27

QUINCANNON

It took him most of the following morning to contact the principals in the Costain case and arrange for them to assemble in the offices of Great Western Insurance at one o'clock that afternoon. All were already present when he and Sabina entered the anteroom on the stroke of one. Penelope Costain, the crackbrain Sherlock in the company of Dr. Caleb Axminster, and the doltish Prussian, Kleinhoffer. He had invited Kleinhoffer not so much in his official capacity but to bask in the copper's reaction to a demonstration of genuine detective work.

Quincannon was in fine fettle. He had slept well, as he normally did when he was about to bring a case to a successful conclusion, breakfasted well, and was eager for the proceedings to unfold. Sabina, too, seemed to have spent a restful night and was in good spirits. He had expected her to ask questions and demand answers, as she had before their sojourn to Andrew Costain's law offices last night. But she had remained curiously silent, a small, private smile lurking at the corners of her mouth, before departing on an unrevealed errand that kept her away from the agency for more than two hours.

In a body they were shown into Jackson Pollard's private sanctum, a large but spartan room with no permanent fixtures beyond a desk, a telephone, and a bank of filing cabinets. Chairs had been brought in to accommodate the group. Pollard wore his usual brusque expression, and behind his spectacles his bugged eyes issued a mute warning when he regarded Quincannon. The little claims adjustor had not been pleased when he'd been refused any advance knowledge of the meeting's purpose.

Everyone sat down except Quincannon. Holmes lit his oily clay pipe and sat in a relaxed posture, his eyes bright with anticipation. Sabina sat quietly with hands clasped in her lap; patience was one of her many virtues. Penelope Costain was like a statue in her chair, her small black eyes unblinking and her head stiffly tipped, fingers toying with a tigereye and agate locket at the throat of a high-collared black dress. Dr. Axminster sucked on horehound drops, wearing the bright-eyed, expectant look of a small boy on Christmas morning. Kleinhoffer's red face was bent into a sneer, as if he considered this business a waste of his time.

Pollard said, "Well, Quincannon? Get on with it. And what you have to say had better be worthwhile."

"It will be," Quincannon assured him. "First of all, Dodger Brown is in custody awaiting formal charges. I tracked him down late yesterday and handed him over to the authorities."

Kleinhoffer stirred and said gruffly, "Not to me, you didn't."

"No, to Sergeant Percy at the city jail. You hadn't come on duty yet."

"Nobody told me about it today."

"The sergeant's fault, not mine."

"You didn't inform me, either," Pollard said. "Not last night and not earlier today. Why not?"

"I came straight here from the Hall of Justice last evening, but you'd already gone."

"You could have told me this morning. Why didn't you?"

"I had my reasons."

"Yes? Well, what about all the valuables Brown stole? I don't suppose you recovered any of them?"

"Ah, but I did."

Quincannon drew out the sack of valuables, which he'd removed from the office safe before coming to Great Western, and with a flourish, placed it on Pollard's desk blotter. The little claims adjustor seemed pacified as he spread the contents out in front of him, but once he'd sifted through the lot some of his ill temper returned. "All present and accounted for from the first three burglaries," he said. "But none of Mrs. Costain's losses is here."

"I haven't recovered those items as yet."

"Well? Do you have any idea what Brown did with them?"

"He did nothing with them. He never had them."

"Never had them, you say?"

"Dodger Brown didn't burgle the Costain home," Quincannon said. "Nor is he the murderer of Andrew Costain."

Kleinhoffer made a noise not unlike the grunt of a rooting shoat. Pollard blinked owlishly behind his spectacles. "Then who did burgle it?"

"No one."

"Come, come, man, speak plainly, say what you mean."

"It was Andrew Costain who planned the theft, with the aid

of an accomplice, and it was the accomplice who punctured him and made off with the contents of the valuables case."

This announcement brought an "Ahh!" from Dr. Axminster. Sabina arched one of her fine eyebrows, but not as if she were surprised. Even Kleinhoffer and the bughouse Sherlock sat up straight in their chairs. The reactions fueled Quincannon's ardor. He was in his element now, and enjoying himself immensely.

Penelope Costain said icily, "That is a ridiculous accusation. Why on earth would my husband conspire to rob his own home?"

"To defraud the Great Western Insurance Company. For monetary gain, so he could pay off his substantial gambling debts. You knew he was a compulsive gambler, didn't you, Mrs. Costain? And that his finances had been severely depleted and his practice had suffered setbacks as a result of his addiction?"

"I knew of no such thing."

"If what you say is true," Pollard said to Quincannon, "how did *you* find it out?"

"I was suspicious of the man from the moment he asked me to stand watch on his property." This was not quite true, but what harm in a little embellishment? "Two nights ago at Dr. Axminster's home, Costain seemed to consider me incompetent for allowing Dodger Brown to escape from the Truesdales'. Why then would he choose me of all people to protect his property? The answer is that he wanted a detective he considered inept to bear witness to a cleverly staged break-in. Underestimating me was his first mistake."

"Was that the only thing that made you suspicious?"

"No. Costain admitted it was unlikely that a professional housebreaker, having had a close call the previous night, would risk another crime so soon, yet he would have me believe his fear was so great, he was willing to pay dear for not one but two operatives to stand surveillance on one or two nights. An outlay of funds he could ill afford, for it was plain from his heavy drinking and the condition of his office that he had fallen on difficult times. He also made two dubious claims—that he had no time to remove valuables from his home and hide them elsewhere until the burglar was apprehended, and that he had no desire to cancel 'important engagements' in order to guard the premises himself."

Dr. Axminster asked, "So you accepted the job in order to find out what he was up to?"

"Yes." Another embellishment. He had accepted it for the money—no fool, John Quincannon. "Subsequent investigation revealed Costain's gambling addiction and a string of debts as long as a widowed mother's clothesline. He was a desperate man."

"You suspected insurance fraud, then," the crackbrain said, "when you asked me to join you in the surveillance?"

"I did," Quincannon lied.

"Did you suspect the manner in which the fraud would be perpetrated?"

"The use of an accomplice dressed in the same type of dark clothing as worn by Dodger Brown? Costain's arrival not more than a minute after the intruder entered the house through the rear door? These struck me as suspicious, though not until later. It was a devious plan that no detective could have anticipated in its entirety before the fact." He added, staring meaningfully at the Englishman, "In truth, a bughouse affair from start to finish."

"Bughouse affair?"

"Crazy scheme. Fool's game."

"Ah. Crook's argot, eh? More of your delightful American idiom."

Pollard said, "Enough of that," and tapped the nib of a pen on his desk blotter after the fashion of a judge wielding a gavel. "So the accomplice pulled a double-cross, is that what you're saying, Quincannon? He wanted the spoils all for himself."

"Just so."

"Name him."

"Not just yet. Other explanations are in order first. Such as how Costain came to be murdered in a locked room. And why he was shot as well as stabbed."

"Can you answer those questions?"

"I can."

"Well, then?"

Quincannon allowed suspense to build by producing his pipe and tobacco pouch. Holmes watched him in a rapt way, his hands busy winding a pocket Petrarch, his expression neutral except for the faintest of smiles. The others, Sabina included, were on the edges of their chairs.

When he had the pipe lit and drawing well, he said, "The answer to your first question," he said to Pollard, though his gaze was on the crackbrain, "is that Andrew Costain was *not* murdered in a locked room. Nor was he stabbed *and* shot by his accomplice."

"Riddles, Quincannon?" Pollard said, purse-lipped.

"Not at all. To begin with, Andrew Costain shot himself."

Kleinhoffer exclaimed, "Hogwash!"

Quincannon ignored him. He paused a few seconds for dramatic effect before continuing. "The report was designed to draw me into the house, the superficial wound to support what would have been his claim of a struggle with the thief. The better to bamboozle me and the police, so he reasoned, and the better to insure that Great Western would pay off his claim quickly and without question or suspicion."

"How did you deduce the sham?" Dr. Axminster asked.

"Dodger Brown was known to carry a pistol in the practice of his trade, but only for purposes of intimidation . . . he had no history of violence. He himself told me he carried his weapon unloaded at all times and I don't doubt that this was the truth; it was empty when I found it yesterday and there were no cartridges in his possession. The revolver that inflicted Costain's wound was new, bought by him that same day, I'll wager, from a gunsmith near his law offices."

Sabina spoke for the first time. "But why the locked-room business?" she asked. "Further obfuscation?"

"No. In point of fact, there was no locked-room ploy."

Pollard growled, "Are you saying it wasn't part of the plan?"

"Precisely. That part of the misadventure was a mix of illusion and accident, the result of circumstances, not premeditation. There was no intent to gild the lily with such gimmickry. Even if there had been, there was simply not enough time for any sort of locked-room shenanigans to have been arranged once the pistol was fired."

"Then what did happen?"

"Costain was in the hallway outside the open door to his

246

study, not inside the room, when he discharged the shot into his forearm. That is why the electric light was on in the hall . . . why the smell of burned powder was strong there, yet all but nonexistent inside the room. The bullet penetrated the arm-chair because the weapon was aimed in that direction when it was fired, through the open doorway into the study."

"Why didn't Costain simply fire the shot in there?"

"I suspect because he met his accomplice in the hallway, perhaps to hand over the jewelry from the valuables case. The empty case was another clue that put me onto the gaff. The time factor again: there was not enough for the phantom burglar to have found his way to the study, located the case, and rifled it before Costain arrived to catch him in the act."

"And the murder, John?" Sabina asked.

"Within moments of the shot being fired, the accomplice struck. Costain was standing in the open doorway, his back to the hall. The force of the single stab with a long, narrow blade staggered him forward into the study. The blow was not immediately fatal, however. He lived long enough to turn, con-front his attacker, observe the bloody weapon in a hand still upraised and—in self-defense—to slam the door shut and twist the key already in the latch. Then he collapsed and died."

"Why didn't he shoot the accomplice instead?" Axminster said. "That is what I would have done."

"Likely because he no longer held the pistol. Either the sud-denness of the attack caused him to drop it, or he dropped it in order to lock the door against his betrayer. In my judgment Andrew Costain was a craven coward as well as a thief. I think, if pressed, his wife would confirm this, despite her allegation to Inspector Kleinhoffer that he was a brave man."

Penelope Costain's face was the shade of an egg cream. "I agree with nothing you've said. Nothing!"

The Englishman said, "Capital, my dear sir. Capital!" and stood to grasp Quincannon's hand. "I congratulate you on an excellent reconstruction thus far—a most commendable job of interpretating the *res gestae*."

"*Res* what?" Kleinhoffer demanded.

"The facts of the case. My learned colleague's deductions coincide almost exactly with mine."

Quincannon stiffened. "Bah," he said.

"My good fellow, you doubt my word that I reached the identical conclusions yesterday afternoon?"

"Then prove it by naming the accomplice and explaining the rest of what took place. Can you do that?"

"I can. Naturally."

Damn his eyes! Quincannon's good humor had begun to evaporate. Glaring, he said, "Well, then? Who stabbed Costain?"

"His wife, of course. Penelope Costain."

28

SABINA

Sabina was the only other person in the room besides John who was not startled by the would-be Sherlock's accusation. Simultaneous gasps issued from Pollard and Dr. Axminster, another piggish grunt from the red-faced police inspector. Mrs. Costain's only reaction was to draw herself up indignantly, her flinty eyes striking sparks.

"I?" she said. "How dare you!"

John stood glowering at Holmes. Sabina supposed she should feel sorry for him, but she didn't; he had been much too sure of himself and the Englishman's inability to match wits with him.

He made an effort to regain command by saying, "Holmes's *guess* is correct. The burglar was known to be a small man, and Mrs. Costain is a woman of comparable size. It was easy enough for her to pass for Dodger Brown in the darkness, dressed in dark man's clothing, with a cloth cap covering her hair."

"Quite so," Holmes agreed before John could say anything more. "While joined in her husband's plan, she devised a counter-plan of her own—a double-cross, as you Americans call it—for two reasons. First, to attempt to defraud the Great Western Insurance Company not once but twice by entering claims on both the allegedly stolen jewelry and on her husband's life insurance policy, of which she is the sole beneficiary. She came to this office yesterday to enter those claims, did she not, Mr. Pollard?'"

"She did."

"Her second motive," Holmes went on, "was hatred, a virulent and consuming hatred for the man to whom she was married."

"You can't possibly know that," John snapped at him. "You're guessing again."

"I do not make guesses. Mrs. Costain's hatred of her husband was apparent to me at Dr. Axminster's dinner party Tuesday evening. My eyes are trained to examine faces and not their trimmings—that is to say, their public pose. As for proof of her true feelings, and of her guilt, I discovered the first clue shortly after you and I found Andrew Costain's corpse."

"What clue?"

"Face powder, of course."

"Eh? Face powder?"

"When I examined the wound in Costain's back through my glass, I discovered a tiny smear of the substance on the cloth of his coat—the same type and shade as worn by Mrs. Costain. Surely you noticed it as well, Quincannon?"

"Yes, yes," John said. But his tone and the way he fluffed his whiskers told Sabina that if he had noticed the smear, he'd failed to correctly interpret its meaning. "But I don't see how that proves her guilt. They were married . . . her face powder might have gotten on his coat at any time, in a dozen different ways."

"I beg to differ," the Englishman said. "It was close and to the right of the wound, which indicated that the residue must have adhered to the murderer's hand when the fatal blow was struck. It was also caked and deeply imbedded in the fibers of the cloth. This fact, combined with the depth of the wound itself, further indicated that the blade was plunged into Costain's flesh with great force and fury. An act born of hatred as well as greed. The wound itself afforded additional proof. It had been made by a stiletto, hardly the type of weapon a professional pannyman such as Dodger Brown would carry. A stiletto, furthermore, as my researches into crime have borne out, is much more a woman's weapon than a man's."

There was no way in which John could refute this logic, and it was plain that he knew it. He sat down in the chair Holmes had vacated and wisely held his tongue.

Penelope Costain once again claimed coldly outraged innocence. No one except Sabina paid her any attention, least of all John and the Englishman. The woman's controlled bluster was a marvel to behold.

"Now then," Holmes continued, "we have the mystery of Mrs. Costain's actions after striking the death blow. Her evidently miraculous escape from the house, only to reappear later dressed in evening clothes." He directed a keen look at John. "Of course you know how this bit of flummery was managed."

"Of course." But John finger-combed his whiskers again as he spoke.

"Pray elaborate."

"There is little enough mystery in what she did. She simply hid until you and I were both inside the study and then slipped out through one of the windows. She could easily have prepared one in advance so that it slid up and down noiselessly, and also loosened its latch just enough to allow it to drop back into the locking bracket after she climbed through and lowered the sash. The window would then appear to have been unbreached."

"Ingenious."

"She may have thought so."

"I meant your interpretation," Holmes said. "Unfortunately, however, you are wrong. That is not what she did."

"The devil you say!"

"Quite wrong on all counts except that she did, in fact, hide for a length of time. She could not have foreseen that both front and rear doors would be blocked. If simple escape had been the plan, she could reasonably have expected to slip out by either the front or rear door, thus obviating use of a window. Nor could she be certain in advance that a loosened window latch would drop back into its bracket and thus go unnoticed. Nor could she be certain that we would fail to hear her raising and lowering the sash, and capture her before she could vanish into the night."

John said heavily, "I suppose you have a better theory."

"Not a theory, the exact truth of the matter. Her hiding place was the very same one she and her husband had decided upon as part of the original scheme. I discovered it yesterday afternoon when I returned to the Costain home while Mrs. Costain was away and conducted a careful search of the premises."

"Unlawful trespass!" This time, Penelope Costain's outrage was not feigned. She appealed to the heavyset Prussian policeman. "I caught him there, Inspector, and you heard him admit to the fact. I demand that you arrest him."

"It's a little late for that, Mrs. Costain," Kleinhoffer said.

"Let's hear the rest of what the limey . . . what Mr. Holmes has to say."

"Thank you, Inspector. I expect that under the circumstances, you'll agree that my actions were justified."

"Maybe. If you can explain how she got out of the house."

"She didn't. She never left it."

"What's that? Never left it?"

Holmes paused as John had done earlier, for dramatic effect. "When you have eliminated the impossible," he said, "whatever is left must, perforce, be the truth. As applied in this case, I concluded—as Mr. Quincannon did—that it was impossible for Andrew Costain's slayer to have committed murder in and then escape from the locked study. Therefore Costain could not have been locked in when the stiletto was plunged into his body. I further concluded that it was impossible for the slayer to have escaped from the house after the crime was committed. Therefore she did not escape from it. Penelope Costain was hidden on the premises the entire time."

Kleinhoffer demanded to know where. "You and Quincannon searched the house from top to bottom, and so did my men. Somebody would've found her if she was there."

"But she was and no one did. Consider this: strangers cannot possibly know every nook and cranny in a large old home in which they have never before set foot. The owners, however, are fully intimate with every inch of their property."

"True enough," Pollard interjected, "but a place large enough for a woman to hide . . ."

"Indeed. And the Costain home contains just such a place. During my search, I discovered a tiny nook inside the kitchen pantry where preserves and the like are stored. The entrance is hidden by the stocked pantry shelves in front of it, so that the Costains could be reasonably sure it would be overlooked by strangers. The nook itself is some four feet square, and while it has no ventilation, its door when cracked open permits enough air for normal breathing."

Sabina remembered the smudge of dirt on the Englishman's cheek she'd noticed yesterday. Her thought at the time had been correct: he really had been crawling around in dark corners. She couldn't help but admire his tenacity. And his cunning deductive powers, which really were quite remarkable.

"Mrs. Costain had no trouble remaining hidden for well over an hour," Holmes went on, "ample time for her to change from the dark male clothing into evening clothes she had placed in the nook earlier. After the arrival of the police, when none of the officers was in the immediate vicinity, she slipped out through the kitchen and dining room to the front hallway and pretended to have just arrived home. The first person to encounter her—Sergeant Mahoney, I believe—had no reason to doubt her story."

John said moodily, "But you did, I suppose."

"Oh, quite. When she first entered the study, I observed the remnants of cobwebs and traces of dust on the hem of her skirt, the fur of her wrap, even the ostrich plume in her chapeau. The pantry room contains cobwebs, dust, and dirt of the same sort. I also observed that a fragment had been torn from one of her fingernails, leaving a tiny wound in the cuticle. Earlier, during my studies of the hallway carpet, I found that same tiny piece, stained with a spot of fresh blood—broken off, of course, when she stabbed her husband. *Quod erat demonstrandum.*"

Penelope Costain said, "There's no proof of any of this."

"Ah, but there is. When Inspector Kleinhoffer consults with Sergeant Mahoney and the officers who were stationed outside your home on that fateful night, I have no doubt that all will swear an oath that no conveyance arrived and no one entered the house through the front or rear doors. As for the missing jewelry and coins, and the murder weapon . . ." He shifted his gaze to Kleinhoffer. "You'll find them where she hid them, Inspector—in a bag of sugar on a shelf in the pantry nook."

"What makes you so sure they're still there? She might've moved them after she caught you poking around the house."

"She would have no reason to move them," Holmes said. "Surely she examined the pantry room and the sugar sack afterward, but I was quite careful to leave everything exactly as I found it. Her natural conclusion was that I failed to discover the room in my, ah, pokings and thus it was still a safe hiding place."

A weaker woman would have crumbled at this point. But not Penelope Costain; her glacial calm and her bravado remained intact. She said flatly, "Even if my jewelry and the murder weapon are where you say they are, I deny putting them there just as I deny your other accusations. None of what you claim to be evidence is sufficient to convince a jury beyond a reasonable doubt that I'm guilty."

Sabina took that statement as her cue. John and the Englishman had had their moments in the limelight; now it was her turn. She cleared her throat, rose to her feet, and said in an excellent imitation of one of John's dramatic pronouncements, "No, Mrs. Costain, but I can prove beyond any doubt that you're guilty of the *other* murder you committed."

Once again there were exclamations from Pollard, Kleinhoffer, and Dr. Axminster. John merely stared at her.

"I have no idea what you're talking about," Penelope Costain said.

"Of course you do. Clara Wilds, your first victim."

"I don't know anyone named Clara Wilds."

"A pickpocket, among other things," Sabina said for the benefit of the others in the room. She glanced at John as she spoke. He seemed somewhat subdued now, broodingly so, but to his credit he made no attempt to interfere. Nor did Holmes, who appeared a bit miffed that a woman had taken his place center stage, but who nonetheless stood regarding her with full attention. "The woman who robbed your husband a few evenings ago."

"Why on earth would I want to murder a common thief?"

"Because you were desperate to recover an item she lifted from him."

"That's ridiculous. Andrew's silver money clip, in which he carried very little cash? You yourself returned it to me yesterday."

"Not the money clip. An item even more valuable to a woman who was an extortionist before she became a pickpocket. A leather-bound notebook that resembled a billfold and contained incriminating information about your scheme to defraud Great Western Insurance."

The last statement was a guess, but a calculated one—the only credible explanation based on the evidence Sabina possessed. The way in which Penelope Costain twitched in her chair, her lips thinning back against her teeth, confirmed that it was the correct one.

"Your husband was an habitual chronicler of his personal and professional life, wasn't he? Names, dates, events, gambling debts—and future plans. You must have been furious with him when he told you he'd committed the details of your scheme to paper and that the notebook had been stolen. And even more furious when you learned Clara Wilds had read his notes and acted on the blackmail opportunity by contacting your husband and demanding one thousand dollars for the notebook's return—the sum he withdrew in cash from his bank shortly before Wilds was killed."

The Costain woman said nothing, her pointy eyes piercing Sabina like stilettos. Or hatpins.

"You were afraid that Clara Wilds would continue to bleed you if you went through with the insurance fraud and your plan to kill your husband. That might even have been her intention from the start, by holding back some of the incriminating pages. So it was imperative that she be stopped and the entire notebook recovered immediately.

"Clara Wilds was too clever to meet your husband anywhere but in a public place, which left you with only one alternative. Once the time and place of the meeting were arranged, you drove a buggy there early, dressed in the same man's clothing you later wore to impersonate the burglar, and waited until the blackmail exchange was completed. Then you followed Wilds to her lodging house near Washington Square. You left the rig in the carriageway behind the house while you killed Wilds, regained the thousand dollars, and searched her rooms until you found the notebook. One of the neighbors noticed the parked buggy, as did another witness when you left the area—"

"It wasn't my buggy! No one can swear it was!"

"No, not your Studebaker—you're too clever to have used your own equipage. A Concord you rented for the purpose."

"That's a lie. I did no such thing." She pointed a finger at Sabina as if she were aiming a pistol. "Can your witnesses describe the driver? State with certainty that it wasn't a man? I doubt it. Anyone could have driven the buggy—anyone could have stabbed the woman."

"How did you know she was stabbed?"

"What? Why . . . you said so . . ."

"No, I didn't. I said only that she was murdered."

"I . . . I assumed it, that's all. All that talk about Andrew being stabbed with a stiletto . . ."

"Clara Wilds was stabbed with her own hatpin, not a stiletto—the very same hatpin she jabbed into your husband when she picked his pocket. A woman's weapon as well, wouldn't you agree, Mr. Holmes?"

"Without question," he said approvingly. "Splendid detective work, my dear Mrs. Carpenter. Capital!"

Penelope Costain stamped her foot. "How do you know so much unless you were there in her rooms? *You* could have killed her!"

"I had no reason to," Sabina said. "You did."

"You can't prove it in a court of law, any more than these two so-called detectives"—she glared at John and the Englishman in turn—"can prove I killed my husband."

"Oh, yes—beyond any doubt, as I said earlier. For two reasons. One is the rented buggy. This morning I visited half a dozen stables in the downtown and South Park areas until I located the one you patronized. The hostler looked closely at you because he thought it was odd that an attractive woman should be wearing man's clothing. He can identify you. As for the second and most damning reason—"

Sabina shifted her attention to Dr. Axminster, who was in the process of eating another horehound drop. "I understand Mrs. Costain had an appointment with you yesterday, Doctor."

Axminster blinked, swallowed, and cleared his throat. "Yes, that's correct."

"For what reason?"

"To request a prescription for laudanum. Her husband's death had made her quite anxious, she said."

"A strong enough dosage that could also be used for the relief of severe pain?"

"Why, yes. She specifically asked for the maximum strength."

"I thought as much. When I spoke to Mrs. Costain at her home yesterday, the pupils of her eyes were as small as arrow points. As they are now and have been since her arrival here. One of the primary ingredients of laudanum, as we all know, is opium, a drug which constricts the pupils of the eyes when taken in a moderately large dosage."

Sabina turned again to Penelope Costain. "Clara Wilds struggled with her attacker before she died, and in that struggle she marked the person—deeply, judging from the amount of blood, skin, and hair under her fingernails. Brown, curly hair of the sort found at the nape of the neck. Yesterday at your home you were wearing a high-collared taffeta dress—an odd choice for a mourning garment—and you held your head at a careful angle the entire time, wincing now and then when you moved, as a woman does when a collar chafes at a painful wound. Would you mind undoing the high collar of the dress you're wearing today, Mrs. Costain?"

"No! I won't!"

"Would you like me to do it? If not, Inspector Kleinhoffer can summon a police matron."

Penelope Costain raised a hand to the left side of her neck, an involuntary gesture that produced a grimace of pain when she touched it. Her calm and her bluster deserted her, and her expression turned frantic. She bounced to her feet and made a panicked attempt to flee—straight into Inspector Kleinhoffer's waiting arms.

29

QUINCANNON

"The man is infuriating!" Quincannon ranted. "Insufferable, insulting, exasperating!"

"John, for heaven's sake . . ."

"Thinks he's a blasted oracle. Sees all, knows all, an expert on every arcane subject under the sun. He's full of—"

"John."

"—hot air. Enough to fill a balloon and carry it from here to the Sandwich Islands. Crackbrain! Braggart! Conceited popinjay!"

"Lower your voice," Sabina said warningly. "The other diners are starting to stare at us."

Quincannon subsided. She was right, he was calling attention to himself. The Cobweb Palace, Abe Warner's eccentric eatery on Meiggs Wharf in North Beach, was a noisily convivial place at the dinner hour, and to draw scrutiny here was no mean feat. The ramshackle building was packed to its creaking rafters on this Saturday evening—with customers partaking of the finest seafood fare in the city, and with the usual complement of monkeys, roaming cats and dogs, and such exotic birds as the parrot that was capable of hurling curses in four languages. Warner had a benevolent passion for all creatures large and small, including spiders; his collection of rare and sundry souvenirs, everything from Eskimo artifacts to a complete set of dentures that had once belonged to a sperm whale to rude paintings of nude women, were draped floor to ceiling in an undisturbed mosaic of cobwebs.

At length Sabina ventured to say, "I don't know why you carry on so about the Englishman. You didn't have to spend all of yesterday trekking through the Barbary Coast and Chinatown with him."

"It was only to get rid of the confounded pest. Besides, I gave him my word that I would, to my everlasting regret." Quincannon's ire began to rise again, and his voice along with it. "The day was interminable. He insisted on seeing every squalid nook and cranny. Opium dens, gambling hells, wine dumps, half the pestholes from Dupont Street to the waterfront. Yes, and the Fiddle Dee Dee and the Hotel Nymphomania, among other parlor houses. He even stopped half a dozen street prostitutes to ask the prices for their services, not only for comparison here but with streetwalkers in London's Limehouse. Faugh! I had half a mind to bribe Ezra Bluefield to feed him a Mickey Finn and turn him over to the shanghaiers—"

"Hush!"

Quincannon subsided again, but not before muttering, "Blasted addlepate."

"Yes, but there's no gainsaying the fact that he has a rare talent for detective work."

"Rare talent! Bah! Just because he happened to stumble upon the correct solution to the Costain murder?"

"Be honest, John. He not only matched your deductive skill, but bettered it in more than one respect."

"I would have come to the same conclusions," Quincannon grumbled, "if I hadn't been out chasing after Dodger Brown."

"I'm sure you would have. But you're still being too harsh on the man. After all, he could have gone directly to the police with his discoveries, in which case you'd have gotten little or none of the credit. Instead he gave us both advance warning of his intentions."

She had a point, but he wasn't about to say so. "Only so he could brag about his alleged genius. He'd have gone ahead with his arrangements if I hadn't stopped him. I still say he had no business poking his nose into my investigation, even if I did unwittingly give him the opportunity."

"I suppose you feel the same about *my* nose."

"Eh? No, of course not. You're my partner."

"But not your equal as a detective?"

"Yes, that, too," he admitted grudgingly. "That was an admirable piece of sleuthing you did on the Clara Wilds matter."

"Well! A professional compliment from the master himself. So you hold no grudge against *me* for what took place in Pollard's office?"

"None. Besides, your investigation and mine were essentially separate."

"So much for compliments," Sabina said.

"You know, you should have told me you suspected Penelope Costain of Wilds's murder, and why. It would have made my job easier."

"And if you'd confided your suspicions to me, it would have

made *mine* easier. Why must you always play your cards so close to the vest?'"

"My father's teachings, and a dozen years with the Secret Service."

"And a colossal conceit."

Quincannon pretended to be hurt. "You wound me deeply."

"Oh, bosh. You'll never change, will you?"

"I might, if you'll agree to accompany me to dinner more often."

"I will—the day you learn the meaning of the word humility."

He wasn't offended. Nothing she said tonight could offend him. He reached over to touch her hand, half expecting her to move it away. When she didn't, at least not immediately, it stirred his tender feelings. He gazed wistfully at her across the table, reflecting again that she had dressed well for him. Beneath her lamb's wool coat, she wore a brocade jacket over a snowy shirtwaist and a wine-colored skirt. Pendant ruby earrings, a gift from her late husband, made a fiery complement to her sleek dark hair and creamy complexion.

"Have I told you how captivating you look this evening, my dear?"

"Three times now. Personal compliments are also well taken, but you needn't overdo it."

"I could tell you fifty times a day how attractive you are and still not be overdoing it."

"You ought to know by now that flattery will get you nowhere."

Flattery—sincere flattery—might get him nowhere tonight, but his ardor and his hopeful determination remained undampened. There would be other evenings such as this. And on one of them . . . ah, surely on one of them . . .

SABINA

Once John settled down and gave his attention to his abalone steak, attacking the succulent shellfish with gusto, the dinner progressed well and she was not sorry she had accepted his invitation. The crab cakes were delicious, the wine well chilled, and his personal compliments, if not his professional ones, well taken despite their underlying intent. He was pleasant company when he had reined in his emotions and allowed his gentle and vulnerable side to dominate. Charming, even. Yes, and handsome, too, with his dark eyes and thick but well-groomed beard, and the gray sack coat, matching waistcoat, and striped trousers he wore.

Not that having dinner with him tonight meant she'd changed her mind about their relationship. But there was no harm in giving in to a minor temptation. But it was there that she drew the line and would continue to draw it. Still . . . she was young and healthy, and while she could never love any man except Stephen, she couldn't help wondering what it would be like if she succumbed, just once, to John's advances. . . .

She felt herself starting to blush and quickly put the thought out of her mind.

If only John weren't so persistent in his designs on her virtue. And so jealous of his prowess as a detective. His self-esteem was justified up to a point—he was almost as good as he believed he was—but it sometimes blinded him to the long view of things. Their recent investigations, for instance. It didn't matter a whit that he'd had to share the limelight with her and a daft poseur. All that mattered was that a cold-blooded double murderess had been apprehended, all the stolen property had been recovered, Jackson Pollard was pleased that his company was not liable for any of the insurance claims, and Carpenter and Quincannon, Professional Detective Services, had been well compensated and were assured of Great Western Insurance's continued patronage. But there was no use in trying to tell John any of this, at least not tonight, his feelings toward the Englishman running as hot as they were. She had no doubt that he would indulge in more grumbling before the evening came to an end.

And of course he did.

He was a jovial companion until they were finishing an excellent rum cake dessert. Then, after a short interval during which his face turned cloudy again, he muttered, "He wouldn't tell me when he plans to leave San Francisco."

Sabina sighed. "I don't suppose I need to ask who you mean."

"The crackbrain, of course. He likes it here, he said. Finds the city stimulating. Might stay on awhile."

"Well? That's his privilege, isn't it?"

"It is as long as he doesn't bother me again with his infernal presence. Why doesn't he go back to England? That's where he belongs—an asylum in England."

The imp in Sabina made her say, "Does he really? We could be wrong about him, you know."

"What do you mean, wrong?"

"Suppose he isn't an impostor. Suppose he really is Sherlock Holmes, the world-famous detective."

John stared at her as if a fiddler crab had suddenly crawled out of the collar of her dress. "You're not serious?"

"It's possible, isn't it?"

"No! The real Holmes is dead. It's folly to think that scrawny, gibbering imitation presuming on Dr. Axminster's hospitality is the genuine article. You know that as well as I do."

"Perhaps. But I have a feeling that whoever he is, neither of us has seen the last of him—personally or professionally."

"We'd better have," John said in ominous tones. "If he tries to interfere in any more of our investigations, I may not be able to restrain myself from strangling, bludgeoning, stabbing, or shooting him."

Sabina rolled her eyes and maintained an eloquent silence.

Authors' Note

While we have taken some slight liberties with dates and geographical locations, the detailed historical background in these pages is as accurate as diligent research can make it. Similarly, the character of the man who would be Sherlock Holmes is as true to Conan Doyle's depiction of the original Holmes as the nature and dictates of the story permitted.

Among the many research tools we consulted, four books were particularly informative and entertaining: *You Can't Win* by Jack Black (Macmillan, 1926), the extraordinary autobiography of one of the era's career criminals; *The Barbary Coast: An Informal History of the San Francisco Underworld* by Herbert Asbury (Knopf, 1933); *Champagne Days of San Francisco* by Evelyn Wells (Doubleday, 1939); and *The Complete Sherlock Holmes* by Sir Arthur Conan Doyle, ed. by Christopher Morley (Doubleday, 1927).

M.M. / B.P.

About the Authors

Marcia Muller is the creator of Sharon McCone and one of the key figures in the development of the contemporary female private investigator. The author of more than thirty-five novels, three in collaboration with her husband, Bill Pronzini, Marcia received the MWA's Grand Master Award in 2005.

Bill Pronzini, creator of the Nameless Detective, is a highly praised novelist, short story writer, and anthologist. He received the Grand Master Award from MWA in 2008, making Marcia and Bill the only living couple to share the award (the other couple being Margaret Millar and Ross Macdonald).